BUSINESS CASUAL

Book 5
Wellington Estates Series

Sunanda Chatterjee

Published in USA

Cover Design: Carrie at www.cheekycovers.com

Editor: Emily Nemchick and Shivani Chatterjee

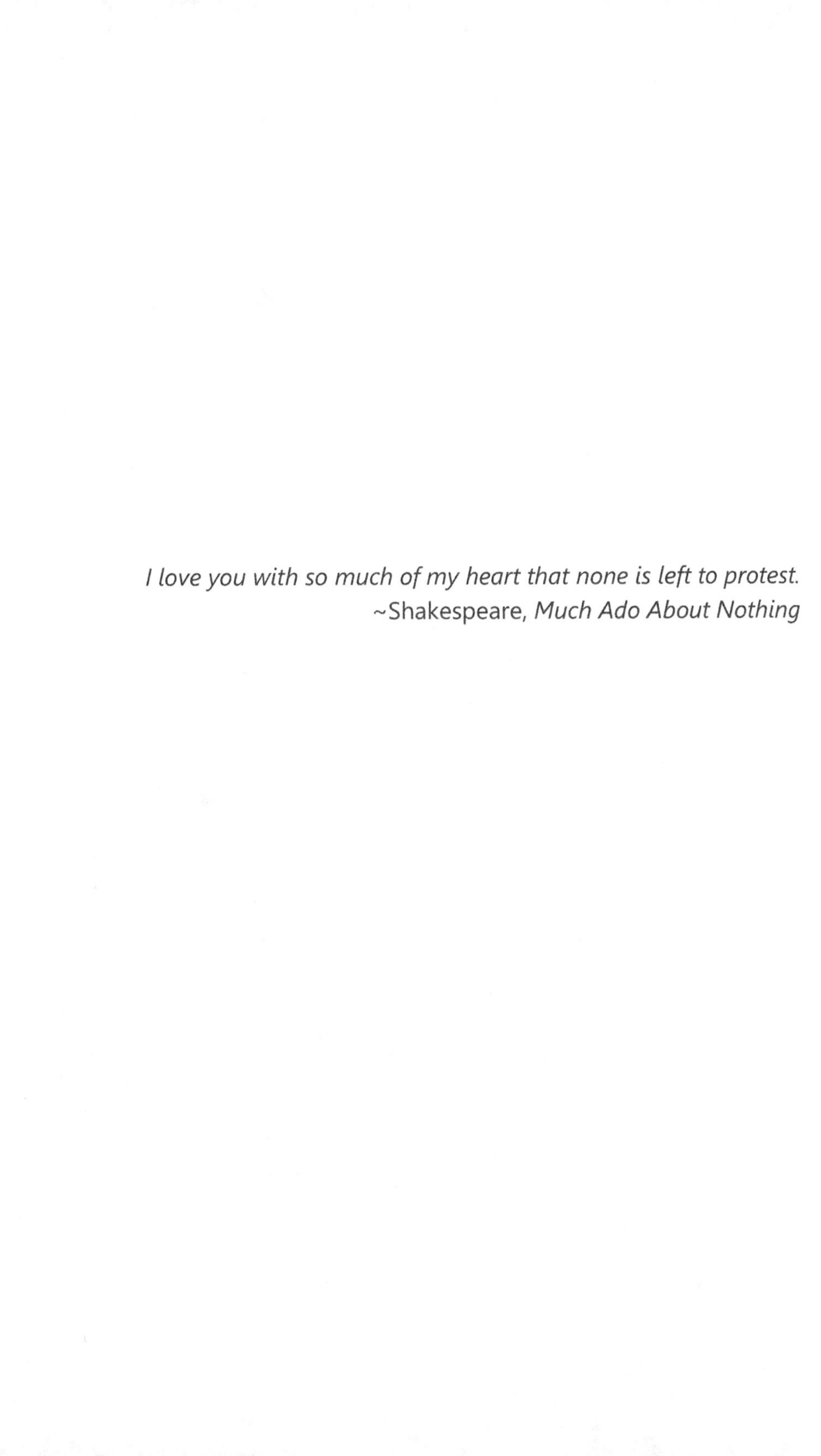

I love you with so much of my heart that none is left to protest.
~Shakespeare, *Much Ado About Nothing*

For Jay

1

AVINASH SINGHANIA cursed under his breath at the stop-and-go freeway traffic, envious of the cars zipping past him in the carpool lane. Damn his date for ditching him at the last minute. Since he was driving solo, he couldn't use the carpool lane. He resisted the temptation to cross the double-yellow line into the carpool lane; he often drove faster than the speed limit, but he was too much of a lawyer to flaunt the law to that extent.

Karina had accompanied him on a few social occasions, and the tabloids had published crazy stories of betrothal. But today she'd bungled the dates, and here he was, on his way to a wedding, dateless. And it wasn't a wedding he could skip. He attended social functions when he had to, but preferred the quiet of his penthouse apartment, peaceful hikes in the mountains, or mornings out on the ocean on his yacht.

He glanced at his watch and honked at a slow driver. He groaned and drove on toward Temecula, about ninety miles south of downtown Los Angeles.

Soon, he took the exit, sped up on the surface streets, and pulled into the Dheer Winery where he screeched to a halt. He hopped out of his Jaguar, tossed his key to the valet, and rushed into the Winery Chateau main hall. A pimple-faced tuxedo-clad young man handed him a program.

Lily Leoni weds Arjun Dheer.

Someone ushered him through the hallway toward the garden, where everyone was already seated. By the entrance he saw the bride--his one-time client--waiting to walk down the aisle. His friend, Detective Harrison McNamara, was waiting with her.

"Hey guys," Avinash said. "Sorry I'm late."

Lily dazzled him with a sunny smile. How different she looked now! The first time he'd seen her was years ago in his office, accompanied by Harrison, with a spectacular black eye and bruises on her arms, seeking his help to escape an abusive relationship with her now ex-boyfriend. She had found love and happiness at last.

"Wow," he said. "You look amazing."

She smiled. "Thanks. Um… and thanks for everything."

Avinash smiled back. "Oh, sure." He wanted to tell her that her ex was now in jail. Avinash had heard from his law school buddy who practiced in Portland. The ex had hurt his new girlfriend, and thanks to the restraining order Avinash had prepared on Lily's behalf, the girlfriend's lawyer was able to get a conviction and put him away for five years. But now was not the time. "Congratulations."

Lily's hazel eyes glittered with joy. "Thanks."

Avinash asked Harrison, "And how's Trevor?" A few years ago, Avinash had helped Harrison and his wife, Laura, adopt a baby boy whose mother had died. That was another thing that had involved Lily; it was she who had somehow convinced Harrison to adopt the baby. Harrison had invited him to the kid's birthday party, but Avinash managed to avoid it, being averse to family functions. It was just too painful.

Harrison laughed. "Trevor is already in preschool. A total brat, if you ask me. But don't tell Laura I said that. She'll kill me. As far as she is concerned, he is an angel. He can do no wrong." Then he took Lily's arm. "Let's get going, coz I'm walking her down the aisle in…" He glanced at his watch. "Five minutes."

"Oh," said Avinash. "You're the bride's dad today?"

A wistful look crossed Lily's eyes. Then she braced her shoulders. "Hah. My Dad abandoned me when I was a kid. He lives in Italy with his new family that doesn't even know about me. I sent him a card. Wasted the postage, if you ask me. I'm better off without him."

Avinash didn't know how to respond, memories from his past haunting him still. But, at least, he hadn't been disowned like Lily had been. He was fortunate. When he'd thought he had lost it all, somehow, he had found a home and a family, foreign and strange though it had seemed then.

Harrison said, "Hurry, now. I saw an empty seat up ahead."

"All the best," whispered Avinash. He rushed down the aisle into the bright sunlight, shoving the scenes of his childhood to the recesses of his mind. He squinted at rows upon rows of white chairs on each side of a red-carpeted pathway strewn with flower petals. The groom, the groomsmen, and the bridesmaids had already assembled under the ornate gazebo decorated with entwined lilies.

He found the empty seat and settled down just as the band started a jazzy rendition of *Here Comes the Bride*. Lily was marrying her college friend after a long courtship, which had followed a longer, tumultuous friendship. Friends to lovers. What a concept.

Avinash blew out through pursed lips. He'd stopped believing in marriage years ago. There was no such thing as true love, or a soulmate. Fairytale bullshit, at least for him. Based on pure statistics and his personal experience as someone who practiced family law, the chances of divorce in any marriage were fifty-fifty, like his marriage to Sierra. But Sierra had been a liar. His clients' marriages were mostly miserable, although he knew a handful of successful ones. From what he knew of Lily, she was honest, considerate, and selfless, and if Arjun was anything like her, they could have a long and fulfilling marriage. Up ahead, the groom grinned, looking pretty pleased with himself, as if he had accomplished the impossible. Maybe this marriage would be a happy one.

Avinash was divorced after a marriage that lasted just twenty months. He was still "single," still "available," and still too busy to date. Magazines tried to feature him as the Most Eligible Bachelor, but he turned them down. He'd tell them, "A bachelor, by definition, is someone who's never been married. I'm the Most *Ineligible* Divorcé."

Still, they featured him as "LA's Best Catch" for three years in a row. He scoffed. He'd never be "caught" again, never marry again. Life had taught him to be a loner, and the unexpected, whirlwind, boozy romance with his college crush made him realize how wrong he'd been to consider that marriages could last. He would always remain a loner. And now, after three years, he preferred it that way.

Up ahead, Arjun Dheer said something to his best man, and they laughed, looking pretty darned happy. Arjun was the proprietor of the Dheer Estates and the owner of the Winery Chateau, where the wedding was taking place. Like Avinash, Arjun was Indian. That was why there were two ceremonies. The Hindu wedding took place earlier—which Avinash had skipped—and was now followed by the Christian wedding.

Avinash looked around him to seek a familiar face. But besides Harrison and Lily, he knew no one else.

He checked his watch and wondered how long he was expected to stay. Despite it being a Sunday, he had a load of work to finish at his office in downtown Los Angeles. As the junior partner at Singhania and Singhania, he had taken his family business in different directions and introduced a section for family law, making it a full-service law firm. His mother, Moyna, managed the corporate and business side of things, and he handled family law, giving preference to clients he deemed most susceptible to being cheated out of money and fairness in the justice system: middle-aged housewives who's been discarded by their husbands for the latest model, no pun intended, siblings who deserved to stay together while being fostered if their parents could not care for them, elderly clients who could no longer think clearly and were likely to be "divested" of their own property by those they had once called darling children.

Avinash's father, Sameer Singhania, was often out of the country as the US Ambassador to the United Nations. Papa had had a successful political career as the governor of California, and then as a two-time US Senator, and Avinash was thankful his father had never wanted to run for President. The scrutiny on their family had been intrusive and hurtful during the elections and the nomination, but would have been unbearable for higher office.

As Lily glided to the altar, radiant and blissful, the priest began his ministrations. Avinash's gaze swept over the bridesmaids. He recognized the maid-of-honor, Danielle Riley, from society magazines, but no one else.

His gaze halted at a stunning face among the bridesmaids. A striking, slender, dark haired woman, who was staring right back at him. His heart skipped a beat. From the color of her skin and dark eyes and lush hair tied in a loose knot at the nape of her neck, she looked Indian. He'd never dated an Indian woman, and the idea enticed him. But would she be willing to accept his no-strings-attached policy? Ethnic Indians generally didn't like that sort of thing. It was always: date to marry or don't be seen in public together. And yet, this was the twenty-first century in the most advanced country in the world. What was the harm in trying? Just to check if she was available and interested in dating for fun. The prospect intrigued him.

His eyes ran down her clinging bridesmaid dress, her full breasts covered with crisscrossing fabric, the narrow waist, and legs that went on forever.

Amid a small commotion behind him, a little boy scampered up the aisle. Wearing a goddamn suit. The kid was barely three or four years old with a wide grin and big ears. He was clutching something in his hands, and that something fell down, and rolled beneath chairs in the row in front of Avinash to rest under a large woman with an ample behind.

People shrieked and squealed and jumped up from their seats.

The boy had been carrying the wedding ring! Who entrusts a kid with something so precious? A wedding ring was a promise not to be broken, a token of undying love, which Avinash doubted could ever be real. But, if you believed in that bullshit, how could you hand it over to a careless kid? Avinash shook his head in disapproval as people stooped and crawled, searching. It was Avinash who spotted the ring, picked it up, and returned it to the boy.

The little boy grinned at him, and Avinash's stomach knotted at a memory, an unrealized possibility from his past, which he pushed back into a dark corner of his mind.

The boy ran up and handed the ring to the groom. After the "I do's", Arjun kissed Lily, and people clapped, hooted, whistled, and made other celebratory sounds. Avinash took in a deep breath and stood up with the crowd. He couldn't wait to get out of here. He planned to skip the reception and head back to work.

As the glowing bride and proud groom marched back down the aisle, people showered them with actual rice confetti, like in Indian weddings, as blessings. Then came the giggling bevy of bridesmaids, jostling and pushing, except for the stunning dark-haired woman, who held the hand of the little ring-bearer.

His phone buzzed. The text was from his mother's best friend, whom he called Auntie Lupe. She was sharing a photo of the latest baby she'd adopted. This was the sixth. He shook his head in wonder and texted back: *How do you do it?*

Her answer came back. *I'm made to be a Mama.*

He chuckled, put away his phone, and looked up at the crowd again.

The stunning woman reached into a cleverly-hidden pocket in her dress and grabbed a phone, gave a tiny smile and then frowned. She looked up. Their eyes met and Avinash's heartbeat quickened.

Work or not, he had to get to know her. Avinash watched her stumble and grip the poor boy's hand harder. Could it be Avinash's "magnetic, intense gaze" described in magazines that had made her miss her step? He tried to hide a smile.

2

UNDER THE ORNATE gazebo, Anila Mallik stood among the bridesmaids and watched her friend Lily Leoni approach the altar. She was positively glowing in her figure-hugging lacy white dress made by their mutual friend Juhi, the proprietor of *Juhi's Dresses*.

On the other side of the aisle, Anila's brother, Arjun, looked radiant in his black tuxedo, waiting for his bride-to-be as she glided up to the altar. The beautician had changed the Indian bridal makeup and hairdo, but the henna on Lily's hands was visible and endearing. Anila smiled with pride and relief for the couple, ignoring the stab of envy.

Anila had experienced this happiness, this fulfilment, the same joy just a few years ago with Vikas, the love of her life, her brave, supportive, loving husband and best friend.

Her mind went back to her days in India as the wife of an Air Force officer. She remembered when Vikas had taken her to the Officer's Mess for the first time, to be introduced to the Commanding Officer at the welcome party arranged for the newlyweds. Anila had been unsure of how to act among the officers and their wives, although everyone had been warm and welcoming. Soon after dessert when the dancing began, Vikas came up to her. "We can leave anytime you want."

She said, "Are you sure?"

"Yeah," he'd said with a grin. "These parties can get a bit wild. And I have a duty to attend them, but now that we've cut the cake and everyone's happy, we can scram."

They had barely finished unpacking, and she was exhausted. She smiled with relief. "Sounds good to me."

They said their goodbyes and returned to the furnished apartment assigned by the Air Force. It was shabby compared to the mansion she'd grown up in, and indeed, what Vikas had grown up with, but he took it in his stride as he sat on the lumpy MES couch and pulled her into his lap.

She giggled and said, "Let me change first."

"Did I tell you, you were the prettiest woman in the crowd today?"

"Yes, twice." She got up from his lap as he held the *palla* of her sari.

"And, your sari is gorgeous."

It was a turquoise brocade Benarasi silk sari, a gift from her mother-in-law, which she'd claimed Vikas had picked himself. "Thanks for the sari too." The blouse was sleeveless, knotted at the back.

Vikas followed her to the bedroom and stroked the bare skin on her arms and back. "Thanks for being such a supportive wife."

She quirked her eyebrows. "All I did was attend a party."

He shook his head. "I know you've sacrificed your career to be a military wife."

She removed the diamond earrings and placed them in the brass-inlaid wooden jewelry box in the rickety dresser. "Maybe one day I'll create some some software for the Air Force." As a computer science major, her skills would be wasted unless she joined the military herself.

He gave a wan smile. "There are many wives here, Masters in Physics, Literature, Mathematics… but since we move around so much, they cannot pursue a stable career. All they can do is teach at the local schools."

She turned to face him. "Or join the Air Force."

He sat on the bed and regarded her. "Anila, I want you to know how much I appreciate your attitude. I know this whole military life is foreign to you. See if you like it enough to actually put on the uniform. These guys? They're family to me. And we take care of each other through thick and thin."

He'd been right. Whenever the unit went out on sorties, the wives gathered in the CO's house for tea and samosas, and waited with bated breath for their husbands to return. The pilots sometimes swung low over their own apartment or dipped the wings to let their wives know they were back. Everyone clapped when that happened. Anila missed that camaraderie, and knew she could have truly belonged with them.

She remembered one afternoon, when six aircraft had taken off but only five returned. Amid the chaos as they tried to figure out whose husband hadn't returned, the CO's wife had been like a mother to them all.

The unit took care of the funeral arrangements for the fallen pilot and the grieving wife, herself a sister of another pilot in the unit. Seeing the widow off when she returned to her parents' home had been heartbreaking. People murmured, "At least she had no children."

When Anila had become pregnant, her mother insisted she visit Los Angeles before the needs of motherhood, child care, karate lessons, soccer, and homework took over. And so, while Vikas went from operation to operation in the Northwest region as a fighter pilot, Anila traveled to Los Angeles and stayed with her parents in her brother Arjun's mansion in Wellington Estates.

Arjun had gone through a lot, and she did her best to support him during tough times. She wanted to believe she had a hand in getting Lily and Arjun together during those times.

She had called Vikas one night to tell him about Arjun and Lily, but his phone had been turned off. A Braxton Hicks contraction hit her and she curled up in bed. After a cup of chamomile tea, she got up for a shower. The warm water always helped her. That's when her phone rang.

She hurried out of the shower, wrapped a towel around her massive belly and padded into the room. It was an unfamiliar number. She had half a mind to decline the call, but then she picked it up. Perhaps it was Vikas calling to tell her his phone had died, and he was calling from a friends' number.

"Hello! Vikas?" she said, gripping it to her ear.

It was not Vikas. As she heard what his commanding officer had to say, her stomach clenched and her knees buckled. She dropped the phone and it clattered to the floor.

Her mother had walked in with a glass of warm milk and saw Anila's stunned face. Alka Dheer frowned, placed the glass on the bedside table, and retrieved the phone from under the sofa. "Hello! This is Anila's mother."

Usually composed and dignified, her mother had gasped. Anila reached for the bed and crumpled into the soft satin sheets. She couldn't believe it.

Vikas had died in an accident. Her husband of three years was dead. She was a widow. Her unborn child would grow up fatherless. Her body trembled as the gravity of the truth weighed upon her, drowning her in tears.

Her mother hung up the phone and sat beside her, stroking her back, trying to console Anila. How does one tell a young mother-to-be that her husband has died but everything is going to be okay? Nothing was ever going to be okay.

As tumultuous thoughts swirled through her mind, her belly tightened painfully. She'd had Braxton Hicks contractions before, but this felt different. She took in a sharp breath, her throat constricted, her chest heavy with emotion. As her belly contracted again, she let out a scream, an animal, visceral sound that penetrated the walls of the house and made the floor rumble. She kept screaming and screaming, as sobs lodged themselves in her throat, her mother ran to call the doctor, and the servants rushed to bring her tea. Her water broke.

The shock of Vikas's death had sent Anila into labor weeks before her due date. It was Lily who had helped Anila get through the agony, the utter gloom that had descended upon the household. Anila had flown to India with her ten-day-old baby for the last rites.

Vikas had left her all alone in the world. He'd never even met his son. When they'd found out the sex of the baby, she'd wanted to name him Aakash, or sky, but Vikas had preferred Suraj, or sun. Now she chose Suraj, and nicknamed her baby Sunny. She bit her lip, willing her tears not to flow as she heard the eulogy given by the commanding officer. Vikas was brave. He was strong. He was a compassionate, caring officer who could have been the Air Chief one day. But his life story had been cut short by a cruel fate that had allowed a bird to hit the engines of his Sukhoi 30. Vikas was flying too low to eject on time.

She tried not to think of the panic he must have felt when his plane went up in flames. The pain. The shock. Did his life flash before his eyes in those last moments? Was there time to ponder the uncertainties of life as he faced certain death? Did he think of her, of their son who was not yet born but now lay fussing in the stroller beside her, fatherless?

She swallowed the lump in her throat. She tried to tell herself that her husband had died doing what he loved to do.

Anila sat motionless through the gun salute, as each shot rang through the air, making her heart flutter with pride and terror of what lay ahead. The airmen marched up to her and laid the folded flag upon her lap. She couldn't bear to look up at them. If she did, her tears would betray her. Vikas had been brave, and she would be too. She needed to set an example for her son, but before that, she had to convince herself she was brave. She was brave. She was so, so, brave. She had to be.

What choice had Vikas left her?

She spent a few months in her in-laws' house in India, and Sunny grew stronger by the day. She had to allow her son the knowledge of his father's family, their influence, their protection.

Finally, her mother-in-law said, "Anila, *beti,* you've been really strong. But you do need to move on with your life."

Anila rocked Sunny in his cradle. "What's life without Vikas, *Maa-ji?*"

Her father-in-law put down his newspaper and removed his glasses. "I know it's hard to even think about it now, but you must get married again. You're too young to live like this."

Sunny fussed and she lifted him out of the cradle. "I inherited enough from my grandfather. I can take care of Sunny." Anila had more money than she could spend in a lifetime. What does one do with money when their heart is empty?

He said, "I am not talking about money. Vikas was our only child. All that's ours is yours now. I am talking about having a life partner, a companion." He raised his hands. "Just know that whatever you decide, you'll have our blessings. And Vikas would want you to be happy."

She looked up at her father-in-law. How could anyone replace Vikas? What she'd had with her husband was precious, incomparable, irreplaceable. How could she risk building a life around someone else only to see it destroyed again? Her heart was already broken in two, and she couldn't bear to see it shattered. Didn't her father-in-law know that marriage was the last thing on her mind? She was a young widow with a little baby to care for.

She shook her head and kissed the top of her baby's head. "Sunny is now the sole focus of my life. I must be both his father and mother, and devote all my attention to him, so he never misses having a father."

In the days, weeks, and months that followed, Anila had tried to get over the shock. She had loved Vikas, even though theirs had been an arranged marriage. He was kind, smart, handsome, and everything a woman could wish for.

Sunny stared at her face intently. He had his father's eyes and smile and even his ears. She used to tease Vikas about his ears, but he claimed big ears meant an intelligent mind. Every time she looked at her son's face, she remembered her husband, and the memory made her heart ache.

With God's grace, she had enough family support and financial security to survive the horrendous days that followed. The Dheers were wealthy. Anila had inherited a hefty sum from her grandfather. Since Arjun had spurned his share by not marrying an Indian girl as was deemed in their grandfather's will, Anila was given the entire estate.

A few months later, Arjun called her from Los Angeles. "Anila, your family is here. I've talked to Papa and Ma and Vikas's parents. We want you to move to America."

She had agreed. Every place in India reminded her of Vikas and sent her into despondence. Sunny deserved a happier life, a happier circumstance. She moved into Arjun's mansion in Wellington Estates. Her parents helped raise Sunny, and Arjun soon moved out. He and Lily had bought a condo closer to her hospital, but they were an integral part of Sunny's extended family.

Her little boy was three years old now, a favorite of his Uncle Arjun, who had delayed his wedding until Anila demanded to know why.

"I don't want my only sister grieving at the wedding," he'd said.

Anila had placed her hands on his shoulders. "Arjun, I'll grieve all my life. I loved Vikas, and I don't think I'll ever love again."

"You'll find someone, someday."

Anila shook her head. "I have no interest in finding someone. Vikas left the most precious gift to me, and I'll devote my life to taking care of Sunny. Arjun, you don't need to halt your life just because I'm not perfectly happy right now. So get married already. Sunny needs a cousin."

Arjun had grinned. "I'll call Lily. And by the way, Sunny will be the ring-bearer."

The next few weeks raced by with preparations for the wedding, and Anila found moments in the day when she didn't think about her husband, as if the sun had momentarily broken through thunderclouds, flashing an ephemeral hope that light still hid behind the darkness.

3

THE WEDDING was the first joyous occasion for the family since Vikas's death. Looking at Arjun and Lily now, ready to exchange vows they meant to keep, Anila passed on a prayer to God, *Please let them be happy. Let them know love.*

Her eyes went to the back of the garden where her son would appear momentarily. Her gaze stopped on a handsome face. He was sitting among strangers, in the rows reserved for Lily's colleagues from the hospital. She'd never seen him before, and as his eyes locked with hers, her heart lurched.

Her son alighted, utterly adorable in his new suit, grinning and striding down the aisle, clutching the ring. And then he dropped the ring.

A collective gasp rang through the crowd, and Anila grasped at her chest. People sprang up from their seats and searched for the ring, which had landed underneath her friend Poorvi's mother.

The handsome stranger with whom she'd locked gazes before picked it up and handed it to her son.

The rest of the ceremony went without a hitch, as Arjun and Lily exchanged their vows.

"I promise to honor and cherish you every day of my life, through sickness and in health, till death do us part."

Death had parted Anila and Vikas prematurely. She hoped Vikas's unused years could be given to Arjun and Lily who would have a long and happy married life.

She gripped Sunny's hand. A buzz at her waist broke her reverie. She pulled out her phone from the convenient pocket Juhi had fashioned into the dress. "Men's tux's have pockets," Juhi had said. "Women need their phones and lipsticks too."

Anila pulled out her phone and saw a text. *"You look beautiful."*

She felt beautiful. Her lips widened into a smile until she realized the number was unknown to her. Who sent it? Couldn't be Arjun, who was busy getting married. Or Harrison, her friend and confidant, who was now sitting in the front row with his wife, Laura.

She glanced into the crowd with a frown and clashed gazes with the handsome stranger. How had he obtained her number?

As Anila and the bridesmaids followed the happy couple back down the aisle, her gaze met the stranger's once more. He was staring at her with caramel eyes. His hair was parted a little off center, with faint brown highlights that looked natural. While everyone was staring at the newlyweds, this stranger was staring at Anila. A surge of warmth and embarrassment washed over her.

He towered over the crowd, his eyes locked with hers, looking splendid in a dark suit and a paisley-patterned Indian silk tie. Anila stumbled and straightened up quickly, clasping her son's hand. The handsome stranger smirked.

The fact that he sent her the text was creepy, but the content sure was flattering. She'd try to figure out who he was later at the banquet. Would he confess that he sent the text?

Amid cheers and rice confetti and applause, they passed through the crowd and entered the banquet hall.

Arjun and Lily went off to take photographs in the vineyard and golf course while the rest of the crowd started enjoying drinks and refreshments, an eclectic mix of chicken tikka, mushroom turnovers, mini quiche, and cocktail samosas.

Anila dropped Sunny off with her mother, Alka Dheer, who was resting in the shade of the late blooming bougainvillea growing on a decorative trellis. Sunny settled in his grandmother's lap as a cool breeze blew in from the west. Alka stroked Sunny's hair back, and his eyes began to droop. Anila brought her mother a cup of hot tea and returned to the hall where the reception was ongoing, and where guests waited until the new couple would make their grand entrance.

Anila remembered her own wedding, when she'd dressed up in a brocade maroon sari, decked in gold and *kundan* jewelry from head to toe. These days, besides a necklace with a little heart pendant Vikas had given her on their second anniversary, she didn't wear much jewelry.

She missed him so much. She clutched the pendant and leaned against the wall, staring at the beautifully decked hall: peonies and white lilies in large planters dotted along the edge, pillars draped with tiny white and pink lights, perfectly representing her petite friend, and now sister-in-law, Lily.

When Arjun had bought the winery, their father had been against it. But now that they had put in so much work into modernizing it while preserving its rustic appearance, renovated and expanded it to accommodate a small wedding party like this one, her father had grudgingly agreed that Arjun had what it took.

Anila and their family friend Poorvi had helped make the dream come true. Arjun had begged Poorvi, who had trained as an event planner, to take the job as the manager of the Winery Chateau. With Poorvi's help, Anila had spent countless hours at the vineyard, trying to dispel the gloom in her heart.

The tall stranger from earlier approached her. His presence made her heart flutter in her chest as she told herself, *I have no interest in men*. She didn't want any distractions to take her attention away from her son. Relationships inevitably led to heartbreak, and she'd sworn to remain single for the rest of her life. No, she was not interested.

But she had to find out how he knew her phone number. And why he'd thought it would be acceptable to text her an inappropriate, albeit complimentary message. God, she'd turned into such a prude.

He stood beside her emanating a whiff of musky aftershave. In a deep, gravelly, *masculine* voice, he said, "Lovely."

So he did send her the text. She cleared her throat. "Excuse me?"

He waved his hand around the hall. "The ceremony, the decor. It's lovely."

"Yes, thanks. It's a beautiful place." She waited for him to tell her about the text.

"I'm Avinash Singhania, by the way." He extended his hand, and she shook it, the warmth of his strong grip seeping into hers, a spark thrumming through her fingers at his touch. She jerked her hand away. What was wrong with her?

Her voice refused to cooperate. But she croaked out, "Hello."

His lips curled into a smile. "Are you going to make me beg?"

"I beg your pardon?"

He grinned, showing a barely-there dimple and lovely little creases around his eyes. Mirth lines. This man laughed a lot. "I introduced myself to you, and you didn't return the favor."

She flushed. She was a savvy businesswoman with a ten-million-dollar business which she'd kept secret from everyone. How had he managed to make her so tongue-tied? Besides, if he had sent her that text, he knew her number, he knew who she was. *Well, two can play the game.* "Anila."

"Nice to make your acquaintance."

"Likewise." She coughed. What the heck was wrong with her?

"Wine?"

Before she could answer, he waved down a passing waiter and picked up two glasses of red wine. "Red okay?" he asked.

"Um… uh-huh. Yeah." So much for the grace and etiquette classes her parents had squandered money on.

He made it a point to touch her hand as he handed her the glass, making her squirm. He was the Devil incarnate!

Her company had come into existence to deal with situations like these, to avoid circumstances in which single women were hit upon by single men at fancy parties. The idea had come to her when the Dheers were invited to events and she had to attend alone. Strange men, like this one in front of her, would approach her and she had to find a way to shoo them off without being rude. She remembered one guy, the owner of a chain of hardware stores, who took an unusual interest in her. She literally had to tell him she had no intention of going out with anyone, ever. Her son was her life. Thankfully, the man had backed off. If only she'd had a date, the hardware store owner wouldn't have tried to get fresh with her.

As Sunny grew up, Anila spent days alone at home and set up the website, *Business Casual.* To find a decent, undemanding date for social occasions like these. She'd never dared to use it herself. Her parents wanted her to get remarried, but they would balk at the idea of no-strings-attached dating just for appearances. Her father knew all about making wine, and was either suspicious or ignorant of other ways to make a living. He would probably tell her all the ways she would fail in her business venture; he was an excessively cautious man. He'd warned Arjun he'd fail at the bed and breakfast venture, but Arjun had made it successful. If all went well with Winery Chateau, maybe one day she'd tell her family about her business. The truth was, she was embarrassed about the whole thing. A widow averse to dating, running a fake-dating site. How ironic was that?

Still, it had been successful so far. Indeed, had she found a date from her website, it would have helped to stave off Avinash Singhania's hot, luscious eyes rimmed by eyelashes a girl would kill for. Those delicious lips above a square jaw. She dropped her gaze and spilled some wine on her dress.

Avinash grabbed a napkin and reached out to her bosom before realizing it was inappropriate. He handed it to her and turned pink. She smirked. Their chemistry embarrassed him too.

He took a sip of the wine and said, "Ah. I taste a hint of Sangiovese."

She regarded him over the edge of her glass. "You know your wines!"

"Indeed. It parallels the delicate, fruity flavors of Tuscan wines."

She tilted her head. He was right. This particular wine was not made here on site. It was from an Italian vineyard Arjun had acquired last year. Was this guy a wine enthusiast or a vineyard owner competing with the Dheers? A spy of sorts?

She found her voice at last. "How do you know the couple?"

He lifted his glass toward the garden where the wedding had taken place. "The bride was my client once."

"Lily was your client? What do you do?"

"I'm a lawyer."

Anila rolled her eyes. She detested lawyers, with the legalese in their language, and the poring over pages upon pages of documents. Everything was a contract for them. A *business deal.* Written, signed, and notarized.

He smiled a rueful smile. "You don't like lawyers." It was more a statement than a question, tinged with regret.

She squinted her eyes and said, "Why does it matter?"

He shrugged. "It doesn't. Um… sorry, I gotta go. Um… nice to meet you."

He turned around abruptly and walked away, leaving her empty and angry and frustrated. Anila cursed herself for being rude to her sister-in-law's guest. She took a few quick steps after him and said, "Hey, Mister…"

He turned around, a slow smile spreading across his face, mirth brimming in his eyes. "Yes, Anila? And it's Avinash."

Color rose to her cheeks. "Look, *Avinash,* I'm sorry. I didn't mean to be rude. After all, I'm the host."

"Oh you are, are you? I thought you were the bride's friend. And how are you related to the family?"

So he didn't know her. "I *am* the bride's friend. But I'm also Arjun's sister." A small frown furrowed her brow. If he didn't know who she was, who'd sent her the text?

Meanwhile, Avinash was looking at her with those warm, inviting eyes. "Ah. The owner of this winery, yes? Do you help him run the business?"

His assumption that she must be associated with a man for work annoyed her. But he was right. She did help Arjun and Poorvi with the winery. Arjun was the overall boss, and Poorvi managed the Chateau. Anila had helped with the interior design and all the furnishings, and helped them with bookings whenever she could. In fact, she had set up the website for the winery and chateau. Customers could book up to three rooms through the site, but for larger groups, they had to call in. Since no one knew about her secret business venture, she decided not to mention it.

She coughed. "Yes, I do. I'm sort-of the assistant manager of the Chateau."

He tilted his head. "Then you're the right person. I wanted to rent this place for my company holiday retreat. For a whole weekend in December. We'd need fifteen rooms."

Anila tried to suppress the whoop of joy. While the chateau was usually booked out during the summer, this was their first winter after the construction of the additional rooms. They served breakfast and dinner with free wine-tasting and golf lessons thrown in. Guests loved it, and several had already booked summer weekends for years to come.

"I can help you with that." She opened her clutch and pulled out a card. "Here. Call me to set it up. Or you can talk to Poorvi, the official manager."

He took the card. "I'd rather talk to you."

She blushed and nodded. "Sure. Okay. Whatever."

He splayed his hands. "Only since I've already met you. It will be easy to go over the contract and such."

Ugh. Lawyers. She quirked an eyebrow and raised her voice in a mocking way. "You mean to cross the i's and dot the t's."

He smirked. "I mean cross the t's and dot the i's, but yes, basically that. So I'll call you?"

She felt color rise to her cheeks. Ugh! He must think she was inept even though she was a successful businesswoman. Not that she could tell anyone about it. "Sure."

She would save Poorvi the trouble of dealing with this flirtatious hunk of muscle, whose physique was clearly evident through his well-fitting suit, his broad shoulders, and strong back begging to be noticed.

He grinned and glanced at her card. The smile slowly disappeared. "Anila Mallik. I thought your family name is Dheer."

"Yeah. I took my husband's name."

"Oh! You're married?" Disappointment washed over his face, and Anila felt a glow of power over him.

She raised her eyebrows. "Why? Is that a problem?"

His face turned crimson. "No, no. Of course not. I… I mean, I didn't see a ring." His eyes went to her ring-free hand and she covered it with the other. He glanced at the heart-shaped locket at her neckline and said, "Your husband gave you that?"

She nodded. Sunny chose that moment to leave his grandma's lap and seek his mother. He ran toward them and clutched her legs, making her splash her wine once again.

Sunny said, "Mommy, I'm tired."

Avinash turned a darker shade of red. "Oh, and the ring-bearer is your son!"

She chuckled. "Is *that* a problem?"

"No, of course not. Not at all. No problem."

She said, "Sunny, say hello to Avinash Uncle." Anila had never gotten used to the American way of prefixing the name with the relationship title. In India, they used the name followed by the relationship. It wasn't Uncle Avinash. It was Avinash Uncle.

Her son stared at the stranger. "You're Ring Uncle."

Avinash gave an embarrassed laugh and pocketed the card. He bowed down and shook Sunny's hand. "Nice to meet you, young man." And then he walked away stiffly.

Anila grinned. Served him right. Making a pass at her like that. It was all the better that she didn't tell him she was a widow. Let him assume her husband was right around the corner.

Watching his retreating back, though, her heart sank a little. His interest in her was enthralling, but her attraction for him scared her more. It was best that he'd walked away.

And he was so annoying with his dotting of the i's and crossing of the t's. Who did he think he was? Didn't she look professional and capable enough to make sure the contract would be fine? Then she stared at her dress. Cleavage exposed in the low cut, clinging maroon bridesmaids' dress, with dark stains from the spilled wine. She sighed. *Whatever!*

If Avinash was serious about booking the chateau, he would show up again, and she would be dressed more appropriately. But perhaps it was best if they spoke on the phone. Distance was what she needed from this powerhouse of a man who made her heart race and her knees melt.

He had good taste; that was for sure. His dark suit and shoes looked Italian made. It was the first time her heart had quickened this way since Vikas.

She bit her lip. It had been three long years. And she had her whole life ahead of her. Were her in-laws and her family right? Should she even allow her mind to consider the possibility of a relationship? But what about Sunny? No one else in this world could love him as much as a real parent would. And he had only one of them. Sunny didn't need a new father. He needed a mother who was solely focused on his wellbeing, his needs.

She hefted her son in her arms and planted kisses on his cheeks, a spark of guilt jolting her back to her reality. "You were absolutely wonderful, Sunny. But now you need your nap."

Her phone buzzed again. Holding Sunny in one arm, she pulled out her phone and saw another text from a different unknown number. *"Who's that man?"*

Her heart hammered in her chest as she scanned the crowd. Avinash was shaking hands with Harrison. If he didn't send the text, who did?

She considered answering the text, then slipped the phone in her pocket. Then she pulled it out again. Her mouth became dry, and she licked her lip. She moved her son on her hip and typed with one hand, *"Who is this?"*

The answer came a few seconds later. *"Don't pretend, Anila. You really don't know? How many other hearts did you break?"*

4

AVINASH TOOK OFF his Rolex and dropped it on the bedside table. A memory from his childhood in India made him smile. He was seven. They were poor. His grandmother was in a panic because she'd lost her ancient wristwatch. Avinash had helped her search every nook and cranny of their tiny low-ceilinged apartment in suburban Mumbai, then called Bombay, where he'd grown up with his grandparents.

After upturning all sofa cushions and pillows and blankets and cupboards, Didima had finally given up. That night at dinner, over *macher-jhol* and *bhaat*, she glanced at her husband and said in her sing-song voice, "I lost my watch today. The leather strap must have broken somewhere in the fish market. I need a new watch."

His grandfather mashed the fish into his rice with his fingers and rolled it into a ball. "It's either the watch or Avi's school tuition."

The word "school" triggered fear in Avinash's heart. He hated his school. He was terrified of it. He had been homeschooled by Didima until a month ago. She'd been scared of the sectarian riots that shook the country when he was born and refused to let him step outside alone. But his grandfather had finally convinced her to let Avinash go to school. A placement test determined that he was ahead of his peers, and was sent to a classroom with nine-year-olds. As the tiny, skinny, scared new kid, he'd been bullied those first few days.

Avinash swallowed a mouthful of rice. "You should get the watch. I don't want to go to school."

Didima turned her glare at him. "You'll go to school if I have to sell my very last breath."

"You're always so dramatic," his grandfather had said. "First, you say you'll never let him go to school. Now you want to sell your last breath."

Didima ignored him. "Avi, why don't you want to go to school?"

Avinash stared at the rice on his plate. His classmates asked about his parents, but Didima had never told him a thing.

One of the girls had mocked him. "You don't know your parents' names?"

When he'd asked his grandmother, she'd said, "One day I'll tell you."

The kids in school claimed Avinash's father had died during the riots when someone stabbed him. Whenever he raised the issue with his grandparents, their stony faces and sullen looks dissuaded him from pursuing it further.

Didima plopped another mound of rice and a piece of *hilsa* fish in his plate. "Eat it. You need to grow up strong."

He glanced at her. "Like my father?"

She frowned. Then she said, "Why don't you want to go to school?"

He looked at his grandmother, trying not to ask the question that was foremost on his mind. "They don't like me."

She cupped his chin, and her voice softened. "They will grow to love you. Who wouldn't?"

Avinash got busy with school and did make friends. They stopped asking him about his parents. His best friend's father ran a community group, *Dosti ke Haath*, or "hands of friendship," and Avinash joined them when he was older, helping cook food for neighborhood families, if someone was sick or hurt, to shop for groceries and essentials.

Years later, after his grandfather died, Didima told him, "If anything happens to me, you must call your mother, Moyna. She lives in America."

That was the first time Didima said anything about her. So his mother's name was Moyna. The only problem was, he'd never met her.

And then Didima was diagnosed with cancer. He was just fourteen years old when he lit her funeral pyre. Dadu had died a few years prior. Following his grandmother's instructions, he called his mother in America. Moyna did come to get him, but when he called her "Ma," she was visibly shocked.

"Please call me 'Auntie'." She told him her husband and daughter didn't know about him.

He took in a sharp breath, the shock of this rejection unbearable. How could a mother abandon her child as a baby, never visit him all this time, and then deny him a place in her heart, in her life? She seemed affectionate, though. Something told him her relationship with his grandparents had been rough.

Avinash was uprooted from everything familiar, and transplanted to one of the richest places on earth, in Beverly Hills, unwanted, unloved. Except by his "Aunt." Moyna's husband was suspicious of him, and their four-year-old daughter Tanya was jealous of him. And as a teenager, he struggled to fit into his environment, which was steeped in secrets and scandals. The drama of his arrival nearly destroyed his new family.

As days passed, he wondered if he was born out of wedlock. Confused, directionless, and rudderless, he tried to make himself invisible and unobtrusive.

Still, as it happens often with untruths, bit by bit, the layers of deception fell off. After a turbulent time with his new guardians and his new little sister, Avinash finally learned the truth.

His family history was one for the movies. His biological mother was his grandparents' daughter, Moyna's cousin. It was his unwed mother who died during the 1992 riots of Bombay. To avoid the scandal, Moyna had "adopted" him, to give a name to her little nephew. She was just eighteen. After a terrible fight with his grandparents, Moyna took off to America for further studies, leaving baby Avinash with them. Didima wanted Moyna to have nothing to do with Avinash, and Moyna had stayed away. Indeed, Moyna had no idea Didima had told him she was his mother.

His visit to Beverly Hills had nearly destroyed his new family and almost broken his aunt's marriage. And now his new "father" was running for Governor of California.

Avinash's arrival was one of the bigger scandals in California politics. Every single thing his Governor Father and First Lady Mother did was splattered across tabloids with innuendo and gossip. Amid much heartache, separation, and tears, things settled down, and Sameer Singhania accepted Avinash as his son, right at the podium as he delivered his victory speech.

Caught up in his new family's political world, Avinash vowed never to have secrets. His life would be an open book. Until he'd opened his heart out to Sierra, who had crushed it in the palm of her hands.

He stared at the scar she'd left on his wrist when they'd argued that last time. That was the reason he wore wrist watches in the age of cell phones, to hide the scar of his ruined relationship. The scar on his heart throbbed each time he thought of what could have been.

He took in a deep breath. Sierra was history. He was better off alone, free to conquer the world, so-to-speak.

He'd bought the Rolex in part because he'd been told the watch never lost time. His eyes moistened at the memory of his grandfather bringing Didima a used watch from the *chor-bajar*, a second-hand market that often sold stolen goods. The watch lost ten minutes every hour.

Didima started coming to school thirty minutes before the last bell rang, just to avoid being late. Kids teased him relentlessly, until his friend Rafik said they could walk home together. He was bigger and stronger than Avinash, and Didima agreed.

She'd have sweet, fluffy, hot *rosgollas* ready for him when he returned from school. He wasn't fond of that dessert made of syrupy cottage-cheese balls, but he loved that she tried. He smiled at the memory.

When he moved, he'd kept in touch with his school friend Rafik, writing letters every week. Rafik graduated from engineering college and came to Los Angeles for his Master's degree. They'd remained friends.

Avinash grabbed a beer from the fridge and called his friend's number. He was surprised when Rafik came on the line; as the CEO of a start-up, Rafik made his own schedule, but was often busy. "Rafik! I'm so glad you picked up."

"Ah! You sound like you're in turmoil. How can I help?"

Avinash smiled at his friend's reassuring voice, a calm tome telling him no problem was unsolvable. He settled on the leather recliner and took a sip of beer. He wondered why he'd really called his friend. Not just for old time's sake. Not to chat about his grandmother.

He sighed deeply, as he realized the thing foremost on his mind. "I met a woman."

"Ah-hah! About time. And where did this meeting take place?"

"At a wedding, believe it or not."

Rafik laughed. "So ask her out on a date."

"I'm meeting her in a couple of weeks."

"Good. Let me know how it goes."

Avinash took another sip and placed the bottle on the side table he'd bought with Sierra from a garage sale in the Bradbury Estates years ago. A photo of him and Sierra in Laguna Beach stared back at him. Sierra was a stunning beauty, and in the background, a couple of guys were visible gawking at her. "It's not that simple. She's married."

After a pause, Rafik said, "Come on, Avinash. You know you can't go there."

"I never saw the husband, though."

"You mean she's divorced?"

"I'm not sure. She didn't seem interested in me, but her body was responding…"

"No means no."

"I know, Rafik," he said, annoyed. "She has a kid too. She seemed to enjoy my discomfort when I found out."

"Was she flirting?"

"No, she wasn't interested."

"But you are?"

Avinash paused for a moment, asking himself that question. Then he turned the photograph upside down as he came to a decision. "She's very attractive. Her personality sizzles." He laughed. "I sound like a school boy! I don't know, though." He ran his fingers through his hair. "She doesn't seem like the kind to date for fun."

"You want to date for fun?"

"All this time, yeah."

"But?"

"I don't know, man. I'm conflicted. She is so starkly different from Sierra that I want to get to know her."

Rafik paused for a moment before answering. "Find out from a friend if she'd still married. If she is, forget all about her. You know better than to get involved with a married woman."

Avinash took a deep breath, knowing Rafik was right, but needing to hear it nonetheless. "How is Zoya?"

"Still sad about the miscarriage. One of these days…" Zoya and Rafik had been married for five years, and for the first two years they didn't want kids because of their busy work lives. When they did decide it was the right time, fate had other plans. And yet, after two in-vitro treatments and two miscarriages, they hadn't given up hope.

"Best of luck." Avinash hung up the phone, wondering how God, or fate, or destiny, or whoever was in power, decided who deserved a child and who didn't.

5

AVINASH LOGGED into the website, *Business Casual*, a word-of-mouth, secretive website, the perfect place he'd stumbled upon two years ago. During one of the parties he'd attended—alone—his colleague had shown up with a dazzling, vivacious woman he hadn't seen before. When he asked, his colleague took him aside and told him about the website. He'd said, "It's perfect for no-strings attached dates for social occasions. My date is a VP at a bank and has no interest in dating. Perfect for me." Women threw themselves at Avinash at such parties each time his photo came up in society magazines, and a casual date with a woman who was not interested in him in any meaningful way seemed like a sensible, feasible, and mutually beneficial idea.

Intrigued, Avinash had done his research. Most of the clients of Business Casual were businessmen and career women who didn't have the time or interest in relationships, and just needed a "date" for formal occasions. Once they chose a "date" they had to be inactive on the site for the duration of the "relationship." If a few dates led to more, that was their prerogative. The idea was to tell the world they were well adjusted professionals in "committed" relationships, although most had no time for a love-life. No drama of *why-didn't-you* or *why-can't-you* or *how could you*. Just fun—and safe—dates with a decent, successful professional, background-checked and vetted by the website, interested only in being seen together and expecting no long term commitment.

For the last couple of years, Avinash was happy with the occasional lady escort the site had found for him. He was a wonderful "boyfriend" and prided himself on treating the ladies well. Not that they expected or wanted anything more. Still, he was seen shopping in Sacks Fifth Avenue with models, at Beverly Hills with actresses, and at holiday parties and banquets with other professional women. It was working out just fine.

Karina hadn't ditched him; she hadn't bungled the dates, but had apparently moved to Spain from where she'd sent him a gift basket with a bottle of port and jars of locally grown olives. Popping an olive into his mouth, Avinash activated his status, seeking someone new for the holiday parties coming up in a few weeks. But each profile he'd view brought memories of a certain dark-haired beauty. *Anila Mallik.*

He logged off from the website, turned off his computer, and locked his office. He bobbed his head at the door of his mother's office, adjoining his. Auntie Lupe was sitting in the overstuffed chair, her feet crossed on Moyna's desk. A dozen cupcakes in a pink and white striped box stood enticing on the side. He smiled. Auntie Lupe always brought them her famous cupcakes. Beside the box stood two coffee cups from *Lupe's Java Mocha.*

Lupe owned a chain of eponymous coffee shops across Los Angeles, a popular Mexican restaurant, and a bakery famous for its cupcakes. The bakery supplied all the snacks at the coffee shops, and Lupe was most proud of her original venture on a busy street in downtown Los Angeles.

Lupe said, "Hey, handsome. Have a cupcake."

He came into the office and stood beside her. "Any new babies in your life?"

She grinned. "Any new woman in yours?"

He grinned at her evergreen question. Besides Rafik, Auntie Lupe had been his biggest support during the divorce; his parents had been on a Mediterranean cruise when Sierra left, breaking Avinash's spirit. If it hadn't been for Auntie Lupe and Rafik, he'd be a basket case.

He picked out a blueberry cupcake. "Oh, you know, same old, same old. How's everything with you?"

She winked and said, "Oh, you know. Same old, same old."

Moyna laughed. "You two! You never change."

He took a bite of the cupcake and grunted in delight. Then he said, "Opening any new *Java Mochas*?"

She smiled. "A dozen more planned across the state, thank you very much. Your mother is helping me with the legal stuff."

He shook his head in admiration. "I don't know how you do it, being so busy with the kids and all." Lupe's husband, Aaron, was an anchor for a local TV station. They didn't have their own children, and over the years, they had adopted six kids. Avinash shuddered at the thought. Lupe's family looked happy enough, but that life, tethered to the house because of so many children, wasn't for him.

He had been dangerously close to it once, but now his mind was made up, and his heart locked away in a safe space.

He'd mentioned it to Sierra once, when Auntie Lupe had adopted her fourth baby. "How can she handle all these kids?"

Sierra had said, "Some people are born to be parents. Others aren't."

He certainly wasn't.

He took a sip of coffee from his mother's cup and nodded his appreciation. "Ain't no coffee like Lupe's coffee. Seriously, though, how do you do it?"

Lupe said, "My hubby makes it possible, and the kids make it worthwhile."

He rolled his eyes at her mantra.

She pointed a finger at him. "Once you have a kid you'll know. Right, Moyna?"

"You're right," said his mother, a smile that held pleasure and sorrow in equal measure. She straightened a photo of Avinash, Tanya, and young Sonia taken years ago in Disneyland.

Avinash's stomach knotted. When Moyna got pregnant with her second child, Avinash was sixteen years old and struggling to fit in. Still, when the baby came, and his sister Tanya took to the new member of the family, he started to enjoy the company of his new sister, Sonia. She was an adorable baby, never fussy, never annoying, and as she grew up, Avinash became like a third parent to her, often accompanying her to her piano lessons, and preening himself for her recitals like a proud parent would.

During the summer after his first year in law school, he'd been interning at the family law firm. He shared an office space with another intern, right down the hall from Moyna's office. Large glass doors allowed them to see who was visiting, and enabled the partners to keep an eye on the interns. It was usually businessmen dressed in fancy suits that went to his mother's office, since she handled corporate law.

That day he'd glanced up through the glass doors to see two cops walking down the hall. One was a pot-bellied middle-aged policeman, the other, a petite, younger policewoman. Avinash was curious.

He watched them enter his mother's office. He heard the scraping of a chair. And an anguished scream.

Avinash rushed to his mother's office, where the cops stood, squirming. His mother was visibly upset. He said, "What happened?"

She glanced at him and crumpled like a piece of paper, sobbing into her hands. "It's Sonia."

"What?" Avinash turned to face the cops. "Tell me. I'm Sonia's brother."

The policewoman said, "My name is Officer Maria Garcia. I'm sorry to be the bearer of such news, but your sister was in an accident."

His knees began to give way, and he held the edge of the table for support. "A… and?"

She cleared her throat. "Um, your nanny was walking her back from school. A teenaged driver made a fast turn and went over the curb. He hit Sonia."

"Is she okay? Where is she? Which hospital?"

Officer Garcia shook her head. "I'm sorry."

"No!" he shouted, ire raging through his body like he'd never experienced before. "No! It can't be. You're wrong. She's barely eight years old."

The cops remained silent. Somehow, he managed, "Where is she?"

Avinash drove Moyna to the coroner's office. Inside the white hall, with polished tiled floors where the coroner rendered verdicts of how someone had died, they walked down the silent corridor, their footsteps echoing hollow. Someone pushed open a metal double door, and they turned into another corridor. Harsh fluorescent lights lit the hallway and reflected off the square-tiled floor. For some reason he still remembered those tiles. Six-inch, square, white, reflecting the lights above. They lined the walls up to a height of four feet. Around how tall Sonia was. Another door. And behind that door was a small room with a gurney on which a small body lay under a white sheet.

It couldn't be Sonia. It couldn't be. They had to have made a mistake.

He crept toward the gurney, Moyna a step behind him, as if she was unable to handle what was to come. Officer Garcia lifted the cover gently to expose the child's face. The same forehead as Avinash's. The same nose as Tanya's. The same curved lips of Moyna, the same split chin of Sameer Singhania. Strands of wispy dark hair strayed out of two pigtails. The pale, ashen, grayed face, devoid of color and life.

He felt Moyna's knees melt as he struggled to stay upright. He had to stay strong for her. He held her to prevent her from falling on the shiny white floor, her shoulders shaking, her body bent over, her throat croaking out silent sobs. He swallowed hard. He looked up at the policewoman and nodded.

She covered the beautiful face of his sister, who would never see another day, never celebrate another birthday, never graduate from school or play the piano again, and never grow taller than four feet.

He knew that day, that despite all the pleasures a parent got from the birth of a child, the pain of loss was always worse. There was no weight heavier for a parent than the limp body of a child, no agony worse than her death. Having a child was just too much pain. Being a parent was just too much of a burden.

After a private funeral ceremony, they cremated his little sister. The urn was so tiny it made his heart clench. They took the yacht out onto the Pacific that day. His parents were unable to function, holding each other for comfort and strength. It was up to Avinash to scatter Sonia's ashes into the water.

He stood portside as cool breeze whipped up his hair, the deep blue water beneath him hiding secrets in its unknown depths, the sound of the waves lapping against the boat as the captain turned off the engine. Avinash stood there, leaning on the railing, the tiny urn in his hand, unable to let go. Clouds swirled above him, and a lone seagull called.

Finally, he opened the lid and saw the granular gray dust in the dark depths of the urn. He bit his lip and shook off the ashes into the water, and they disappeared into the expanse, absorbed by the ocean as its own. Ashes to ashes, dust to dust. Some gray powder blew back from the breeze, and he watched it make patterns on the back of his hand.

Avinash had held it in until now, but this was Sonia, telling him she wasn't ready to let go, wasn't ready to leave just yet. His heart clamped into itself, as hot tears stung his eyes and his breath caught in his throat. He had to let her go. His body shook as he dusted the last mortal remains of his baby sister into the water.

Goodbye, Sonia. I'll love you forever.

Later on, when one of Lupe's multiple kids had their piano recital, he attended it with a heavy heart, a lump forming in his throat as he imagined the lovely sister he should have had, sitting in a pretty dress on the little red bench, playing Mozart.

The loss had left a deep void within him. Someone had once told him a parent can only be as happy as their least happy child. What if the child wasn't alive anymore? Was it possible to ever be happy again?

Moyna had never fully recovered from the loss of her little girl. But she still had Tanya. And she had him.

Avinash dropped the cupcake wrapper into the wastebasket and placed a hand on Moyna's shoulder. He straightened the photograph of the three siblings. More to distract her than anything, he turned to Lupe and said, "So, how's Aaron?"

Auntie Lupe grinned. "He's fine. But don't change the topic. It's time you settled down, young man."

Moyna squeezed Avinash's hand acknowledging his concern, accepting his love. Then she smiled at Lupe. "Oh, it's wasted effort, Lupe. He does what he wants. We're tired of telling him. It seems Tanya will settle down before him."

Tanya was a vivacious, brilliant seventeen-year-old, who had already graduated with her Bachelor's degree, and working towards her PhD. She wanted to be a doctor, but she was too young to start just yet. Hence the PhD.

He grinned. "I pity the guy who dates Tanya. She'll have him in knots, or the double helix!"

They laughed, because Tanya's wit and love of science could put anyone to shame.

He nodded at the box of cupcakes. "That was fantastic, Auntie Lupe. And Ma, I'm off to check out the B and B for the retreat."

Moyna's forehead creased. "The one Temecula? Drive safely, Avi. You always drive too fast."

Lupe said, "Let him be young, Moyna. Remember when we were in college?"

Moyna raised an eyebrow. "We had a crappy old car that barely went up to fifty miles an hour."

Lupe laughed. "But we took chances. Remember our trip to my farm? I let you drive the car even though you didn't have a license yet!"

Moyna grinned. "Shh!"

Avinash said, "Ah! A new story I must hear about later. If I'm going to avoid traffic, I better be off now."

Lupe said, "Oh, you look happy. Seeing someone interesting?"

He winked. As the elevator sang its familiar, dull, monotonous tune going down to the basement parking garage, he hummed along.

6

AVINASH WAS IN great spirits during the long drive to Temecula: the air was crisp, the sky a brilliant blue, and the freeway not too crowded for a workday. But mostly, he was excited at the prospect of seeing Anila again.

But Rafik's warning pricked his mind. He needed to know if Anila had a husband in the picture. If she did, Avinash would walk away like a dieter passing by the window of his favorite bakery. Stealing a glance away from the road, he quickly scrolled the contacts on his phone and clicked on Lily Leoni's number.

She answered in two rings. "Avinash Singhania, to what do I owe this pleasure?" After a pause, she said, "You know I'm so excited for the cruise you bought for me and Arjun. But you'll have to wait for the thank you cards."

He coughed and said, "Hey, no, it's not that. So um… I wanted to ask about your friend Anila. I know she has a kid. But I didn't see a husband at the wedding."

Lily gave a long sigh. "Ah. I saw you two talking at the reception. It's a tragedy, what happened to her husband." She told him he was an Indian Air Force pilot, and he'd died in an air crash before Sunny was born.

Avinash gripped the wheel, unable to fathom the extent of Anila's grief. He'd sensed a flash of pain in her eyes when she watched the married couple enter the banquet hall, but maybe it was his overactive imagination.

He heard someone paging Dr. Lily Leoni over the phone. She said, "Hey, I have to go. But tell me, are you into her?"

Avinash said, "Yeah, no. I was just curious."

Lily said, "Ask her out, Avinash. She's lonely. She's a lovely person. She deserves better than what fate has given her."

After his disastrous marriage, he didn't believe in fate, or destiny, or kismet, or karma. He and Sierra were supposedly destined to be together, but Sierra was off somewhere in New York, performing on stage in some Broadway show. "I don't believe in fate. I make my own."

"So make hers as well. She's worth the trouble."

He laughed. The idea of seeing Anila, now known to be available, sparked excitement in his heart. He'd never dated anyone who'd ever been married before. But Anila's dark eyes were hypnotic, their magnetic draw pulling him in like the string of the kites he used to fly as a child in India.

"She's definitely worth it, but is she interested?"

"You can't know unless you ask. I gotta go, Avinash. Call her!" Lily hung up.

Avinash rolled down the window and drove for an hour along the highway, his mind on her dress at the wedding, the crisscrossed plunging neckline revealing just a hint of cleavage, the delicate curve of her waist, and her full hips. He gripped the wheel until his knuckles turned white. The coastline whizzed past him, the sapphire ocean to the west blurred with the sky over the horizon as seagulls squawked overhead.

Then he saw the massive billboard advertising the new musical starring Sierra Smith and some guy. She hadn't aged one bit. So she wasn't in New York; she was in town. But she hadn't called, and that was just fine by him.

When he reached the Winery Chateau, the receptionist told him Anila was on a conference call and would see him shortly. Already annoyed from Sierra's stupid advertisement, Avinash frowned and glanced at his watch. He was a few minutes late for his appointment, and Anila wasn't even ready. Still, he nodded and took a seat in the visitor's area.

The receptionist was a lovely, voluptuous woman with elaborately coifed hair, bright red lipstick, and heavy mascara. "Would you like some water?" she asked. "Tea? Coffee?"

Time to put on his magic persona. He gave her a sly grin. "A glass of wine would be nice."

Flustered, she said, "Oh… um…"

"I'm kidding," he said with a wave. "Given this is a Winery Chateau."

She giggled, a high pitched, tittering laugh, returned to her seat, and ran her tongue along her lower lip.

He had that effect on women. Sometimes he flirted with them just to check if he still had the mojo. It was on today, it seemed. He wondered if Anila would be susceptible.

The office door opened, and Anila stepped out, looking gorgeous in a black pin stripe pant-suit, with a long-collared white shirt, the top button open, the heart-shaped pendant dangling where his eyes shouldn't wander, red toe-nails peeking through black open-toe shoes. Hell, even her toes were sexy.

Anila walked up to him, and he stood up. "I am sorry to keep you waiting, Mr. Singhania. I trust Peggy took care of you." Her voice was seductive as hell.

"She sure did." He turned to Peggy and winked.

Peggy giggled, batted her eyelashes, and returned to her computer.

Anila grew rigid and extended her hand, which he took, a thrill running up his arm. Avinash cleared his throat and said, "Thanks for seeing me at such short notice."

"We aim to please," she said with a smile that didn't reach her eyes. Those eyes! Smoldering hot coals. And that voice of shimmering, liquid silk. "Please come in."

Sunlight streamed in through large bay windows. The light was magic to her skin, which seemed to glow from within. The desk was polished wood, and the furniture black leather and dark wood. Luxurious, classy. The kind he liked. On the side was a leather couch, a light jacket strewn over it. Her jacket. He wanted to touch the fabric. He took in a deep breath and clenched his fist. He was here on business.

"Please have a seat." She settled in her chair and faced him, leaning forward. Avinash sat across from her and watched her movements. She clasped her hands in front of her, then held the edge of the table, leaned back and crossed her legs, hitting her knee on the table. She didn't wince. Her eyes spoke volumes about her confusion at his request and the mutual attraction she tried to deny. "So, do we have a specific weekend in mind?"

He told her, and she glanced at the computer screen, typed something, and frowned ever so slightly. If he hadn't been staring like a love-struck teenager he'd have missed it. She tucked a strand of dark hair behind her ear, exposing a delicate teardrop pearl earring, which dangled, its tiny shadow dancing on her neck, camouflaging her racing pulse. "We can probably work something out. Four rooms are booked for a bachelorette party, but they were tentative dates. I'll confirm with the party and get back to you."

Avinash watched her as she bit her lip. Then she said, "If you're flexible, we can do the weekend after. But I won't be here. It will be Poorvi."

He could have easily changed the weekend, but he wanted to see Anila again, and again, and again. He shook his head. "I'm afraid it has to be that weekend. And I'd really rather prefer that you're there for the event. Just to make sure everything runs smoothly, since I already know you and we have a rapport."

She didn't answer.

He said, "We do have a rapport, don't we?"

Color rose to her cheeks, and she nodded.

He pumped his fist mentally. "*Yes!*"

He hid a smile. "Please see if we can arrange all the rooms, and get back to me."

She nodded, subjecting him to the full power of those eyes. They seemed to cover almost a quarter of her face. He stared at their depths, in awe of those lush eyelashes that needed no mascara. She had a bit of makeup on, but was blushing underneath it, as evidenced by the color of her neck and the little snatch of skin he could see above her collar.

He enjoyed this part of a dalliance, watching his effect on the woman of interest. Then he controlled himself. She was a widow. And a mother. And although he was interested, at least perfunctorily, he didn't know if she reciprocated. And then a thought struck him. What if he led her on and she reciprocated and he realized he wasn't ready to jump into the complications she presented? He pushed his chair back and got up.

She followed suit.

He said, "If you can confirm in a week or so, we can sign the contract and go from there."

Another tiny frown, then a forced smile. "Of course."

Avinash hummed all the way back to Los Angeles, feeling like a teenager whose "promposal" has been accepted by the hot girl in school. He chided himself; that was not how a guy unsure of his emotions behaved. Did he truly, definitely want her? He hardly knew her. Wind whipped past him on the highway as the answer came to him. He wasn't sure. But a crack had formed in his beliefs about true love and soul mates. Just because his marriage hadn't worked out, it didn't mean it was impossible. He thought of Rafik and Zoya, his Auntie Lupe and Uncle Aaron, and even his parents.

Anila Mallik had cast a spell on him. She and Sierra shared some qualities but differed in others. Anila was equally stunning, equally driven, but there was a look of honesty in her eyes, a tone of authenticity in her voice, and for some reason, her utter devotion to her son made her irresistible to him. He was drawn to her like bees to the lavender bush in the planter on his balcony, a gift from Karina that he watered religiously. While Sierra had been like a shallow pond, Anila was a deep, unknown sea of mystery, of intrigue.

Driving back to Los Angeles, he called his friend Rafik again, who picked up after a few rings.

Rafik said, "I was going to call you. Come over for dinner on Eid."

"I didn't know you had to invite me. I always show up for your biryani and Zoya's *seviyan*."

He laughed. "Zoya would kill me if I didn't make sure you're not off on some party or other. So you're free next Sunday, right?"

"Yeah. It's penciled in my calendar."

"Now, what did *you* want to talk about?"

He passed a truck with a sticker that said "Make Your Own Fate." Avinash smiled and said, "Rafik, I think she likes me."

"Ah. The woman from the wedding. And the husband?"

Avinash honked at a slow driver and passed him from the right. "She is a widow. I mean, it's sad, but it happened three years ago."

"Three years is a long time."

"It is, isn't it? But she is so reserved."

"You're a charmer, Avi. If you can't get her out of her shell, I don't know anyone who can."

Avinash chuckled, hoping his friend was right. But how could Anila be ready for such a major change when she still wore the goddamn pendant her husband had given her? Sierra had sold off the diamond earrings he'd got her two days after breaking up with him.

Rafik said, "But before you go any further, you must realize that she may not be into casual relationships. So unless you're sure about your feelings, don't pursue her."

"Yeah. You're right."

"She's lost her husband and may not be ready for someone else."

"Yeah, yeah, I know."

Rafik persisted, "Avi, you must ask yourself, what do you really, truly want?"

Avinash sighed and hung up. Anila had lost her husband, and he had lost his wife. Both death and divorce separated two people, both were cruel, both left an indelible mark on the heart. But there was a vast difference. Divorce was by choice.

Death, although irreversible, left an unbreakable connection to the lost love, a hook of sorts that tugged and pulled forever. After a divorce, a new relationship would likely be with someone who was a polar opposite of the ex. How did separation by death differ? If Anila was ever ready, would she seek someone similar to her husband, who reminded her of her lost love? Avinash could never be like the military man. He was a free spirit. Besides, he didn't want to pretend to be someone else.

But he was getting ahead of himself.

What do you really, truly want? Easy, casual relationships had worked out well for him, but did he want to grow old coming home to an empty penthouse every night, watching TV, drinking beer, eating out of take-out boxes, and falling asleep on the couch? Why did his heart lurch every time he saw a home in the suburbs with a nice yard and white roses growing on a picket fence, a tricycle in the porch, a swing on a tree branch, a minivan in the driveway? He had lost that chance once, and perhaps he was afraid it would not happen for him, so he refused to try.

But Anila made him want it all. She had made a home in his heart, burrowed herself deep in the recesses of his brain, such that everything he saw reminded him of her.

His methodical lawyer mind told him he had to introspect whether he was so drawn to Anila that he wanted to explore the possibility of a long term relationship with her. But he also knew how to take things one at a time. First, he decided, he would try and get to know her. If she was truly someone he wanted in his life, he would take step two, and decide whether the package she came with, her previous marriage, her child, was something he could handle. And third, if he really, truly wanted her, he would figure out a way to make her want him back.

But one thing he was sure of: he wanted, *needed* to see her again.

7

ANILA LIFTED SUNNY out of his car seat, picked up his backpack, and closed the door. Holding him by his hand, she entered the preschool. As usual, his best friends, Megha and Trevor, were on the swings.

"Sunny!" yelled Megha in her high-pitched voice. "Come here!"

The kids' fathers, Connor and Harrison, were chatting as Connor pushed Megha higher and higher. Anila's heart caught in her throat at a distant memory.

Vikas and Anila had met in a park after they had been introduced by their parents. He wanted to make sure she was happy with the marriage proposal. "Life as an Air Force officer's wife isn't easy."

She had smiled, taken by his honesty and his considerate, chivalrous attitude. "Whoever said life is easy lied."

They walked on the rubber jogging-track along the perimeter of the park, under the dazzling orange and yellow blossoms of *gulmohar* trees that rimmed the edge as hordes of kids played cricket in the center.

He said, "Still, you're marrying into the Mallik family as well as into the Air Force. My unit is like a second family to me."

She turned to stare at his earnest eyes, the wide forehead, the strong jawline, dreaming that one day, she would have children that looked like him. "I like large families."

"You're sure?"

She'd smiled. "Are you trying to dissuade me? Is there someone else?"

He said, "Hell no! I fell in love with you the moment I saw you. I just want to be sure you're one hundred percent on board."

And in that moment, she was. "I am."

Since then, the park became their favorite place to visit, a place Vikas called the Proposal Park. Late in the evenings after kids had left the park and the sun began to set, Vikas would push her higher and higher on the swing, waiting for her to protest. But she loved it all, the breeze rifling through her hair, the creak of the chain straining against the swing bar, the sound of Vikas's voice telling her about everything under the sun, the sight of the orange-yellow flowers of the *gulmohar*, the birds tweeting in their heights, clouds skimming across the sky above.

Sunny tugged at her hand, tugged her back to the present. "Mommy, where's *my* daddy?"

Anila swallowed hard. For a moment she wondered if her thoughts were so transparent that Sunny could read them. They she saw him looking wistfully at Megha, being pushed by her father on the swing. No matter how many times and how hard Anila pushed Sunny on the swing, she could never take the place of a father. She knew this topic would keep coming back. "You know where he is, honey."

He pointed to the wide blue sky with wisps of white clouds, a kite scanning the earth from high above. A jet flew overhead, leaving a white streak in its wake. "Up there?"

She croaked out, "Yes. He's in heaven now."

"He cannot come back from heaven?" He shook his head as he said it, as if confirming what he already knew to be true.

"No, honey. No one can."

"Why can't I have a *new* daddy?"

Anila crouched low and took his face in her hands. "It doesn't work that way, okay?"

He stuck out his lower lip in defiance. "Why not? Julie got a new daddy. He brought donuts for our class yesterday."

A few months ago, Sunny's classmate Julie had a birthday party, where Anila met a man flipping burgers on an outdoor grill. She had embarrassed herself by assuming he was Julie's father. He'd winked and grinned. "One day soon." It turned out that Julie's mother was divorced. She had been dating the new man in her life for the past year.

So they'd already got married. And he'd bought donuts for the kids in Julie's class.

Anila sighed and got up. "We'll talk about it later, okay? But right now, you've got me, and Uncle Arjun and Auntie Lily and Nanima and Nanaji."

Sunny's voice was wistful. "Julie said she's getting a baby sister."

A sob formed in her throat. Vikas and Anila had talked about having a family. As an only child, he was envious of the close and friendly relationship Anila shared with her brother. He'd said, "I missed growing up with siblings. I've always wanted a large family. If you're okay with it, I want three kids, even four!"

She'd wacked him on his arm. "I'll be so fat, you'll leave me."

Her husband had turned to her and taken her face in his hands. "I love you so much, Anila, it hurts. I will never leave you."

But he *had* left her, and Anila wondered if it was ever possible to be loved like that again.

They approached the swings, and Sunny ran off to play with his friends.

Anila's phone buzzed. Again, a text from an unknown number, which was different from the one at the wedding. *"Blue is your color."* She had blocked that number, but like spam callers, someone was using fake numbers to harass her.

She swallowed hard. She was wearing a royal blue fitted top over black dress pants. Was this person watching her? She scanned the area for any suspicious person, but there were a dozen cars in the parking lot, and she couldn't peer into each. With a shiver in her back, she straightened up and walked ahead.

She considered telling Harrison about the strange texts, but there had been no threats so far. As a detective, he would have little to act upon. As her friend, Harrison would get overly concerned and make a big deal of something that she could handle. Ignoring the texts was her best option.

She put her phone in bag just as another text came. *"Anila, you deserve a life apart from your son."*

Her heart hammered in her chest. Whoever the texter was, he was following her, watching her. He knew what she was wearing, what she was doing.

Up ahead, Megha's father, Connor Riley, turned to face Anila. "Hey, I'm glad I ran into you. You know about my exhibition, right?"

As a world famous photographer who exhibited his award-winning pictures all over the globe, Connor traveled a lot. He often accompanied his wife Juhi for her fashion shows. Anila watched young Megha when her parents were traveling, and the families had gotten close. Still, she had been hoping not to be invited, because these functions were always attended by couples and she felt left out.

Still, with the strange texter somewhere out there, she was relieved to linger at the preschool for a bit and gather her nerves. "I'm not sure. I'll have to check my calendar." If only she dared to use her own website to find a suitable escort.

Connor tilted his head. "It's weeks away. Please pencil in the date. Juhi and Danielle will kill me if I didn't invite you personally. You'll know so many people there. It will be a blast."

Harrison chimed in. "The venue is spectacular. The rooftop of the Swanson building downtown."

She raised her eyebrows. "Wow. That's the one with fifty floors, right?"

Harrison grinned. "Fifty-five floors. And I'll be there too. In fact, the kids will visit for a short while with Megha's nanny, and she can watch all of them. Come on. Say yes."

She made an awkward gesture and nodded. "I'll try." If Harrison left the school and walked to the parking lot with her, she'd tell him about the texts.

After kissing her son—who scrubbed off his cheeks in defiance—she waved to Connor and Harrison. They were still chatting, and Anila took it as a sign not to tell Harrison just yet.

But her hands were shaking as she got into her car. She pulled out her phone, but there were no more texts. She entered an address in her phone. Anila pulled out of the parking lot and followed the GPS directions to a location in downtown Los Angeles, watching the rearview mirror to see if anyone was following her. She made unnecessary turns like she'd seen in movies, confusing the GPS. No suspicious vehicle made the same turns as her.

Billboards along the roads advertised TV shows and radio channels and the new musical in town. She'd watched it with the bridesmaids after the bridal shower for Lily. The lead actress, Sierra Smith, with unearthly talent for music and dance, had mesmerized them with her award-worthy performance. Anila breathed out through pursed lips. Some people's success was advertised on billboards, while others kept it secret.

Anila came to a stop in front of a two-story building in an upscale locality. She pushed her sunglasses to the top of her head and got out of the car. Her realtor, Jonas Howard, was already waiting. He gave her a wide, confident grin and waved. As usual, he was in a long-sleeved polo shirt to cover his tattoos, but one peeked above his collar. A sunflower. She waved back.

They had looked at several spots for a possible office for Business Casual, which had grown too big not to have a physical address. Anila had decided to rent an office for the clerical staff and the programmers, with an area for clients to meet and greet.

She still smarted from the recent lawsuit; one of her clients had sued another client for harassment in a pub where they'd met, and wrapped Business Casual in its tentacles.

Anila had asked Harrison to work as a freelancer to run background checks for her new clients just to prevent a repeat of that episode. Harrison had been surprised at Anila's secret business venture, and promised not to tell anyone. He'd agreed happily, since he and Laura were expecting a baby, and he needed all the money he could get. It was an unexpected pregnancy, almost four years after they'd adopted Trevor. Wait until Sunny found out Trevor too was going to have a sibling! She sighed.

Anila had banned the offending client from her site. The suit against Business Casual was eventually dropped, but Anila decided to find a suitable, lighted space where her clients could safely meet before deciding to "date." Since most of her clients were professionals, a location in downtown Los Angeles would be perfect.

She wondered if it was the guy who had been sued who was now stalking Anila. But it couldn't be. How would he know of her association with the website? Besides, she was sure she'd never met him, let alone break his heart!

She turned her attention to Jonas as he led her toward the building. He had shown her several warehouses with potential, but high-class businessmen and businesswomen probably wouldn't want to meet for the first time in a warehouse, however posh the interior. Anila envisioned large glass windows, indoor plants in massive brass planters on plush carpets, tasteful paintings and photographs on the walls, soothing music, and elegant furniture.

Jonas grinned. "I think I've found the perfect place."

Anila turned around in a circle and assessed her surroundings. The location couldn't be better. It was within walking distance from many skyscrapers filled with law offices, corporate headquarters, and small businesses. The street was lively and well lit, with wide sidewalks for pedestrians, and plenty of parking for those who preferred not to walk. The two-storied building seemed to have apartments above, and office spaces on the lower level. There were two shuttered stores, a smaller space which used to be an accountant's office and a larger, L-shaped bookstore. Right in the center was a busy bakery.

"We're looking at this one." Jonas opened the door to the vacant accountant's office and led her inside. Anila stared at the layout to decide what would stay and what could go. It would be tight, but with a bit of remodeling, she could place the clerks and the programmers here. But there wasn't enough space for a meet-and-greet. Besides, she realized that clients might not want to be seen by the programmers, who themselves preferred to work behind the scenes.

She needed a larger space which she could partition off for her clients. "What about the bookstore?"

Jonas said, "Oh. I didn't think you'd like it. It's in the corner, with heavy foot traffic in the evenings."

"Let's check it, if possible."

While he was on the phone, Anila called home to ask her mother to pick Sunny from preschool. This was going to take longer than she'd hoped. The new nanny she'd hired a couple of months ago had asked for a day off. "Myra won't be in today."

Her mother said, "Sure, Anila. Where are you anyway? I called the Chateau, but they said you wouldn't be there today."

Anila knew she'd have to tell her family about her business once the office was leased and running, but until then, she wanted to keep it secret. "I came to the mall to pick up some things. I'll be home soon, Ma."

Jonas returned with a smile, and Anila hung up.

He said, "The owner is delighted for us to see the bookstore. It's a bigger space." He rubbed his thumb over his fingertips. "More moolah for him!"

Anila and Jonas entered the bookstore. By itself it was still too small, but if she leased both the spaces, the clerks and programmers could be in the larger space, and the clients could meet in the accountant's office, although it was not as attractive a space as this one.

She took in a sharp breath. It would have been far better to have a larger contiguous space, just for ease of rent payments, and general upkeep. But was it worth looking at more properties? She did love the location. She tapped her chin and tilted her head. "What about the bakery?"

Jonas said, "It's a long-term lease. Twenty years, I think. You'd have great neighbors."

Anila nodded. "Let me check something." She stepped outside the bookstore onto the sidewalk. A couple walked into the bakery, and a woman walked out with a giant pink and white striped box filled with something that smelled delicious. Anila waited for her to pass, and then she entered *Lupe's Cupcakes*.

The aroma of chocolate and vanilla, freshly baked pastries, and coffee filled the room. Old, yellowed photographs of celebrities and important people who'd visited the bakery were plastered on one wall in tasteful black-and-white frames. Anila recognized the ex-Governor of California, a smattering of movie stars and TV personalities.

Anila beckoned to a flustered Jonas and settled in a corner table beside massive mirrors to watch the crowd. A college student in a pink and white striped uniform complete with a pert hat took their orders and smiled extra-long for better tips.

Anila asked, "What's good here?"

The waitress grinned. She spoke in the young women's way to ending each sentence in an upswing of tone, as if asking a question. "Everything! But if it's your first time here, I'd recommend the blueberry cupcakes. It's all fresh ingredients. In fact, the fresh shipment of blueberries came early this morning."

Anila smiled. "Blueberry cupcake it is. And a cappuccino, please. Extra cinnamon and a dash of nutmeg. Jonas, what would you like?"

Jonas frowned in confusion. "Um…" he said. "Same."

Anila was staring at the space with a grin.

Jonas rubbed his forehead. "What are you thinking?"

The waitress brought their orders. Anila took a bite of the muffin and nodded with approval. Then she took a sip of coffee, which was strong, hot, and flavorful. She settled back in her seat. "Delicious as promised. Try it."

Jonas had a bite of his cupcake and said, "God, it's yummy."

She smirked at the use of the typically young-American term. "I'll buy you a box for your kid sister." Then she said, "Check with the owner if this space is available."

His face darkened. "I said it isn't."

She took another sip of her coffee. "Everything's available for a price."

"Okay," he said, frowning. "But you know, I *can* find other office spaces."

Anila shook her head. "I'd like to lease the whole three-store area. If not, I'd like the bakery to move over, maybe to the bookstore. I need a common, contiguous office space."

"But..."

She gave him a cold look. "Call him. No harm in trying."

Her phone buzzed again. Her heart hammered in her chest as she read the text from yet another unfamiliar number. *Ah, you do have a life apart from your son.*

She answered: *Who the hell are you? Stop harassing me.*

The reply came instantaneously: *You still like cappuccinos?*

Her hands shook as she typed: *Stop this or I'll report you.*

I can't. I love you. Don't you know that by now?

Who the hell are you?

You'd said once that great minds think alike.

She frowned. *Noah Katz?*

8

A FEW MONTHS AFTER Sunny was born, Anila was lying in bed clutching Vikas's photo to her chest. She stared at the swirling, shimmering patterns of light from the reflection of the summer sun from the swimming pool. Vikas would have loved the pool; he was an ace swimmer. Where was he now? Was he watching over her and his son?

Her mother walked into the room, holding a sleeping baby Sunny. Anila didn't greet her mother. Alka placed Sunny in the crib, braced herself, and then smiled at Anila. She took the photo from her hands and placed it on the nightstand. "Your Papa and I were thinking. Why don't you take up a class or get a job? I know you don't need the money, but maybe it will help take your mind off Vikas."

Anila scoffed. "I'll never stop thinking about Vikas, Ma. He was my husband. I loved him, and I love him still. I'll never stop loving him. Besides, I'm helping Arjun with his Chateau business. I'm setting up the website, but..."

"But what?"

She pulled herself upright and waved her hand. "I ran into some trouble with the code, but I'll figure it out."

Her mother folded her hands across her chest, a stance she used for not taking "no" for an answer. "Why don't you take a class then? Coding? Website development?"

"Ma! Stop it! I have a degree in this stuff. I'll figure it out."

"Yes, *beti*, but this is not healthy. You need to meet other people too, you know."

With some reluctance, Anila signed up for a computer programming class to brush up her skills. And Ma was right. She'd meet new people, and maybe that would help her out of the blackness that had engulfed her mind. Maybe it was the gloom that prevented her from figuring out what was wrong with the website.

It was in that class that she met Noah Katz for the first time. He was a shy young man with a short, straggly beard, a mop of long, unruly hair, and dark eyes behind horn rimmed glasses. He always wore ripped jeans and shabby T-shirts, and carried a battered messenger bag that had belonged to his father. The shabby exterior couldn't hide his brilliance.

For the final project in the class, the instructor asked them to work in pairs. Anila was sitting beside him. She turned to him and asked, "Want to work on this with me?"

"Um… yeah. Whatever." He stammered and dropped his gaze to his nails, bitten to the nub.

They worked well together. He used to be quiet in class, but opened up to her. He told her he'd been adopted as a baby. He didn't know his biological parents. His adoptive parents had been elderly, and his father had recently passed away. He dropped out of community college to care for his ageing mother. He worked part-time at a coffee shop, but his first love was computers.

She said, "You don't need classes. You could teach this one."

He smiled shyly. "So could you, Anila." He pronounced her name in a peculiar way, with a shorter middle syllable. *Anilla.*

While working out a problem, he imitated their Russian instructor with a strong accent and had Anila in splits. She hadn't laughed so much in months.

"Stop!" she begged.

He switched to a British accent and asked, "Is that better?"

"Very funny. Can we focus on this now?"

He imitated Gollum and Yoda, and she couldn't stop laughing. Finally, she said, "I have a baby at home, Noah. I need to finish this."

He stared at her for a long time, and then nodded. "I'm sorry. I didn't know."

"About my baby? He's five months old."

His face reddened a little. "And the father?"

"He died five months ago." And just like that, the cloud descended upon her once again. Noah didn't push her for more information, but didn't attempt to make her laugh either.

Over lunch and programming, Noah and Anila shared their grief and the ways each was trying to deal with the loss of a loved one. He told her about group therapy he'd tried that didn't help him.

She said she'd never believed in such things. "I like to do things alone."

One Saturday when they'd come to a dead end in the project, she'd said, "Let's try to brainstorm. I need a coffee."

They went to the coffee shop where he worked, and he insisted on buying. With a wink, he said, "I get employee discount. What would you like?"

"A cappuccino. Extra cinnamon."

He returned with their coffees, and said, "Have you tried it with a dash of nutmeg?"

She hadn't. So he added some, and Anila took a sip. She nodded her approval. "Wow… This is my new favorite flavor."

He grinned like a little boy whose teacher liked the card he'd made for her birthday. They set up their laptops on a high table at the corner, the sun streaming into the café, pop music playing in the background. Around them sat customers with their laptops open, a mother with her toddler and a baby in a stroller, and a couple huddled together in a quiet booth, middle-aged, clearly in love, and somehow emanating the impression that they were having an affair, as the woman kept staring over her shoulder.

Anila wondered what people thought about her and Noah. He moved his coffee cup, and for a moment their hands touched. He turned pink and stammered his apology. It was perfectly innocent. He was a kid, really, at least eight years younger than her. She didn't want to embarrass him by showing that she'd noticed. She concentrated on the project, and for a few minutes, they worked quietly.

Then she took in a sharp breath just as an idea hit her. "Hey, I think I've got it."

She told him what she'd come up with, and he grinned. "I was thinking the same thing."

She smiled. "Great minds think alike."

A week later, Noah didn't come to class. Anila texted him. *Hope you're okay. Do you want me to present our project tomorrow or will you be in class?*

He texted right back: *Mom has the flu. I think I'm sick too.*

I'm sorry. Do you have help?

We haven't eaten in two days. Ran out of bread.

Text me your address.

Anila bought sandwiches and soup from a deli and took the food to his tiny, shabby apartment. Coke cans, beer bottles, pizza boxes, and sandwich wrappers were strewn all over the cramped living room. Something rotted in the kitchen, giving out a rank stench. He didn't seem to notice. He hadn't shaven in days, and looked terrible. His face was flushed, his nose red and swollen, and he blew his nose on a crumpled tissue. He was wearing worn pajamas and a hooded sweatshirt that smelled of moth balls. From somewhere inside, Anila heard the sounds of coughing. Must be the mother.

Noah thanked her for the soup, his voice shaking with emotion.

She moved the pizza box and placed the food on the coffee table. "That's what friends do."

He leaned into the hallway corridor, watching her from a distance. "Never had any. So I have no idea what they do."

Anila felt a flash of pity for this lonely boy. "Listen, let me know if you need anything. I can handle the presentation or ask to postpone to next week when you can be there. Is that okay?"

He went through a coughing fit. "Can you ask to postpone?"

Anila nodded. "I think you should see a doctor."

"Naah. Mom's getting better. I'll be fine too."

"You sure? I can drive you to urgent care."

"No, I don't want to get you infected. You have a kid."

Their presentation the following week got them an "A." And just like that, the course was over.

It was two years later that she saw Noah again. She didn't even recognize him. It was at a high society event that she had no choice but to attend. He brought her a glass of champagne, which she refused. She wanted to drive home as early as was polite.

He said, "You prefer a cappuccino, Anila?" *Anilla.*

That's when she recognized him. He looked different now. He'd shaven his beard. His hair was styled. He was wearing a goddamn tux.

She smiled. "Noah? What a surprise. I didn't recognize you."

"But I recognized you like that." He snapped his fingers. "I mean, that's not a face you can easily forget. You look stunning."

She laughed. "Thanks. What are you up to now?"

"Mom passed away last year. I still worked part-time at the coffee shop while I made my first app. Apple bought it. Now I make apps for Apple. Full time. I've made a fortune, and I'm looking for someone to spend it with."

"Still single, huh?"

"Not if you say I do."

That took her by surprise. She'd been aware of his crush on her two years ago, but she'd hoped it had passed. She cleared her voice. "Beg your pardon?"

"Anila, I cannot get you out of my mind. I couldn't ask you out earlier, but now I've got money. I'm successful, and you deserve that. Go out with me, even if just for a coffee. A cappuccino with extra cinnamon and a dash of nutmeg."

His desperation to be with her and his utter confidence in assuming she'd be interested annoyed and scared her in equal measure. "I'm so sorry, Noah. I'm so much older than you. I'm a mother, for God's sake."

He leaned in toward her, his face inches from hers. "I have enough money for all of us. Say yes."

She took a step back. "My life is devoted to taking care of my son. I am not interested, and will never be interested in another relationship. I'm sorry if I gave you a wrong signal."

Stunned and abashed, he took a step back. "You don't know what you're missing."

That look of hurt in his eyes made her heart melt. "Please try to understand, Noah. It's not you…"

"I know the drill." He nodded and made circles on the marble floor with the tip of his shoe. "I understand."

After that, she did see him occasionally at social events, but he stared at her from afar, never approaching her or offering her a drink.

But now, it seemed, things had changed.

9

AVINASH SINGHANIA steepled his fingers and faced his client, nineteen-year-old Stella, who clutched her little girl in her arms.

Detective Harrison McNamara sometimes sent clients his way, including Lily, a doctor, who had been abused by her boyfriend. Avinash didn't have to second-guess Harrison's opinions. Harrison had said, almost apologetically, "Stella is poor, Avinash. But she needs help. I can think of no one better than you."

Avinash had agreed to hear her out.

Stella's eyes darted between his face and the window behind him. She coughed. Then she said, "The view is lovely."

He turned around and stared out the window of his office in the high-rise building in downtown Los Angeles. A few high clouds hovered in the sky, the Pacific Ocean calm and expansive to the west. He knew she was stalling. "Yes, it is."

Stella squirmed in her seat, clearly unsettled to be in the plush law office, sitting in a soft leather chair, wearing cheap denim shorts, a well-worn tank-top, no-show socks with a pair of fraying knock-off Converse. Tattoos covered her arms, and her dirty blonde hair was tied in a ponytail, a few loose strands framing her disarmingly youthful face. Her daughter was in a pretty dress and nice shoes. Clearly Stella put the needs of her little girl above her own. Avinash took it all in.

Stella's eyes flashed, as if picking up on his judgment. "Look, Mr. Singhania. I can pay, but not a lot. I need to keep Nina. They can't take her away from me."

Stella's ex-boyfriend—Nina's father—was in jail for selling crack at street corners. Stella had been an addict herself, and been to rehab while her mother took care of the little girl. But last month Stella's mother died of complications from undiagnosed, uncontrolled diabetes, and now the ex-boyfriend's parents wanted custody of Nina.

Avinash said, "Nina's grandfather, your ex's father, works in the city government, you said?"

She nodded.

"A year away from retirement, with full pension?"

"Yes."

"And her grandmother retired last year? Where do they live?"

"Yes. They live in a small but nice house in Glendale. Picket fence, yard, rose bushes, central air, everything."

"I see." This was going to be hard. Who would pit a poor, recovering addict against a stable, middle-class couple to be the suitable guardians for this beautiful child?

Her eyes grew wide. "But Mr. Singhania, I have a job. I am clean. I will take care of Nina. I promise on my mother's grave." She made the sign of the cross over her chest.

He glanced at the file in front of him. "You're working at the Goodwill store?"

She nodded, her hoop earrings bobbing in the air. "It's temporary, but I am a good worker. The manager told me I'll get the first full-time opening they have."

Nina reached up to grab one earring. Stella clasped her daughter's hand, kissed it, and then detached the earring from her earlobe, slipping it in her purse. It was a small, intimate, calm action of a mother lightly disciplining her child, and a trusting child, acquiescent of the gentle reprimand.

Avinash's heart clenched at the memory of his mother grabbing baby Sonia's hand when she used to tug at her earrings. Tanya, who was about seven years old, would ask, "Ma, did I do that when I was a baby?" Moyna would smile and nod, making Avinash realize he could never ask that question to anyone. Brought up by grandparents, now dead, his childhood was a mishmash of memories, where truth blended with make-believe, and nothing was certain.

In that moment, Avinash vowed to do everything in his power to make sure little Nina got to live with her mother, and be able to ask those questions as she grew up, and have someone who could answer them with authority. *Yes, you used to jump on the bed and ruined the springs. Yes, you hated broccoli. No, you loved lentil soup.*

He swallowed hard. "Look, Stella. It looks challenging. The court always wants what's best for the child, but you have everything stacked against you."

Her eyes widened. "What's best for Nina is to be with me. She doesn't even know her grandparents."

He nodded. "I'll do my best. The one thing in your favor is that the court always wants the child to be with her parents first. So let's hope it works."

She pulled out a coin purse and extracted a stack of rolled up twenty-dollar bills "How much do I owe you?"

He waved his hand. He planned to represent Stella pro bono. "Later. Use the money to buy yourself a nice outfit for the court. And um… I know this is petty, but wear a long sleeved shirt to court to cover those tattoos. People can be weird about stuff like that." He stood up and smiled.

Embarrassed, she got up and hefted Nina into her arms. "Thanks. It means a lot."

Avinash pointed his finger at her. "In the meantime, take care of Nina. Make your shifts. Do not be late. Do not give your boss a reason to fire you. And for heaven's sake, do not use!"

She shook her head. "I won't! I promise." Somehow, he knew she was telling the truth.

Avinash's phone dinged a reminder. *Meeting with Anila Mallik at Lupe's Cupcakes in twenty minutes.* He smiled in anticipation as Stella and Nina left the office. Avinash had told his secretary to cancel his afternoon appointments. He got up with his briefcase. His phone rang, and he saw it was his mother.

She'd been out of the country for the past few days, leaving him to handle the firm. "Ma, how is the trip? Enjoying Zurich?"

She sounded happy. "It's going so well. Took a couple of skiing lessons. Twisted my ankle, so that's over. I also met lots of big shots, your father's colleagues that I've forgotten already."

He laughed. "You needed the break. When will you be back?"

She said, "In a week, I hope. Your Papa wants to travel. He wants to do a driving trip through northern Italy."

"It's a lovely place. You'll have lots of fun."

"You're handling everything there?"

"Yeah, of course. Did you, for a moment, doubt that?"

She laughed. "No, of course not."

"So the reason for the call?" He glanced at his watch. It was late in the evening in London.

She yawned and said, "Listen, Lupe called about her lease for *Lupe's Cupcakes.*"

He closed the venetian blinds of the windows and left his office as the motion-detector lights turned off. "And?"

"It seems the landlord wants her to move over to the corner spot."

He waved to the secretary and walked to the bathrooms. "The old bookstore? It's a bigger space, isn't it?"

"Maybe by a little, but that location is her first-ever venture. She's attached to it."

"What do you want me to do?"

"Can you talk to the landlord?" After a pause, she said, "It's Roger Chu. Have you worked with him?"

"No, but send me his contact."

She sent it within seconds. He pushed open the bathroom door and called the landlord.

Roger Chu's secretary said, "He is in meetings all day. I'll have him call you. Can I ask what this is about?"

"It's about the lease on the bakery in his downtown building."

"I'll let him know."

After hanging up, Avinash splashed cold water on his face and ran his fingers through his hair, patting down a wayward strand. He never cared how he looked, but somehow, he wanted to impress Anila Mallik. He drove eight blocks, parked his red Lamborghini, and entered *Lupe's Cupcakes*. The location was perfect for Auntie Lupe. No wonder she didn't want to move.

He'd been surprised when Anila had suggested meeting in *Lupe's Cupcakes* for signing the contract for the holiday retreat.

"I have a meeting later nearby," she'd said.

Avinash entered the café. The servers were new, and thankfully, no one recognized him. It would have been embarrassing, because he came here with his sister Tanya often, and they were treated as royalty.

He scanned the bakery and realized he was a few minutes early. Finally, he chose a corner booth and settled down. A new, long-legged waitress sauntered up to him and handed him the menu.

He said, "I'm waiting for someone."

She walked away just as the door dinged open and Anila Mallik walked in. She moved her sunglasses to the top of her head and gazed at the well-lit space, her eyes widening in recognition when she spotted him, which made him feel like he was glowing. She glided to his table in a regal, graceful manner fit for a queen. He stood up.

She was dressed in a charcoal pantsuit, with a pale pink scoop-neck shirt. The damn heart-shaped locked dangled at her neck.

Avinash ran his fingers through his hair to avoid staring. He offered her a smile, which she returned. His gaze flew to her lips, soft and plump, which would taste so good. A nervous wreck, he blew out through pursed lips and shook that urge away. She did things to his heart that few had managed before.

Except Sierra. But Sierra was history. Sierra was stylish like a coiled serpent ready to bite, and Anila had the grace of a wildcat.

He gestured to the seat opposite him and Anila sat down, placing her LV satchel on the side.

He said, "What would you like?"

"Um…" she hesitated. "I've tried their blueberry cupcake…"

"You've got to try the pumpkin-spice cupcake. It's their holiday special."

She shrugged. "Sure."

He waved down the waitress, who returned with a smile. "Coffee?"

"Sure," said Avinash.

"Yes, please," said Anila.

The waitress smiled at Anila and tapped her pen on her chin. "Let me see if I remember. A cappuccino. Um… with extra cinnamon and a dash of nutmeg."

Anila flushed a deep shade of red. "Just cinnamon."

"No nutmeg?"

Anila shook her head. "*Definitely* no nutmeg."

Avinash frowned at the exchange. The waitress seemed to know Anila's coffee preference, but the mention of nutmeg had changed something in the dynamic. She was so full of mysteries.

The waitress nodded. "Anything to eat?"

Avinash ordered the cupcakes, and the waitress left.

Anila pulled out a folder from her leather satchel and placed it in front of her. After scanning a few pages, she handed them to him. "You've reviewed the emailed version, am I right?"

He nodded, wanting to prolong the meeting. A strand of hair had broken free from her sunglasses and hung in a spiral at her chin. The delicate gold chain with the pendant glittered at her collarbone.

She said, "This is the same thing. If you don't trust me, you can read it again."

"I trust you." He took the pen she offered and signed on the dotted lines in four places.

Anila's phone buzzed and she frowned at it. It must have been something unpleasant, because she ignored it and shoved it into her bag with unnecessary gusto.

The waitress returned with their order. Avinash moved the paperwork to the side and made space for the coffee and cupcakes.

"A regular coffee for you, and a cappuccino with cinnamon, no nutmeg for you."

Anila's eyes flashed as the waitress left again. He watched Anila take a bite of the cupcake and close her eyes. Her pleasure at his suggestion of the pastry brought him uncanny glee; he wanted to make her happy, to make her smile. So far she hadn't displayed the slightest hint of pleasure at seeing him. He had seen her smile only once, and that too, at her son when he'd shown up at the banquet and called her "Ma," catching Avinash by surprise.

After she finished the last sip of her coffee, he handed her the contract. Their hands touched, and her body jerked like she'd received an electric shock.

So the chemistry was mutual...

Before he could consider the implications of what he was saying, he blurted out, "Would you like to go out with me, sometime? A coffee, maybe? Cappuccino with cinnamon, no nutmeg?"

She paused for a few long, agonizing moments, holding him in her steady, deep gaze. "We're having coffee now."

"I mean, not for signing contracts and such. Just for fun. Or dinner, maybe?"

Her eyebrows rose skyward. "Like a date?"

He smiled and nodded, resisting the urge to run his fingers through his hair like he did when he was nervous. Why was he so awkward around her?

The tiny frown on her lovely forehead made his heart twinge. She cleared her throat. "I don't think it's a good idea."

"Why not?" His heart hammered in his chest. There. He had laid his heart bare. He had to jump through hoops just to get to know her better. But he realized with a tiny frisson of pleasure that he wanted to.

She regarded him with dark, unfathomable eyes, which now glistened from a film of moisture. Or was it just the light? She swallowed hard. "I'm married. I thought you knew that."

He jutted his chin toward her hand, ringless, bare. "Yes, you'd told me. But I also know about your husband."

Her eyes moistened a little more as she bit her lip. Darn it. She was still grieving. He'd hoped three years was enough time for her to be over it. But the pendant gave it away. She wasn't ready.

When she didn't answer, his voice softened. "I also know he was a patriot. And I know of his accident three years ago." He considered his words carefully before saying, "You can't put your life on hold forever."

Anger flashed through those ebony eyes. "Why not?"

He said, "It's not healthy."

She straightened up in her seat and said, "Who are you to tell me what I should or should not do?"

Avinash stared at her for a while. So she wasn't interested. *At least not yet.* And it made him even more determined to get through to her, to hurl himself at the wall she'd created around herself. Without the slightest tone of apology, he said, "I'm sorry to have asked. It was impudent of me."

Her voice was hoarse, like she was talking past a lump in her throat. "Yes, it was. And let's keep this strictly business."

A sardonic smile curved his lips and he said, "As opposed to *business casual.*"

Her eyes flew open and she stared at him, the mild tremor of her hands all too visible. Had she heard of the website? Had she used it herself? She was a single woman and no doubt got asked to parties.

She stood up and abruptly shook his hand. "We'll see you at the retreat."

Later that night when Avinash got home, he turned on his laptop and browsed through the website, *Business Casual.* But Anila Mallik was not a member.

This feeling of being obsessed with someone was unfamiliar to him. He had deluded himself into thinking that he'd loved Sierra. But it had been an infatuation, a physical attraction. With Anila, though, he realized now, the attraction was magnetic, inevitable, from an ancient, irrefutable law of nature. Something deep and visceral connected her with him. There was no escape. She had rewired his brain and entangled herself into every synapse, every thought.

He was tired of no-strings-attached casual relationships. He needed more. He went to bed dreaming of her sleeping beside him, her head on his shoulder, her silken hair tickling his face. Soft, warm, and loving, knowing fully well that pursuing her was a battle he was likely to lose. As an attorney, he was used to winning. The realization struck that losing her was not an option he was willing to accept.

10

WHEN AVINASH mentioned Business Casual, Anila's heart jumped into her mouth. He had a smirk on his face when he'd said it, and she wondered if he knew she was the proprietor. Unsure of how to react, she stood up and extended her hand. "We'll see you at the retreat."

He looked stunned to be cut off like that, but maintained his composure. He got up, took her hand, patted it with his other hand as if they'd been friends for years. "Looking forward to it."

Avinash walked out of the bakery and got into his flashy car. She rolled her eyes. Then she glanced at her watch and sat back down. She had a few minutes before her meeting with the owner of the building, a meeting she'd decided to take without her agent present.

Her phone buzzed. It was a text from the nanny, Myra. *Sunny is napping after a bath. Had a good snack.*

Anila texted back. *Thanks.*

Her phone buzzed again. This time it was from the same number that had texted her minutes earlier with: *You're cheating on me.*

This new message read: *Did you enjoy your cappuccino with that man?*

She frowned. She had no doubt now that it was Noah. He was watching her! A small spark of fear rose in her heart. She scanned the café, searching for him. But besides a group of high school girls doing homework together, an old man reading a newspaper, and two young women in athleisure gear with sleeping babies in strollers, the café was empty. She glanced out through the large glass panes for a parked vehicle with someone inside, but found no one suspicious. A row of cars lined the street, but she saw no one in any of them. Except perhaps a BMW with darkened windows. She bit her lip. Let him watch her. She lifted her middle finger in a discrete way that only someone watching her could see.

Noah was being a pain in the neck, but she wasn't scared of him. She wasn't. She just wanted him to stop bothering her. She called Harrison's phone and left him a message. "I have an issue I wanted to discuss. Please call me back when you have a moment. But text me first." That was just in case she was home when he called. She didn't want to worry her family; Arjun had just returned from his honeymoon, and she didn't want to scare her parents.

Anila ordered another cappuccino and turned on her laptop. Glancing at the crowd to ensure privacy, she opened up Business Casual and browsed through the profiles. There were fifteen more members since last night. If she'd been doing this solely to make a living, she'd be rich. But since she had more money than she knew what to do with, she donated all her profits anonymously to the Air Force Wives Welfare Association in India, to help widows of soldiers who had died in the line of duty.

She skimmed through the older profiles, searching for Avinash Singhania. And she found him in all his glory. The photograph was professionally taken against a plain, warm background. He was stunning in a dark suit, an open collar shirt, and a winning, enchanting smile, tiny laugh lines around his eyes. And somehow, he managed to look better in real life. From reviews—which were not seen by the client himself—she discerned him to be courteous, chivalrous, generous, and always dependable. He treated his dates with dignity and never shopped around for anyone new unless his "regular" date was somehow permanently unavailable, such as through matrimony or relocation.

He liked to go fishing in his yacht on weekends where he took his dates even if there was no "event" to attend, just to get to know them better. He shopped in expensive Beverly Hills stores and gifted diamond bracelets to his dates, he tolerated the opera, liked movie premiers, enjoyed snowboarding, and loved to hike in Griffith Park and the Santa Monica Mountains.

He had recently made his status "Active."

Anila would probably not enjoy most of the things he liked. But what did it matter, anyway? She tapped her fingers on the table and hid a smile. What were the odds that he was her client and didn't even know it?

She saw a note under "Special Comments." She clicked on the internal link and cupped her chin. Avinash Singhania was divorced. She frowned, wondering what had gone wrong. He seemed like a wonderful guy, universally liked by people around him.

Anila's phone rang. It was Lily. She smiled and answered, "Welcome back!"

Lily said, "You still haven't picked up the stuff we got you. I could drop in later today."

Anila said, "Ma wanted to have you both over for dinner anyway. So, how was it? But spare me the lewd details."

Arjun and Lily honeymooned in Italy, to the same village where they'd suffered trauma a few years ago. Lily's father lived there. "The place is just too beautiful to connect to fires and kidnapping and all the awful stuff that happened years back. We planned to make new memories there, and boy did that work! It was lovely, Anila. We should do a girls-only trip there one day."

Anila laughed. "Sounds good."

After a pause, Lily asked, "Did Avinash Singhania call you?"

Anila tapped her fingers on the table. "Why would he call me?"

"Oh!" Lily giggled before continuing, "He called me after the wedding, asking about you."

"He did, did he? And was it you who told him about Vikas?"

"Yeah. I'm sorry, Anila, but um… I don't know how to put it delicately. You're so young. And three years is a long time. Think about the thirty or forty years ahead. I know it's hard to see right now, but Avinash is a great guy. He helped me out with, you know… Anyhow, if he calls, give him a chance."

"I'm not looking for a—"

"I know, I know. Just if you're up for making a new, dependable friend."

She heard conversation in the background, and Lily giggled. "It's Arjun saying something crude. I gotta go. Bye, Anila. See you tonight."

Anila put her phone into the satchel and continued searching Avinash's dating history. He'd been a client almost since the website went live, and had just five "dates." Karina Geula, the woman Avinash had been "dating" for the past three months, had suspended her account. Which meant that either things were going too well for the couple and they planned a more permanent relationship, or that she was unhappy with the service, or that she had moved out of town.

Losing a client was always hard, but having an unhappy one was worse. Anila made a mental note to check in with Karina later in the day.

So Avinash was *sans* his regular date. By asking Anila out, had he hoped to make her his "regular" date? The woman in her was flattered to be asked, and excited at the possibility, but the businesswoman in her wondered if he was unhappy with either Karina or with Business Casual.

She sighed. Once she secured a physical location, her venture would be more grounded and hopefully offer better customer service. If it worked out well in Los Angeles, she'd consider leasing office space in other major metros.

She was half-way through her coffee when a portly Asian man with a scruffy salt-and-pepper beard walked in, scanned the restaurant, and approached her table.

"Ms. Mallik?" he said with a little frown. His breath smelled of garlic and onion.

Anila got up to shake his hand. "Mr. Chu."

"Your agent said you'd like to meet me personally. I don't meet clients without their agents unless they're serious about the contract." He gave her a cheesy smile. A tiny fleck of spinach was stuck between his teeth. He was clean shaven but for a spot on the left side of his jaw. A faint coffee stain ran down the middle of his shirt. A sloppy man, but wealthy.

She smiled. "Thank you for meeting me. How did it go with the owner of this bakery? Are they willing to move to the corner? I'd really rather have a large contiguous space."

"I'm sorry. I did tell her, but she wasn't happy. She said she'd get back to me. She's been a good tenant for over twenty years."

"But she seems amenable?"

He shrugged.

"You could give her a discount on her rent for the bookstore, and I'll make up the difference."

He shook his head.

She leveled her gaze at him. "Okay. If she doesn't want to move over, I'd ask her to move out."

"What do you mean?"

"I'll lease the entire first floor from you. Above asking price. It's an offer you cannot refuse." She wrote an amount on the paper napkin and slid it toward him, knowing it would be too tempting for him to pass up.

To her surprise, he glanced at the number, shook his head, and raised his hands, palms out. "I'm sorry. But the bakery is a popular place here. I can't ask her to leave. I cannot evict her without cause."

"Name your price."

He squirmed in his seat. "She's a long-term tenant, Ms. Mallik. Please try to understand. You could lease both locations and let her remain in the middle. I'll give you a deal."

Anila swallowed the last of her coffee. "I'm afraid that won't work for me." His face fell. From the way his jaw sagged, she knew she was in a position to squeeze him a bit more. "However, I do have another offer."

He looked up eagerly.

"Would you like some coffee?"

He shook his head. "Just had lunch."

She nodded. "I'll buy the whole property from you. The whole building."

"The whole building?"

"Yeah."

He shook his head with vehemence. "It's not for sale."

She smiled. "I've learned that everything's negotiable. There's no deal-breaker in real life, except death." That was a lesson she'd learned the hard way. She clutched the pendant at her throat, hoping he would fall for the ploy.

Roger Chu frowned. "I'll have to think about it."

She nodded. "How many units do you have upstairs?"

"There are six apartments."

"Perfect."

"What do you mean?"

"I mean my employees can live upstairs and work downstairs. No one likes the traffic in LA."

He squirmed in his seat, a deep flush spreading across his face. "I'm not selling."

She gave him a sweet smile. "That's what you say right now. Quote me a price and we can go from there. My agent will get in touch with you."

"But they're long term tenants."

She tried to convey her determination through her eyes, with a firm, unwavering gaze. "I'm not stupid, Mr. Chu. I saw 'For Rent' signs for apartments, so do not bluff. Either you're charging too much rent, or the apartments are in a state of disrepair, and therefore, unrentable."

He rubbed his forehead, his defiance losing steam. "I've had trouble keeping people here. Rents are high. Mortgage is high. I can't afford to have empty apartments or to refurbish or remodel."

"How many are vacant?"

"Four."

"I have at least four employees who would live here, as a perk for working in my company, but only if I own the property. And I'll let your other two tenants stay if they want. Same rent."

"Ms. Mallik. I…"

"Look, I'm giving you a way out. I'll give you two weeks to think about it. Send me an offer. If I don't hear from you, well, there are other properties in Los Angeles."

After he left, Anila ordered a dozen blueberry and pumpkin spiced cupcakes to go. She stepped out of the cafe, excited to embark on her new venture for the prime downtown property. She had driven a hard bargain, but it was a win-win for them both.

Anila's phone buzzed again. The text said: *You're hurting my feelings, going out with so many men.*

11

ANILA'S HEART HAMMERED in her chest. She carried the box of cupcakes and got into her car. Once inside, she took deep breaths. As a young child, Anila had learned to compartmentalize her emotions well. She could stonewall her agony about being called fat from her happiness at excelling in school. She whispered, "Build the shield around yourself, Anila." She considered calling Harrison again, but decided against it. If this was Noah, she knew he wouldn't hurt her.

She slipped the phone back in her bag and turned into the on-ramp. As she pulled into the freeway, Anila's phone rang yet again. She frowned. Was Noah calling her now? But it was her mother's photo that popped up, grinning into the camera, holding Sunny.

She smiled and picked it up. "Hi, Ma. I'm on my way home. Is Sunny up yet? Ask Myra to play ball with him until I get home."

"Myra's mother was sick, and she had to leave. She said she can't come tomorrow, but I can pick him up from preschool."

"Did he have a good day?"

Her mother said, "Yes, but..."

She merged with traffic on the freeway, her heart skipping a beat. "Yes?"

"It's okay. I'll talk to you later over *chai*." Anila and her mother enjoyed the evening tea ritual in the rose garden every afternoon, sometimes accompanied by biscuits, or samosas.

"No, Ma. Tell me."

Her mother hesitated. "Sunny was talking about getting a new daddy."

Anila sighed. So he hadn't given up on that. "I'll talk to him."

"*Beti*, maybe it's time you at least considered it."

She gripped the wheel. "What?"

"You know... shall I ask around for you?"

Anila knew what her mother meant. She'd try to find Anila a husband. "Absolutely not. Even if I was interested—and I'm not—I'd do it myself."

Her mother's voice quivered. "I'm sorry the first time didn't work out. They had matched the horoscopes."

Before the wedding, Vikas's parents had brought in a priest, who made a show of peering at the birth charts and nodded appreciatively. Who knew what he saw and what he approved of. It was only after he said, "It's a perfect match," that his family agreed to the wedding. How had he not seen Vikas's death?

Anila's grip tightened. "I'm sorry, Ma. I didn't mean it that way. It's not your fault. How could you have predicted the accident? But things have changed. I've changed… And I don't want to talk about it, okay?"

"Okay, *beti*. Drive safely."

Anila drove along the highway and took the exit toward Wellington Estates. Nestled in the hills south of Angeles National Forest, the estates boasted quiet, exclusive luxury few could afford. An acre sized lot was considered small, and the mansions spread over several thousand square feet. Industrialists and politicians and old money thrived there, and vacant lots or "For Sale" signs were rare.

She weaved through the winding streets around the lake and the golf course and was surprised to see that the only "For Sale" sign she'd seen in the last three years, in the mansion across her street, was now labeled "Sold." On a rare occasion when a mansion sold in Wellington Estates, it usually came with a massive housewarming party as neighbors got to know each other, to gauge each other and size them up, establishing the social status. But this sale had been quiet. Probably some recluse of a once-famous author or a washed up Hollywood star. The property had a tall hedge, and the ivy covered walls of the gothic style stone castle made her think of torture and ghosts.

Anila pulled past the cast iron gate of the Dheer home, enjoying the popping sound of gravel under her tires. Grabbing her satchel, she walked indoors.

In the family room, sunk into a large beanbag, her son was sobbing, his grandmother hovering over him.

Anila ran to them. "What happened? Are you hurt?"

He looked at her tearfully. "Trevor is going to have a baby sister."

She gulped. She already knew about it, but now Sunny knew it too. "That's wonderful."

"If I can't have a daddy, why can't I have a baby sister?"

Tears sprang to Anila's eyes. No matter what she said or did, this was a wish she could not fulfill.

Her mother said, "Oh, a letter came for you while you were out."

It was anonymous, but before she read it, Anila knew who'd sent it.

> *Dearest Anila,*
>
> *I see you drifting too far from me. I cannot bear it. If you went out with that man, I don't know what I'd do. I could spread rumors online about him. I could expose your association with Business Casual. Did you find that man through your site? I know he's a member.*
>
> *Why don't you want people to know about your site? It's fantastic. I'd use it, but I'm not looking for a "date" with someone I don't know.*
>
> *Yours forever.*

Anila crumpled the letter and threw it in the trash. Then she picked it up, flattened it, and slipped it into her leather satchel to show Harrison later.

She asked Sunny to play ball with her in the backyard, thanking the easy distraction of children. They played catch until he stopped complaining and started laughing, tea with Ma forgotten.

Later, she opened her laptop. Multiple searches did not get any hit on Noah Katz. It was as if he didn't exist. Even his community college didn't show him as an ex-student. Anila knew she was hacking into the site illegally, but she had to find out.

She came up with nothing.

She called Harrison again, and luckily, this time he picked his phone. "Hey, what's up? I got your message and was about to call you."

She closed her door so no one could hear her conversation. "Someone's stalking me." She told him about the texts. Luckily, she hadn't deleted them from her phone, although she'd been tempted to. "I'm pretty sure it's someone I used to know from a coding class. I've tried to look him up on the internet, but it's as if he doesn't exist."

"You think he's moved out of state?"

"He knew what I was wearing, Harrison. He knew I was dropping Sunny off to preschool. He's been following me. He's a whiz with technology. Like some sort of evil genius. He's somehow managed to scrub the internet of his existence."

He asked, "Has he made any threats?"

She considered that. He hadn't threatened her physically. He'd only said he would expose her association with Business Casual, which she'd planned to do anyway, once she secured a location for the offices. "No, not really."

"Where are you right now? Are you safe?"

"Yeah, I'm home. Arjun spent a fortune on the security system. No one can break into the house."

"I'll come over tomorrow and collect everything. You can file a report."

Anila didn't want her parents to worry, so she said, "No, I'll come to the station myself."

"What if he follows you and realizes you're making a report?"

"Well… He's never threatened anything physical so far, but you're right. Don't come to the house though. I don't want to worry my parents. Let's meet for lunch?"

Dinner with Arjun and Lily took her mind off Noah, and Sunny's mind off new daddies and new siblings. Looking at all their photos was heartening. She remembered those heady days with Vikas and knew the cloud Lily must be on right now.

Over dessert of *gajar halwah*, Arjun asked, "Any new bookings for the chateau?"

Anila tried to control her blush as she said, "The Singhania and Singhania Law firm have booked a holiday weekend. So we're all full. The bachelorette party moved to another weekend."

Arjun said, "Thanks a lot for all your help."

Later that night Anila returned to her bedroom to update the holiday bookings for the Winery Chateau. Sunny was already asleep.

Alka Dheer came to her room with a tall glass of milk. "Anila, it's been three years."

Exasperated, Anila said, "I know, Ma." Sunny wanted a sibling, her mother wanted her to be remarried, Avinash wanted to ask her out on a date, Noah wanted God knows what, all while Anila just wanted to buy a building for her business. It was her way of coping with the stresses all around her. Instead of thinking about life, she obsessed over material things. Pulled in every direction, she felt irritable and helpless.

But she saw the dismay in her mother's face and said, "I'm sorry. I didn't mean to be curt."

Alka waved her hand and sat on her bed. "You have a long life ahead of you, *beti*."

"I'll be just fine. I have you and Papa and Arjun and Lily…"

Ma rubbed her thumbs over her nails, a nervous tic Anila recognized. "But you don't have a life partner. It's a long and hard life ahead of you. Sunny is lonely and…"

Anila flashed her a smile. "Soon Arjun will have a baby, and Sunny can have a baby cousin."

"You know it's not the same."

Annoyance rose through Anila like a serpent. "So what would you have me do? In vitro from donated sperm?"

Her mother sighed. "I think it's time you at least considered a relationship."

That was the last thing on her mind. "I can't, Ma. I can't have my attention and love divided between Sunny and some guy. No one can put Sunny first except me. *No one.* You, of all people, should know that."

Her mother bristled at the harsh words. "What… what do you mean?"

"Papa never treated Arjun right. Papa favored me. Always. And it hurt Arjun. I can't have Sunny go through the same. Ever. Can you understand that?"

Her mother rose and patted Anila's back. "Drink the milk while it's hot."

Anila knew she'd hurt her mother's feelings. "I'm sorry, Ma."

Her mother sighed and hesitated by the door. Her hand still on the doorknob, she turned to face Anila. "It was different in my time. And not everyone's like Papa."

"How? Humans don't change. Everyone would put their own child first. You see it all the time in books and movies."

"They don't show you in movies how lonely life can get. Please, for your own sake, just go out there. Date. Maybe there's a perfect guy for you who will also put Sunny first."

Anila sighed.

Her mother persisted. "Besides, don't you think it might be better for Sunny, too? To have a father in his life. Kids do best when they have both parents." With that, she left the room, closing the door gently behind her.

Her mother's words echoed in her mind. She wanted what was best for Sunny. But was having a stepfather in his best interests? On the other hand, a stepfather was better than no father.

What would that feel like, going out on a real date with someone? How would it feel to have another man's lips on her mouth, another man's hands on her body? How would it feel to utter someone else's name, to create a space in her heart for someone new?

Could she forget or diminish Vikas's imprint on her mind and her soul? *Till death do us part.* He had left her, but her heart hadn't parted from the memory of him.

She logged off Winery Chateau's site and logged onto Business Casual. She stared at Avinash's profile photo. In those kind, twinkling eyes, could she see a future for herself and for Sunny? From those perfectly shaped lips, could she bear to hear her name whispered in bed? She closed her eyes, thinking about the current that flowed through her when their hands had touched. The excitement tinged with terror when he'd asked her out for coffee. The disappointment when he'd given up too soon.

The door opened and Sunny entered, rubbing his eyes. "I can't sleep, Mommy."

Heart racing, Anila shut off her computer, caught in the betrayal. "You can sleep with me just for tonight."

She clutched Sunny to her chest. *I'll always be faithful to your father!*

12

ANILA WALKED INTO *Roy's*, the popular downtown café where Harrison had asked to meet. As the door dinged, Harrison looked up from a corner table and waved. She sat across from him as a plump waitress in a frilly apron appeared and filled two mugs with coffee without being asked. Anila smiled at her gratefully. She had slept fitfully, with Sunny kicking her in his sleep and her own mind flitting from issue to issue like a butterfly on wanderlust. She'd finally fallen asleep at 4 AM.

When her alarm rang at seven o'clock, she hurried out of bed, woke Sunny from his sleep, and dropped him off to preschool. She'd skipped breakfast, because Harrison wanted to meet her before work.

She had driven through downtown traffic on surface streets, careening into one-way lanes at the last minute, slowing down until the signal turned yellow before crossing, just to shake Noah off her trail.

"I don't think he followed me here," she told Harrison. "*If* he's following me. I didn't see any strange car following me, anyway." She sighed.

Harrison nodded his approval. "Okay, show me what you've got."

Anila showed him her phone, scrolling up to the first text she'd received from Noah. Then she showed him the now-crumpled anonymous letter. She told him how they'd met during the computer programming course, and how he'd been infatuated with her, but had seemingly got the hint.

The waitress appeared again with a little notepad. "You know what you want?"

Harrison didn't open the menu. Instead, he said, "The usual."

The waitress nodded. "Okay. Breakfast burrito with everything. And you, Miss?"

Anila shrugged. "Um… breakfast burrito, no meat?"

As soon as the waitress left, Harrison picked up her phone again and frowned. "You answered his text?"

Feeling foolish, she mumbled, "Just to find out who it was."

He took in a sharp breath. "First things first. You need a new phone number. Unregistered."

She scoffed at herself. "Why didn't I think of it?"

He smiled. "That's because you're a decent person. And second thing, we need to ask Avinash for a restraining order."

"No, not Avinash. I'm in a business relation with him. He's booked the chateau for his firm's holiday party. I don't feel comfortable."

Harrison said, "Fair enough. We can do a Cease and Desist order. I just need this Noah Katz's address. I'll deliver it myself."

She shook her head vehemently. "I told you, I can't find him anywhere. It's like he doesn't exist."

"Okay. I can have someone look into him. I know a hacker, actually. He's helped me out before."

"Won't you or he get into trouble?"

He smiled. "No. He's a professional hacker. He gets paid by companies to find bugs in their software. If anyone can find him, it's Haller. He helped crack a Russian prostitution ring a few years ago. Now he's a consultant with our police department."

"Money is not an issue."

Harrison nodded, picked up his phone, and made a call to his hacker friend just as the waitress brought two humongous plates and slid the bill under Harrison's plate. "Whenever you're ready."

Anila shoved a credit card into the waitress's hand without Harrison noticing. Buying him breakfast was the least she could do. She ate her burrito as Harrison told his friend what he needed. He hung up. "He will call me when he finds something."

After eating a hasty meal, Harrison asked the waitress if Roy was in. "I need to print something."

Anila assumed Roy to be the proprietor. The waitress said, "He had to run an errand. But he said to use his office."

Harrison led Anila into a back office, where she settled with her laptop, and he dictated a Cease and Desist letter.

"In the end, add these words. *Please note that your behavior is a violation of the California Penal Code Subsection 646.9 - Stalking and 422 - Punishment for Threats.*"

Anila looked up from her screen. "He hasn't threatened me with physical harm."

"Yet. Besides, whatever he's doing can be considered a threat. He threatened to expose your business, right?"

"Yeah."

"I still think he'll be scared off if we have a lawyer write it."

Anila shook her head. "The less people that know, the better."

After half an hour, Harrison's phone rang. He put it on speaker. "You're on speaker. I have Anila here with me."

"Hey Anila, this is Haller. So I found your guy. Sneaky bastard. He's scrubbed his identity off the surface of the earth. Now he goes by the name of Isaac Abbott. He's a big shot venture capitalist. Wealthy beyond measure. Lots of shell companies. No bank accounts in the US that I can find… must be all off-shore. It will take some time."

Harrison said, "Where does he live?"

"No residence under his name. But there are three residential properties in the name of one of his shell corporations." There was a pause. "One is in Beverly Hills. One's in La Jolla. And the third is in Wellington Estates. The last one was bought a couple months ago. I'll text you the addresses."

Anila took in a sharp breath. Wellington Estates? That had to be it. Only one property had come on the market and had been swapped up quickly. A cold shiver ran through her at the thought of how daring and how forward he'd been. How could she keep her movements private with him lurking so close-by? He had made his intention clear, and that clarity scared her. But she wouldn't tell Harrison; he'd just add patrols near her home and not only scare her family, but also warn Noah.

"Thanks." Harrison hung up the phone and squeezed her hand. "Don't worry, Anila. I'll take care of it. You just need to sign the Cease and Desist letter. And don't forget to change your phone number."

"How am I going to explain a new phone number to my family?"

He shrugged. "Prank calls. Spam. Whatever. I still think your family should know about Noah. At least Arjun."

She shook her head. "No, I don't want to bother him."

"You like doing things in secret, don't you? Business Casual, and then this."

She managed a smile. "Since childhood. If I got Arjun involved, it always got him in trouble with our father. We're really close still, but I keep him out of my issues."

"Well, I'm glad you reached out to me. And I promise not to tell anyone."

Anila attached the USB cable to the office printer and printed out the Cease and Desist letter. Harrison put it in an envelope, sealed it, and said, "I'll take it over and make sure he gets it. Also, I'll put an officer by your house."

"Please don't. My parents will…"

He waved his hand. "Don't worry. My guys will be discrete. Even you won't notice them. And this Noah or Isaac won't know what hit him."

Before heading out to the Winery Chateau, Anila got a new phone number, transferred the numbers of all her family and friends, and sent them a text.

This is Anila. Got fed up of spam calls. I'm texting all friends and family. Here's my new number.

As texts began to flood her screen acknowledging her message, she noticed one from Avinash. *I'm honored to be included among friends and family. So… coffee sometime?*

She slipped the phone in her bag without answering, but her heart was singing as she pulled into the freeway.

And then the recurrent thought hit her again. Could she allow her truant heart to get attached to someone else? Didn't her heart belong to Sunny first? Was it humanly possible for a man to truly love another man's child?

13

SEVEN-YEAR-OLD ANILA was thrilled to be on the family road trip to Mahabaleshwar, a hill station in the Western Ghats in India. She sang songs all the way, annoying Arjun.

"Stop it!" he complained.

Papa said, "Let her sing. You could join her!"

But Anila's older brother Arjun sat in the car, his arms crossed over his chest, glaring out the window. His irritation was surprising, because he usually sang right along with her.

She found out at the end of their trip. After spending the weekend in the clean, crisp mountain air, watching monkeys climb on their car and on the roof of the hotel, with the lush green forests all around, eating delicious locally-grown food, the Dheer family would return home. Everyone except Arjun, who was to attend a summer camp.

When Anila found out, she knew she'd miss her brother desperately, but she also looked forward to spending time with her mother while Papa was at work.

Her brother didn't want to go to camp. "Papa," he pleaded. "Please let me come home. I promise I'll be good."

Anila didn't know why he was being sent to summer camp while Anila wasn't. She would have loved to hike, sing songs around the campfire, play games and maybe learn horse riding.

"You need to man up," her father told Arjun. "You're turning into a sissy."

Ma patted Arjun on his back. "It will be over in four weeks, Arjun. We'll come to pick you up. You'll make new friends and learn new skills."

He whined, "I already have friends and skills."

Papa had laughed. "Skills?"

Seeing Arjun's face fall wrenched Anila's stomach. She doted on her brother, and never wanted to see him like this. "Please, Papa?" she said.

Papa told her to go sit in the car. With one last look at her brother, Anila went to the car. Her father followed.

Once she was seated, Anila stared out the window. Her mother was hugging Arjun, whose shoulders shook as he wept. Her father scoffed and drummed his fingers on the steering wheel.

After a few minutes, Ma let Arjun go and came to the car. Her face looked pale, her eyes shiny from unshed tears. Anila waved at Arjun, who stared at his family driving away, his hands tucked behind him, a lonely boy in a big, scary world. A camp counselor led him away.

As they drove out, Papa said, "He's turning into a crybaby."

Young Anila could not take it anymore. "Papa, Ma told me I must respect my big brother. But how can I respect him when you talk to him like that? I… I look up to him."

Her father glanced at her reflection in the rearview mirror and didn't answer. After a few minutes, he said to Ma, "Anila is such a kind and sensitive child. I'm so proud of her."

Ma said, "And of Arjun?"

Papa didn't answer. After half an hour on the highway, Anila's eyelids drooped and she fell into a light slumber, the kind when each sound makes you aware that you'd been asleep for a few seconds. It was going to be a long drive home. She kept her eyes closed.

Ma said in a soft voice, "She's right, you know."

Papa turned to Ma. "What?"

"You need to go easier on Arjun. He's just a kid. You treat Anila so much better. It's obvious she's your favorite."

Papa gave a long sigh. "I'm trying, Alka, I really am."

Her mother's voice had a catch. "You'd promised me."

Papa didn't say anything. Anila wondered what promise Papa had broken. Why was Anila his favorite? She made as much a mess as Arjun while playing, talked back as often– if not more–, didn't complete her homework, didn't win swimming and tennis tournaments like him. Then why was she Papa's favorite?

***

Papa's favoritism continued as Anila and Arjun grew older. Anila had always been chubby, but by the time she was eleven years old, the kids in school started teasing her.

When the school bell rang, Anila grabbed her book bag and got up from her seat. The boy sitting behind her chanted, "*Moti, moti, double roti. Moti utth gayi, bhago, bhago!*"

The fat girl has got up, run away, run away. Anila bit her lip. She wouldn't cry. She wouldn't. Two other boys joined in the chant. She hurried out of the class, but they followed her all the way down the hall. She tried to run, but her heavy book bag didn't allow her that respite. They laughed and scattered off in other directions.

Anila stood by the gate waiting for her brother's class to be let out. They often walked back home together unless Papa was sending a car.

Arjun walked toward her and smiled. How strong he looked, how muscular and fit. They ate the same food and while he became strong, she got fat. Why couldn't she look like her brother? She turned her face away. Being tuned to her emotions, he frowned. "What happened, Anila?"

If he hadn't asked, she would have been fine. But the sound of the brotherly concern in his voice was too much to bear. Big, fat tears rolled down her cheeks.

Inches taller than her, he took her by the shoulders. "Tell me! Did someone do something? Say something! I'll break their bones."

She shook her head. A big brother coming to her rescue would just make it worse. "It's nothing."

"I've known you all your life, which is more than you can say about me."

She tried to smile at his perpetual taunt, that he knew her all her life but she didn't know him all of his, because he was two years older.

He said, "Anila, tell me now or we're staying right here. We're not going home."

"Papa will get angry."

"I don't care. You have to tell me now." He shrugged, a steely glint in his eye. Whatever happened, it would always turn out to be Arjun's fault. As far as Papa was concerned, Anila could do no wrong. She hated it, and tried to tell Papa it wasn't always Arjun's fault, but Papa would not listen. There was no other way.

Anila looked at him with tears jiggling in her eyes. "Some boys tease me."

"About what?"

Her lips trembled. "I'm fat, Arjun. There. I've said it."

He scoffed. "That's it?"

"You won't understand. You're an athlete. You play cricket and football and everything. I'm not good at sports."

"You have other talents."

With a spark of hope, she turned to him. "Like what?"

"You're so smart."

"And fat." The sobs began in earnest. Didn't he know that being smart didn't take away all her other miserable qualities?

"Hey! Who are these boys? I'll have a word with them."

"No! Please don't. They'll think of something else to harass me."

They started walking back together. Arjun turned to her. "Maybe they are jealous because you always get A's."

"That doesn't change the fact that I'm fat."

He stopped walking. "You know what can change that?"

"What?"

He grinned. "Working out. Let's do it together."

"But you have sports after school."

"Not everyday." He pinched her cheek. "Besides, I can work out extra for my chubby cheeked baby sister."

"Stop it!"

He said, "I'm serious! I don't have football practice today. So let's start after homework."

That's how they started playing jump ropes, climbing the stairs at home ten times in a row, short sprints in their driveway, sit-ups, and with great difficulty for Anila, *pushups.*

Arjun would make her sit on his back as he did his pushups while she chatted about her day.

In a few weeks, she was able do full push-ups instead of what he called knee-pushups.

Arjun said, "It's time for more." He stood with his feet on both sides of her and pressed down on her back. "Now do it."

He was too strong. She said, "No! Stop."

He laughed. "Come on, Anila. You can do it. Try harder. No pain, no gain."

She tried her best but she couldn't. "Stop it! Stop!"

The door flew open, and Papa stood, horrified. He yelled, "What's going on? Why are you hurting her?"

Arjun, defensive as usual, said, "I… I was trying to help her."

"Help her? You were attacking her." Papa ran to Anila and helped her to her feet. "Did he hurt you?"

Anila was so angry with her brother that she wanted to say yes. But she shook her head in alliance that comes with sibling love. "He's trying to help me lose weight."

Papa's eyes flashed. "Did he call you fat? Is he teasing you?"

She shook her head, but she didn't tell Papa about those boys. In fact, she'd begun to lose weight, her clothes already loose around her waist. She felt good, and the boys had stopped teasing her.

Papa turned to Arjun. "Stop it at once. You don't want her to get huge muscles like a man. Now leave her room."

Arjun left her room, his fists clenched.

For her brother's sake, Anila decided from then on not to involve him in her life so much that he got in trouble with their father. She loved them both, and couldn't stand it when Papa treated Arjun with disdain.

Later that night, she crept into her brother's room. He was in bed already. "What is it?"

She stood in the doorway, wringing her hands. "Arjun, the boys don't tease me anymore."

"Good for you." He turned his back to her.

She climbed on his bed and shook him by the shoulder. "I wanted to thank you."

He sighed. "You'll get fat if you don't keep up the exercises."

"I like feeling slim and strong. Do you think Papa will let me play sports? Maybe tennis?"

He said, "No harm in asking. He can never say no to you. I'll get back to playing football with my friends."

"I love working out with you, but I don't want you to get in trouble."

"I know."

"So, I'll work out on my own, and you can test me from time to time."

"Okay."

"Want to feel my muscles?" She flexed her biceps, and Arjun prodded them like a devoted brother.

He grunted. "Are you making it tight, like this?" He got up in bed and flexed his biceps to show off a nice mound.

She groaned and tried harder. "Yes!"

He almost chuckled. "You're getting there."

She hopped off his bed and tugged at her pajamas. "See? It's loose."

She saw a small smile on his lips. As he covered his ear with his pillow, he mumbled, "Great! Now go away."

She grinned and returned to her room. She was so happy she wasn't an only child like some of her friends. Who did they talk to when they were feeling low? Who did they have to be their confidant, their friend, their rival, all in one?

***

Many years later when Arjun left for college in Los Angeles, Anila was busy with her high school finals. She only had one paper left, and she was working on the last calculus problem in the practice set.

Papa's uncle was planning to visit from Australia, and he was to stay in one of the many guest bedrooms. Papa chose the smaller one adjacent to Anila's bedroom. Ma was cooking up a storm in the kitchen, the aroma of hot spices and ginger wafting across the house.

Papa tiptoed across the hall in an attempt not to disturb Anila, opened the creaky door to the guestroom, and started pottering around, tidying up the room, although it was already tidy and an army of servants had already dusted the dresser and wiped down the windowsills.

Anila heard the cupboard door open, and then a loud clatter, as things fell out on the Italian tile floor. She heard a yelp and a shuffle, and then her Papa bellowed, "Alka!"

Anila's heart raced. She closed her book and ran to the guestroom, thinking Papa was hurt. But he stood there, glaring at the floor, where over a dozen giftwrapped boxes of various sizes lay strewn. She picked one up and read the label: *For Arjun. Happy Tenth Birthday.* Another box said: *For Arjun. Happy Fifteenth Birthday.*

Why were there a bunch of unopened gifts in the cupboard for Arjun? Had he not opened Papa's gifts? She expected another tirade against her brother, but instead, her father stood there, fists clenched, jaw tight, until Ma scampered in, wiping her hands on a towel. "What happened?"

Seeing the gifts, her shoulders sagged. "Oh! You found them."

Papa said, "You said you'd throw them away. You said it would stop."

"I know. It didn't, and I'm sorry."

"Does he know?" Papa asked.

Ma shook her head, tears trembling in her eyes.

Anila was flummoxed at the exchange. Papa stormed out as Ma started picking up the boxes. Anila squatted down to help. In a few minutes, Papa returned with a large plastic bag, filled it with all the gifts, and threw the whole bag out.

When he left the room, Ma collapsed on the bed, sobbing. Anila sat beside her and placed a hand on her shoulder. "Ma, what's going on? Who sent these gifts? Why is Papa so angry?"

Between sobs, Ma said, "One day you'll find out, and you'll understand."

"Understand what?"

Ma stared at Anila. With a sigh, she said, "You're old enough to know. But promise me you'll never tell Arjun."

Anila nodded, curiosity eating her alive.

Ma said, "Have you ever wondered why you look so much like Papa, tall and slender…"

Anila winced. "I wasn't always slim."

"But your frame."

"It's genetics, Ma."

"I'm tall and thin too."

"Your point being?"

Ma looked into her eyes and said, "Arjun is so muscular. His face structure is so different…"

"So?" Then she frowned. "Are you saying that…"

Ma nodded, tears jiggling in her eyes, her face crumpled in sorrow.

Anila's eyes widened. "Arjun is adopted?"

"In a way. I am his mother…"

Anila's eyes widened. "You cheated on Papa?"

Ma stared at her, frowning. "No! I'd never do that! It was before we were married."

As the truth revealed itself, Anila gasped. "Papa found out?"

"I told him I was pregnant before we got married. I promised Papa I'd keep Arjun's father out of the picture. And Papa agreed to give Arjun his name and a home. But Arjun doesn't know. Please, please do not tell your brother. It will kill him."

It made complete sense now. Papa favored Anila because she was his daughter. He was unkind to Arjun because he wasn't his son. Papa would never love Arjun as much as Ma would. Because blood is thicker than water. No one could ever love as child as much as their real parents. No man could love another man's child as much as he could love his own.

14

ANILA PULLED OUT the folder from her satchel and scanned the documents detailing the contract with Winery Chateau and Avinash's law firm. She wanted to make sure everything was in order before filing it away. She frowned. Avinash had forgotten to sign one page, an important one at that, the one that explained the pricing. She cursed under her breath. Dot the i's and cross the t's, indeed!

He would think she was inept, although it was his fault. Well, it was her fault for not checking. She had left the café in a hurry when he'd mentioned Business Casual.

But maybe he'd done it on purpose so he could see her again. Well, if he had, he'd won. There was no way she could file away the papers without his signature. She considered herself a decisive, confident woman, and yet she couldn't figure out whether she wanted to see him again or not.

She considered calling his cell phone, yearning to hear that gravelly, masculine voice. Her stomach knotted. No. That was too dangerous.

She typed out a text on her new phone: *This is Anila Mallik.*

She deleted her last name. *This is Anila.*

Then she frowned. Why was she shying away from using her married name? She *had* been married. Avinash knew that. Would removing her married name give him the signal that she was interested? *Was she?* She wasn't sure. Why lead Avinash on when her mind wasn't even made up? She groaned. She was assuming facts not in evidence, as a lawyer would probably say. She rolled her eyes and added her last name.

This is Anila Mallik. You forgot to sign one of the documents. When can I get your signature?

He answered in a minute. *I know it's you, I saved your number. I'll be downtown in family court all morning. Perhaps at lunchtime?*

She scoffed. Nice way to ask her out to lunch. Boy, was he persistent. The prospect enticed and terrified her in equal measure. She thought for a few seconds then wrote:

I'm busy at lunchtime. I can swing by the courtroom and find you between cases.

At ten o'clock, she grabbed a coffee from *Lupe's* and drove to the courthouse. She walked up the majestic steps, was screened for weapons, and allowed inside.

In the dull gray hallways, families huddled with their lawyers who gave them last minute advice, policemen strolled with coffee cups in their hands, and a young woman sobbed into a tissue. This is the place where broken families came to pick up the pieces. Fight for alimony. For child custody. She took in a deep breath. At least, for Anila, there had been no custody battle; her in-laws were happy to let her bring Sunny up, even though he was their only grandchild. She felt a stab of guilt. While they'd been considerate, hadn't she taken them for granted? She decided to take Sunny to India to visit them the following summer.

Anila sat down on a wooden bench and sent Avinash a text: *I'm here.*

There was no reply. Perhaps he was in the middle of a case. She waited for fifteen minutes, tossed her empty coffee cup into an overflowing trash bin, and then sent another text. *Will you be long?*

Still no response.

A vision of Avinash arguing in court for a client made her want to see him in action. She picked up her satchel and peeked into courtroom by courtroom. She recognized his voice in the fourth courtroom, arguing on behalf of a young woman.

Anila tiptoed in and sat down in the last row. She saw a few people sitting among the spectators, perhaps reporters or people who were waiting for their turn in front of the judge, who was an older woman with gray hair, a pinched nose, and the kindest, largest eyes Anila had ever seen.

Avinash's voice boomed. "Mr. Carter says the child's paternal grandparents are well settled, and can take better care of her. We say the child has a name. Nina. And she calls *my* client 'Mom.'" He pointed to his table, where the young woman in a high ponytail sat on one of the chairs. The child, Nina, was squirming in her lap. She looked to be about two or three years old.

Avinash turned to the other side in a dramatic flourish. "We all know about nature versus nurture, Your Honor, but let me ask a difficult question. If the grandparents are such good role models, how come they raised a child who sold drugs at street corners and ended up in jail?"

"Objection!" shouted the other lawyer, presumably Mr. Carter.

Avinash raised his hand, as if in surrender. "I withdraw." But his point was made. "However, let me say this. My client in this situation in no small measure due to the father of the child. He is serving time for drug dealing. My client has never been convicted of a crime. She became an addict because of her ex-boyfriend. Since he's been in jail, Stella went to rehab and got clean. Her mother watched Nina all that time. But Stella's mother tragically died a little while ago, and now Nina's other grandparents are claiming custody. Based on what?"

"They have resources!" shouted Mr. Carter.

Avinash took in a deep breath and picked up a green circular chip and displayed it for all to see. "My client has been clean and drug free for six months. And she has the chip to prove it. Her mother passed away, and she has no one in the world except for Nina. Stella has a job with Goodwill. You've heard from her manager that she's an excellent employee who will get the first available fulltime position."

The judge interrupted him. "Who watches Nina while Stella goes to work?"

An older woman in shabby clothes, who had been sitting behind Stella, stood up. "I do, Your Honor."

Avinash jumped in. "Excuse her interruption, Your Honor. This is Natalie Sanchez, a cousin of Stella's mother. She owns the house where Stella now rents a room. Natalie is retired and enjoys spending time with Nina. Nina is almost three years old now, and will soon go to preschool."

Mr. Carter stood up. "Nina may one day want to take art classes. Piano lessons. Tennis lessons. Can Stella afford all that?"

Anila watched as Avinash's shoulders sagged just a little. Then Natalie tapped him from behind and whispered something.

Avinash was on his feet. "Natalie owns a piano, Your Honor. And she was a piano teacher for twenty years until she retired. Nina sits in Natalie's lap while Natalie plays, and Nina hums along. If Nina has the tiniest bit of interest or talent, Natalie has offered her free lessons."

Mr. Carter's face turned red. "But can Stella or Natalie provide Nina a pool? A yard to play in? Great schools?"

Avinash placed a hand on Stella's shoulder and delivered the punch line in a softer, almost velvety voice. "Your Honor, being poor is not a crime."

A collective gasp sounded in the courtroom. Avinash allowed a moment for the idea to settle in the judge's heart. It worked, because the judge bit her lip and jotted something down.

Then he added, "And money is no substitute for a mother's love."

Mr. Carter rose. "Your Honor, this is not time for fancy, abstract words or theatrics. We're here to decide what's best for the child."

Avinash held him in a steely gaze. "What's best for Nina is to stay with her mother. A child needs her mother's hugs more than a pool, her mother's kisses more than a yard. She needs Stella to tuck her into bed at night, read her a book, take her to a movie, and attend parent-teacher meetings. Nina needs her *mother*, Your Honor. No one in the world can love a child more than her parent."

Anila's throat constricted. *Avinash knows. He understands.*

Avinash walked closer to the Judge. "I will personally make sure Stella attends her meetings with the social workers. She will go to AA. She will stay clean. She will earn her next chip and the next. She will keep her job. If not, she would lose Nina. She knows it."

The judge's eyes moistened. She ruled in Stella's favor, and Anila wanted to break into applause.

As people started to stream out of the courtroom, Avinash said, "Stella, I gave my word to the judge. Don't make me regret it."

"Cross my heart," said Stella. "You've given me the most precious thing, Mr. Singhania. And you won't accept money. How can I repay you?"

He grinned. "Just send me a Christmas card with Nina's photo every year." He turned to Natalie. "And invite me to Nina's piano recital sometime."

Anila's heart seemed to burst with affection for this man, who understood a mother's heart better than most. She scurried out of the courtroom and waited in the hallway, her heart thudding in her chest.

When he came out of the courtroom, she pretended to be scrolling down her phone, sitting on the wooden bench.

He stopped beside her and broke into a smile. "Hey! Have you been waiting long?"

She looked up at him and lied. "No, um… not long."

"Okay. What did I miss?"

"What?"

He quirked an eyebrow. "I mean, where did I forget to sign?"

In the past minutes she'd forgotten why she was even here. Anila fumbled through the papers from her satchel and offered him the offending page.

He placed a foot on the edge of the bench, used his thigh as a table, placed the paper on the folder of files he carried, and signed the dotted line. "I'm sorry you had to come all the way."

In truth, she was happy she'd come and seen him in action. She waved her hand and lied again. "It was on my way. No worries."

He regarded her with warm brown eyes and dragged a hand through his hair. Then he glanced at an expensive watch on his wrist. "Um… I have an hour before my next case. Care for a coffee? The cafeteria has a warm black liquid that passes for coffee."

Say no! Say no! She could still see the coffee cup she'd discarded in the waste basket beside her. Her heart was already thudding, albeit from non-caffeine related causes. She glanced up at him. "I would kill for a cup of coffee."

The relief on his face made her heart jump. She followed him to the basement cafeteria, a cavernous, desolate place with dull white floors, a high ceiling, fluorescent lights, gray plastic chairs, and small square tables.

Avinash motioned her to take a seat, and she hesitated, wondering if she should wipe it down. *Don't be pompous!* She slid into a chair and placed her satchel on the table. Finding a sticky residue, she moved it to her lap. Around her, groups of people were sitting at tables, sipping coffee, eating donuts, and flipping papers, discussing their game plans for their cases.

Avinash bought two cups of steaming coffee in Styrofoam cups. "I found cinnamon. Um… and I wasn't sure about nutmeg, but they didn't have it anyway." He stared at her face, but she kept it impassive. It was thoughtful of him to remember cinnamon. And to wonder about Noah's damn nutmeg.

"That's okay," she said. "Thanks." The coffee wasn't as bad as he'd warned, and she enjoyed the acrid flavor as it went down her throat.

Avinash's phone rang and he frowned. "I am so sorry, but it's my client. I have to take this."

She nodded. "I should get going as well."

He looked concerned and kind as he talked on the phone trying to calm down the high pitched, panicked woman's voice. It seemed to be a contentious divorce case.

They picked up their coffee cups and left the building. As she turned left and he turned right, he placed a hand over his phone and said, "Hey, Anila."

"Yeah?"

He smiled. "Thanks for the coffee."

She smirked and said, "You paid."

He blushed. "You know. Thanks for saying yes."

She had turned away with a warm, guilty glow on her face. She got into her car and placed the satchel on the passenger side seat. Her hands were shaking from the caffeine, her pulse racing.

She leaned forward, trying to clear her head. Her heart-shaped pendant dangled forward, got caught in the steering wheel, and the chain snapped. The pendant fell into the crevices of the seat. In a panic, Anila got out, moved the seat back and searched for it. Then she used her phone flashlight and saw the pendant sparkle somewhere deep within. But no matter how hard she tried, she could not reach it.

She sighed and got back into the car. Then she glanced at her watch and called her mother. "I'll be late from the Chateau. Could you pick Sunny from preschool?"

Her mother sighed. "He was crying in school and they called home. I've got him already."

Anila gripped the wheel. "What happened?"

"He was throwing a tantrum. He wants a baby sister like Megha and Trevor."

"Oh, Ma. What do I do? Do you think he needs a counselor? A therapist?"

Her mother's voice was cold. "He needs a father and a sibling."

Anila hung up, annoyed with the world, annoyed with her yo-yoing heart, her flip flopping loyalties, and her confusion about the future. Out of habit, her hand reached for the pendant, only to find it missing.

Overhead, a jet flew into the clouds with a deafening noise. A sob escaped her throat.

What are you trying to tell me, Vikas?

15

THE SINGHANIA AND SINGHANIA law firm's holiday banquet and retreat at the Dheer Winery Chateau started off without a hitch. Anila was the perfect hostess, managing a slew of attendants who ensured everyone's needs were met, pillows fluffed, extra blankets provided, mini-fridges stocked, and spa treatments and wine-tastings booked.

For the daytime events, she wore a business suit, but for the evening banquet, she chose an ankle-length turquoise dress with emerald earrings paired with high heels. Anila had kept the spare sets of clothes in the closet in the office and changed in the bathroom. She'd have used one of the spare guestrooms, but they were all booked for this event.

She checked her phone to see any messages from her mother. But there were none. And after the Cease and Desist letter, Noah– or Isaac– hadn't harassed her. Or maybe he couldn't find her new number. In any event, she'd enjoyed the last whole week in relative peace and quiet. Sunny had settled into a happy routine with Myra and hadn't harassed Anila about a new daddy or baby sister. And all it took was a fish tank. Sunny had been giddy with joy when he saw the goldfish darting about in the tank, the air bubbling through the water. "Can we get more colorful fish?"

That was a request she was happy to fulfill. "Sure. On your birthday."

As guests mingled holding champagne flutes or glasses of wine, Anila took a breather and rested her back against the wall, watching the crowd. Avinash's mother, Moyna, a slender, stunning, middle-aged woman, came for a short time with his sister, Tanya, who was several years younger than him. Anila watched Avinash dote over his sister, protecting her from "unwanted advances" from younger lawyers and office staff, even though it all looked innocent and Tanya seemed fully capable of protecting herself.

Anila had felt Moyna's eyes on her a few times as she'd moved around the banquet hall, ensuring everything was perfect. She took a deep breath and approached Moyna. "Mrs. Singhania, I hope you're having a great time."

Moyna smiled, her face softening as she regarded her with dark eyes. "Yes. Everything's great. Avinash has great taste." If it was meant to be a *double entendre*, it hit its mark; the comment made Anila blush, and Moyna narrowed her eyes.

In a hurry to change the subject, Anila said, "Your daughter is so vivacious and charming."

Moyna broke into a smile and beamed. "Yes. She's also terribly intelligent. She's doing a PhD in neuroscience. She's only seventeen."

Here was a mother proud of her child, much like Anila herself. Anila had informed everyone when Sunny took his first step, spoke his first word, pressed the pedal on a tricycle the first time. She smiled.

Moyna continued, "Avinash and Tanya are alike and yet different. She's such an extrovert, and he's the opposite."

"Really?" Anila frowned. "He looks really friendly and outgoing, too."

Moyna stared at Anila. "He can seem friendly, but he's got his heart hidden behind a shell."

Anila blushed again. That was the opposite of everything she'd read about him in the society magazines. But Moyna was his mother, and probably knew him best. Or, he hid his personality from her.

Before she could answer, Moyna said, "He was coming out of his shell, you know, until Sonia..." As she trailed off, Anila frowned. Who was Sonia? Was she his ex-wife?

Then Moyna placed her hand on Anila's forearm. "Having said that, I hope he's been behaving himself with you. He *can* be a terrible flirt."

Anila didn't know how to respond. "Um... he's fine. Um... charming."

"He keeps people at a distance, you know. Since the divorce. He flirts, but won't... *can't* commit."

Anila didn't know how to react. Was his mother warning her about Avinash? Had she discerned Anila's interest in him, tentative though it was?

Tanya approached them. "Mom, can we leave? I've got an experiment running and should get back."

Moyna turned to Anila. "This is my daughter. Tanya, this is Anila, the manager."

Tanya's face lit up, and she grinned. "Ah! I was wondering. So nice to meet you at last."

At last? Anila blushed. Had Avinash mentioned her? She felt embarrassed, blushing like a teenager. They shook hands. "Very nice to meet you too. Best of luck with medical school applications."

Tanya flashed her a smile. "Thanks. I wish I could stay longer, but I really should get back to the lab."

Moyna said, "I'm afraid that's my cue. It's a long drive home, so we better get going." She held Anila's arm. "It was very nice to meet you."

Anila said, "Likewise. Drive safe."

After they left, the lights dimmed, and the rock band of the daughter of one of the law firm partners came to the make-shift stage. Amid a roar of applause, they began playing loud and slightly off-key music. Anila hid a smile. This was another parent who couldn't see any fault in their kid.

From the corner of her eye she saw Avinash walk toward her holding two glasses of wine. He hadn't brought a date to the retreat, while almost everyone else attending came as a couple.

"You need a break," he said, coming to stand beside her and leaning against the wall. "You've been working for sixteen hours straight."

"I'm still on the clock," she said. "No drinking at work." She shifted her weight from one foot to the other, taking pressure off what was sure to be a nasty blister tomorrow.

He smiled, his eyes crinkling up in the most enchanting way. Her heart skipped a beat. He whispered, "I won't tell. Come on. You could say you were testing the wine before allowing it to be served."

She chuckled and accepted the glass. "Lawyers with their loopholes!"

The music was loud, and the microphones—which were thankfully brought by the band and couldn't be blamed on the chateau—screeched. Avinash winced. "Is there a place we can chat?"

"Chat about what?"

He cleared his throat. "Um… about tomorrow's events."

She turned to look at him. Didn't he trust her yet? Today's events had gone off smoothly. "It's all planned out. Everything will be fine."

"Humor me," he said. "Just because you won't go out with me doesn't mean we can't be cordial."

Her heart raced at the thought of going out with him. If he asked her again, she doubted if she could refuse. He didn't know she'd watched him at work in the courtroom, and that he'd impressed her so much she was reevaluating her priorities in life.

Her hand reached for the pendant as it often did when she was anxious, but her neck was bare. She hadn't been able to retrieve Vikas's gift from under the seat of her car.

Avinash was watching her. Dressed in a very nice Armani, his pale peach shirt open at the collar, he looked so relaxed, so debonair, that she couldn't take her eyes off him.

He took a sip of the wine and grimaced as the microphone screeched again, and the lead singer started her number, the pitch too high for her, which she compensated for with volume.

Avinash turned to her with beseeching eyes. "Have mercy on me."

She smiled. "Fair enough. Let's go." She led him to the office, turned on the lights, and settled on the couch. Staring at him as he stood leaning against the door, she patted the cushion beside her. "Have a seat." It felt terribly bold, and her heart raced.

He sat beside her, reached out with his long arm, and placed his glass on the desk. She could smell a faint musky cologne. Anila held her glass in both hands and turned to him. "What do you want to talk about?"

He seemed awkward too, she noticed with satisfaction, as he reached out and picked up his glass again, twirling it in his hand, not drinking. He looked nervous. Was this what his mother meant?

He said, "Anila, I would love to get to know you. But I know you're not interested in dating or anything like that. Can we be friends?"

Here it was. An offer, a simple proposal, but weighed heavily with unseen implications, like cigar smoke in a dark room. She cleared her throat. "Depends."

"On?"

She twisted in the couch to stare at him, hoping her eyes could hide how vulnerable she felt, how scared. "What are you expecting from me?"

"Friendship. You tell me about you, I tell you about me."

Her heart hammered in her chest. She was desperate to know more about him, to do all the research she had to do if she were to decide on something serious with him. Why had his marriage broken up? Who was Sonia? How long ago was that? Why was he still single?

Finally, she managed, "You start. I heard you're divorced. Can you talk about that?"

He grimaced, as if the memory of his ex-wife lanced him. She regretted the question instantly and raised her hands in surrender. "Unless it's too painful."

He sighed deeply. "Oh, you have no idea. What can I tell you about Sierra?"

Sierra? So his wife's name was Sierra. Who was Sonia, then? She said, "Why you broke up, for starters."

He shrugged, the weight of the world shifting as he did. "We got married too young. It didn't work out."

Anila had married young and made it work. "Because you grew up? That doesn't make sense."

He ran his fingers through his hair, ruffling up the top. He looked youthful, playful, *vulnerable.* "You might not believe this about me, but I was a shy kid growing up. So when I went to college, I met all these people and was intimidated by some, enamored by others. I was secretly in love with Sierra from the day I saw her in the corridor of my dorm. She was on her way to some party or something. The heel of her shoe broke just as I stepped out of my room. I heard her curse. I was tongue-tied, but I somehow managed to offer help. She came into my room. I super-glued the broken heel while she stood barefoot in my room, staring at my shaking hands. When it was done, she gave me such a striking smile."

He was quiet for a few moments, as if reliving those moments. Then he said, "She was a theater major. Vivacious, drop-dead gorgeous, chatty, extroverted… And I was this love-struck teenager. She lived two rooms down in my dorm." Then he shook his head. "But, after that one time, she didn't seem to know I existed."

"That's awkward."

He scoffed. "Yeah. And then a few years later, before the start of my second year of law school, after…" He trailed off. She wondered what he'd been about to say.

He continued without explaining. "Well, I went to Vegas with a group of friends. I saw her there, but she didn't recognize me. Someone introduced us. She asked if I was related to the ex-Governor of California, who'd been in the news recently. I said yes and somehow found the courage to ask her to dance with me. To my surprise, she agreed. I'd been in love with her, rather, the idea of her, for so long that it seemed like a gift from heaven, to bump into her like that. And she didn't even remember me from college. So my awkward heel repair job stayed secret."

Anila was touched that he was opening his heart out to her without asking for the details of her life in return. Did he share his story often? "Then what happened?"

He swallowed a large gulp of wine and placed the glass on the desk. "One drink led to another, and she got really tipsy. So I led her back to her room. She was leaning in for a kiss but I... I sort of pushed her into her room and went back to mine. She was drunk. I couldn't do that."

"That's gentlemanly of you."

"We saw each other again the next couple days, and my friend group got along with hers. A few nights later, she kissed me on the dance floor. She said I was like no one she'd met before. We drank and danced well into the evening, and at the end of the night I asked her to marry me. And what do you know? For some weird cosmic reason, she agreed. We were both very drunk. We were married in the casino by a minister dressed as Dumbledore. He waved his cheap plastic magic wand and pronounced us man and wife. Dumbledore was a bit drunk too, I think. He made sure we kissed." A wistful smile hovered over his lips, as if he missed her still. "We had a fun-filled honeymoon that lasted the rest of the weekend."

Anila laughed. "That sounds kinda romantic, actually."

He ran his fingers through his hair again, something he seemed to do when he was nervous. "It was too sudden, too soon. I really thought she'd call the whole thing off in the morning, after she'd had her coffee and the hangover was gone."

"But she didn't?"

He shook his head. "I was stunned too. I realized only later that every single thing she did was premeditated, preplanned. I suppose she was seducing me. She was quite an actress, letting me believe I was seducing her. The only thing that makes sense is that she wanted some security."

How could anyone blame Sierra for trying to find a place to belong? Anila said, "Nothing wrong with wanting security."

He scoffed. "She didn't want me. She wanted the status. We were trying to fit a square peg in a round hole. We didn't gel. She came from a lower middle class, broken family. My family was rich, powerful, political." He drained the last bit of wine before saying,

"My parents weren't too happy about the marriage, but they accepted her into the family. But I'd refused to let them pay for my tuition. I was working two jobs to support myself. And I had a tiny studio apartment. I think Sierra had assumed I was living the life of a wealthy man. She didn't complain about the apartment, though. Her waitressing job was close by, and she freelanced on and off as an actress. An extra in a musical, or an occasional gig with a band." He thumbed over his shoulder, as the off-key music carried into the office. "She was way, way better than that one."

Anila giggled.

He continued, "Sierra's real passion was musical theater, though. She had a beautiful singing voice, but man, could she dance!"

"Sounds like a lovely picture."

He made a sound that was half scoff, half laugh. "Until she started hanging out with her college friends again. All the time. They partied late into the night…"

A wave of female loyalty swept over her. "But you were busy with your job and school. She has a right to have a life."

"Yeah, you're right. But we were a bad fit. What we had couldn't be called love. It was the stupidity of youth, an infatuation. And then the lying started. She deceived me one too many times. She stabbed me in the heart. Figuratively. I had to let her go just to survive." He rubbed his wrist and twirled the expensive watch. "We got divorced before I finished law school."

"I'm sorry to hear that."

"If it wasn't for my childhood friend, Rafik, I'd have gone crazy."

"What became of Sierra?"

He sighed. "She's a star now."

Anila turned to look at him. "Wait a minute. Are you talking about Sierra Smith?"

Avinash shrugged his shoulders dejectedly. "The one and only."

"You were married to Sierra Smith." It was more a statement than question.

"That's me."

Her eyebrows rose. "God, she's gorgeous!"

He scoffed. "If you're wondering what she saw in me, I wonder the same too."

"I didn't mean that." What she wondered was, after being married to Sierra, what did Avinash see in Anila?

They stared at the opposite wall for a few minutes, each lost in their private thoughts.

16

AVINASH REMEMBERED Sierra's blissful face, her smile, her curvaceous body underneath him when they made love. He squeezed his eyes shut. Their relationship was doomed to fail. But sitting beside Anila, who was still in love with her husband years after his death, made him realize not all relationships would fail. After all these years, Avinash had finally got over Sierra, but talking about her brought back all the chaotic emotions, interspersed with a rare pleasant memory.

They had learned to live under the same roof, with routines so disparate that days would go by and they wouldn't see each other. Often, when he returned from class or his job, he'd stumble over her heels strewn across the bedroom, their bed littered with clothes she'd rejected for whatever function she'd decided to attend. Exhausted and annoyed, he'd put her clothes away in the closet they shared, where his clothes were pushed aside into a quarter of the space. He didn't mind not having space in the closet; he minded not having space in her heart.

He'd open the fridge to find expired milk and no food. He'd munch on Cheerios. Once in a while he put on a pot of rice and made a lentil-vegetable soup. But Sierra didn't like the smell of Indian spices. Just to avoid an argument, he'd cook pasta and open a jar of store-bought sauce.

Sierra didn't like to cook. She usually ate at the restaurant where she waitressed all days of the week, on occasion bringing him a slice of cake or penne pasta. "For my love," she'd announce. "Whom I miss very much." She said it as if trying to make herself believe it.

And yet, she spent all her spare time with her friends, going to bars and nightclubs, or going out on weekend trips. She'd return with the pungent smell of pot clinging to her clothes. Often her breath smelled of alcohol early in the morning.

His friend Rafik told him Sierra was acting out because she missed him. "Why don't you plan a nice trip for the two of you?"

During spring break, instead of studying or taking extra shifts, Avinash planned a surprise trip to Hawaii.

When he told her, she frowned. "I had plans with friends for next week. You should have asked me before."

"I'm sorry." He apologized for planning a wonderful week on a beachfront property he could barely afford, but that's how their relationship worked. She'd done him a favor by marrying him, and he had to pay obeisance forever, like a convict in prison for life.

It wasn't fair. And so, for the first time in their marriage, he started an argument. "But Sierra, we're married. I wish you'd spend more time with me."

She placed her hands on her hips and tilted her head, stunned that he would challenge her decision. But she said, "I do spend time with you. We live in the same shitty apartment, for God's sake."

He would have backed off, but her use of the words "shitty apartment" awakened an uncharacteristic anger. He clenched his jaw and raked his fingers through his hair. Taking a deep breath, he said, "I want you to *want* to spend time with me."

She pouted. "You're never available."

"That's not fair. I am home almost every evening."

"That's when I work."

He squeezed the bridge of his nose. "That's true. But Sierra, I miss you."

"Don't be so clingy." She hugged him and said, "I'm sorry, okay? I'll spend more time with you." Another favor doled out by the queen, as if she was dropping her handkerchief he should accept gratefully. It annoyed him.

Emboldened by winning the first argument with her, he said, "And Sierra, I don't like that you smoke pot. It messes with your mind, you know."

She stiffened and took a step back. "Are you calling me stupid, Mr. Brains?"

"No, I just don't like it when you do that."

"Well, I don't like that you study all the time. So we're even."

Her comment meant she wouldn't stop smoking pot, because there was no way he would stop studying. Irritation pricked him like a bug bite. His voice rose. "I study so I can get a good job and support both of us."

"Fine."

The chill in her manner made him desperate to please her yet again. He placed his hands on her hips and pulled her close. "I'm sorry for raising my voice. It won't happen again. Um… do you want to go away just the weekend? San Diego, maybe?"

She took a step back. "Didn't I tell you? Um… my aunt is sick. She wants me to spend the weekend with her."

"The one in Denver? The one I've never met? I could go to Denver with you."

Her voice softened. "Her apartment is smaller than this one. Let me go alone. But I'll make it up to you. I promise."

That weekend, after seeing her off at the airport, Avinash visited his parents' home in Beverly Hills. His father was out of town, and his mother was at work. So he hung out with his half-sister Tanya, who was altogether too mature for her age. "Sierra kicked you out, huh?"

"No, she didn't. She's visiting her sick aunt in Denver."

"Oh. Sorry to hear that. Want to get cupcakes at Lupe's? Like old times."

He laughed. He and Tanya used to share one half of each flavor of cupcake until they were queasy. Then he'd have an espresso, and Tanya would drink hot chocolate. It was their special bonding activity whenever they hung out together, something they had started after Sonia died, and that happened less and less often since he'd got married.

"I've missed you, Avi," said Tanya. "Sleep over at home tonight. We could make pancakes for breakfast tomorrow. I found a great recipe for oatmeal, apple, cinnamon pancakes."

He smiled. Cooking with Tanya was one of the household chores he enjoyed. She always prattled away about how she'd learned that a pinch of this or a dash of that could enhance or ruin a dish. "Sure."

That night he went to bed in the same bedroom he'd occupied when he'd come to America at the age of fourteen. The room still smelled of fresh paint, although it had been years since he'd left home. The scratches on the wall from the Kobe Bryant poster he'd ripped off to take to college still showed. Moyna had still kept some of his trophies from the school in India. A photo of his grandmother holding him as a baby graced the table. A few other photos of him and Tanya, and the one with him, Tanya, and Sonia, which his mother had in her office.

He fluffed his pillow and lay down on the bed, covering himself with the duvet. This bed was so much more comfortable than his studio apartment, where he shared a full sized bed with his wife, where she hoarded the comforter and he often lay shivering.

He stared at the ceiling remembering those days when he'd been desperate to fit in. How was it that he still yearned to fit in? Why couldn't he find his place in the world? When he married Sierra, he thought this was it. He had arrived. Avinash Singhania was *somebody*. He sighed deeply.

He turned over in bed, reached for his phone, and called Sierra. She should have landed by now. She hadn't called him from her aunt's place. It went on voicemail. After a long time he fell into a fitful sleep, until urgent knocking on the door woke him up.

Avinash stared at his watch. 2 AM. He climbed out of bed and opened the door. Tanya stood in the doorway in her pajamas, frowning at her phone. He cleared his throat. "Too early for pancakes."

She looked up at him with large eyes. He frowned. "Tanya, what's wrong?"

She bit her lip and said, "Um… Sierra is not in Denver."

"What?"

"She's in Las Vegas. I saw a video of her dancing on pool tables. Here!" She handed him her phone and together, they watched the racy video. Sierra was wearing a short red dress, her friends on the table with her. Men clapping and egging them on. Drinks flowing all around. On the walls behind them Avinash saw the name of the casino. The same one where they'd got married fifteen months ago.

His voice cracked. "Must be from before."

Tanya shook her head sadly. "Look at the time stamp."

17

ON THE LAST day of the holiday retreat at the Winery Chateau, the central atrium had been converted into a ballroom, and a DJ played trendy rock and pop music. Employees of the Singhania and Singhania law firm danced without inhibition as strobe lights sparkled from the center of the ceiling and waiters circled the perimeter with champagne and *hors d'oeuvres*.

Anila excused herself, went into the office, and closed the door behind her. She called home. "Ma, how's Sunny?"

Her mother said, "Arjun and Lily took him to the park. They had fun, so don't you worry. He missed you, but a bit of separation is good for him."

"Is Myra coming back? Is her mother better?"

Her mother said, "Seems to be. Myra is... how do I say it... adequate. There are nannies who love kids, and those that do it as a job. For Myra, it's a job. Her mother is sick, and she needs the money. She hasn't developed much of a bond with him."

"Yeah, but he spends most of his day in the preschool and then takes a nap at home. She doesn't have much time with him."

"That's true."

Anila smiled. "Can I talk to him?"

"He's already gone to bed."

Anila sighed. "Thanks, Ma."

"It's the last day of the retreat, right?"

"Yes."

A knock on the door interrupted her call. "Ma, I gotta go. I'll be home late. Don't wait up for me."

Avinash peeked into the office. "Thought I saw a light. Care to dance?"

She tilted her head. "Me? I'm not part of your firm. You go have fun."

He squinted and then grinned. "What? Have fun while you slave away? You must think poorly of me."

All through the retreat, Avinash had been sweet and generous, yet kept his distance from her. And from that distance, the interactions seemed fine, safe even.

She smirked. "I'm not slaving away. I'm okay."

"Come on. Just one dance."

A familiar tune from a popular single sounded from the atrium, and Anila stood up. "That's my favorite song."

Avinash had a naughty grin on his face. "I know."

She frowned at him. "How do you…"

"I found out at Lily's wedding."

She rose from the chair. "Who told you?"

"No one. I saw you dancing with your son. You didn't dance to any other number. So I guessed you like this one a lot."

She hesitated.

He said, "Come on! I asked the DJ to play it only twice."

She laughed and followed him to the dance floor. He was an elegant, graceful dancer, and she was grateful for all the dance lessons her parents had forced her to take as a child; Papa had claimed she was getting big, manly muscles from all the workouts, and he thought dancing would help her stay lean. After that spate of chubbiness as a preteen, she'd remained slender.

Soon, the floor cleared out, and it was just the two of them in the center. Avinash held her close, and she felt the power in his arms, his legs, and the sensuousness of their coordinated movement as they glided on the floor. Nothing else seemed to exist but his body touching hers, his hands on her waist, his breath on her cheek. Vikas couldn't dance if his life depended on it, but Avinash was skilled as he maneuvered her around the floor, bent her backwards, twirled her around, and then pulled her close. For the next few minutes, her mind went blank.

After the second rendition of the song, applause exploded from the guests. Blood rushed to Anila's face just as a slow number started. She tried to step away, but Avinash pulled her closer.

His voice was hoarse. "Stay!" It was a request, a demand, an entreaty, all rolled into one.

She wasn't sure what made her agree: the magnetism of his personality, the enchanting lights, the wine she'd consumed, or the glow on his face as he beheld her with gentle brown eyes, eyes that assured her she was deserving of attention. Confusion clouded her mind, as if she was drunk on momentary pleasure, a temporary high until the crash would surely come and bring her back to earth. But for now, she floated on clouds, and she wanted to remain there just for a little while longer.

They danced well into the night. She wondered if his night with Sierra in Vegas had been as enthralling as this was for her, but she shook it out of her mind. He was older now, more mature, and they were not drunk. Tipsy, maybe, but not drunk. Passion clouded her mind, but she wasn't slurring her speech or missing her steps. The song switched to a fast pop number, and they jived together, laughing. The evening drew on. She was impressed to learn he could waltz. His stamina and grace were tremendous.

She was exhausted after the long night, and her feet ached, but she couldn't bear to move away from him.

The crowd around them thinned, and slowly, everyone else began to retire to their rooms. Soon, the DJ started packing up, and Anila said with a little catch in her voice, "Party's over."

He said, "Join me for a drink."

"Oh, I don't know…"

"Come on. Last night I told you the sordid tale of my miserable marriage. Tonight, tell me about you. What makes you tick."

"Just one drink." She laughed, but it may have been the wine or the utter comfort she felt in his company. His dates had been right in their reviews of him.

He picked up a bottle of wine, hooked two glasses in his fingers and quirked his eyebrow in the most seductive way she'd seen. "Where?"

She didn't want to return to the office where the space was so limited that his knees abutted against the desk. She led him to the wine tasting room, and they settled down on the low, plush couch. Avinash poured two glasses of wine.

Before he could ask her about her past, she said, "When did you come to America?"

He poured wine in the glasses and handed her one. "At the young, impressionable, awkward age of fourteen. My family was rich and famous, and the media made it the talk of the town when I showed up. I tried to fit in, but it was hard."

She took the glass from him. "I came as an adult, and it was hard. I can't imagine how it must have been for a teenager."

"It worked out in the end. I mean, look at me now!" He waved his hands over his body and grinned.

"Humble, much?" She grinned back. He could be such a kid!

He turned to her and changed the subject abruptly. "Tell me about Vikas."

That startled her. She looked up at him, but his eyes spoke of openness, of honesty and genuine interest, and not the macabre curiosity of someone who wants to hear the nasty details only to feel grateful their own lives.

Her hand reached for the pendant once again, and not finding it there, dropped to her lap. Finally, she said, "Vikas was a wonderful person."

"What was he like?"

She settled deeper into the couch, resting her head on the soft cushion. "He was sweet and funny and kind and talented."

"Do you have a photo?"

She dug through her purse and pulled out the photo from her wallet. It was taken on the first day of their honeymoon cruise, with both smiling at the camera from the back deck of the ship, wind whipping their hair as the waves arrowed away from the ship and settled into the depths behind them, land receding further and further. She could almost smell the sea and Vikas's cologne. She didn't tell Avinash she'd suffered from food poisoning through their honeymoon and that the other photos showed her lying in bed in their cabin, holding a cup of soup or a dry toast.

Avinash took the photo from her, stared at it, and then returned it. "He's handsome. You must miss him a lot."

Missing him had transformed from agonizing, piercing pain, to a dull ache, and finally now, after three years, she could remember an anecdote here or a story there, without the desperate gloom that would follow. An odd morning would go by without her thinking of her husband. Then she'd see the twinkle in her son's eye, an exact replica of her husband's. Sometimes it would bring dismay and sorrow, while other times it would bring a smile to her face. Each day the pain eased, until she felt guilty for not feeling sad. Wasn't that being selfish, moving on, when Vikas hadn't been given the chance? Her voice was soft. "Yeah, I miss him a lot."

"What's your best memory of him?"

She smiled. "A bit like your story, but mine was happier. Vikas had been really busy with the air exercises, and I hadn't seen much of him. So I complained that we didn't have fun anymore. He felt terrible and asked me what I'd like to do. I said, I don't know. Hang out together, go for a movie…"

He gripped his glass and took a tentative sip. "And?"

Anila stared at the ceiling. "He didn't say anything, but the next day he showed up early from work with his pockets full of movie tickets. Different theaters, different show-times, different movies. He asked me which one I liked. We could watch one or a few…" She laughed. "Some were overlapping times. He'd sent out an orderly to buy tickets for as many movies as he could."

Avinash smiled. "So which movie did you end up watching?"

Her smile faded. "I don't remember what we finally decided…" She frowned. "I'm beginning to forget those little things." She couldn't recall the exact color of his favorite shirt or the name of his favorite restaurant. She did remember the way he'd frown while reading the news or watching an intense cricket match, the way he'd smile when she sang in the kitchen while cooking. He'd join her in an off-key rendition, but she'd forgotten the songs.

Tears stung her eyes, and she swallowed hard. "As the years pass by, I can't remember every line on his face, every nuance of his expressions… I fear it will all fade away."

He held her hand. "Hey! You love him. That's all that matters."

Anila noticed how he said "love" instead of "loved." But it *was* in the past, wasn't it? Does one eventually stop loving a person after their death? Do the memories start to fade away into oblivion, never to be reclaimed? And does life, at some point, create an empty space to be filled with something else in its place? Someone else?

Refusing to consider that last idea, she said, almost hotly, "I will always love him."

He didn't answer.

She said, "It's not fair that I had such little time with him. It's not fair he didn't get to see his son grow up. It's not fair his son doesn't know him."

After a moment of silence, he said, "How does Sunny take it?"

"He asks about his father. He wants a sibling. A baby sister. It's hard to even think about it. I'd sworn never to marry again." She bit her lip, as she realized she'd used the past tense for that thought.

Somewhere in her subconscious, had she started to change her mind, at last? That while she had sworn never to marry, the idea wasn't entirely out of the realm of possibility now.

But no matter what happened, it would be unfair to Sunny. She added, "I'll always put Sunny first. How can anyone else do that except for his father?"

Avinash said, "His father isn't here."

"Exactly."

She heard the catch in his voice when he said, "That must be hard."

Anila took a deep breath. "Sunny was born when I went into labor at the news of my husband's death. One day we mourn, the next day we celebrate his birthday."

"Do you think you'll ever be ready for more?"

The weight of that question hung in the air like the scent of a fragrant rose, the offer in it invisible but not imperceptible.

She shrugged. "I don't know. Vikas was an only child. He and I had wanted our child to have what I had. A sibling, who understood how it was growing up in the same family, with unconditional love for each other even if there's some rivalry. To know you have a sibling who'll always have your back." She paused. "Arjun and I were inseparable growing up. Now that little Megha and Trevor will both have little siblings, I know Sunny's going to want more."

Avinash paused. He cleared his throat. "And you?"

She glanced at him, but his face showed no emotion. She took in a sharp breath. "Maybe one day I'll be ready for more."

"More what?" His eyes sparkled with delight, with hope. She didn't want to push him away, because if she did, she wasn't sure if she'd ever get him back. Here he was, in his full glory, demonstrating his interest in her. How could she resist that?

She dropped her gaze, unable to offer him what he clearly wanted, and yet unwilling to shut out the possibility. "More from life. Maybe have more kids someday. But, like I say, there's no Season 2."

"What do you mean?"

She gave a sardonic laugh. "You know like in a TV show… the first season shows the hero and heroine, and everything's going fine, and we expect a season two. We look forward to it. But maybe the actor had a falling out or asked for too much money, so the director has to cut him out. Accident. Death." She snapped her fingers. "Just like that, there is no season two."

He took the last sip of his wine and poured out another glass. She waved her hand, refusing a refill. After a long pause while he seemed to weigh his words, he said, "There *can* be a season two. With a different actor."

She turned to stare at him, as a pulse throbbed in his neck. Her voice was soft. "It can never be the same."

"No, it won't be the same. But it doesn't have to be worse."

Their gazed clashed. In those words and those eyes, she read his intent, his proposition, his hope. She didn't know how to respond, feeling guilty for neither discouraging him, nor letting it go forward.

She took in a sharp breath. "Enough about imaginary TV shows. Tell me about you. What do you want from life?"

He leaned back into the soft leather and stared at the opposite wall.

18

WHEN ANILA asked Avinash what he wanted from life, he couldn't tell her the truth. He wanted her. That's what he wanted. But it was impossible; she'd made that amply clear. She wasn't ready, and it was just too complicated. He'd mentioned a season two, suggesting it be with him, but she hadn't responded. What was he supposed to say now?

He cleared his throat. His armor was on, his defenses up. "My life is great as it is. Why would I want to change anything?"

She scoffed. "So much for being frank and friendly. It's fine if you don't want to tell me."

"Oh, I do. That's just it. I take life one day at a time. Make space for whatever to happen. No obstruction, not resistance. Just go with the flow. No worries for the future, no regrets for the past."

She repeated after him, "No worries for the future, no regrets for the past."

"Yup," he said with a smile.

"Does it work?"

"It has, so far."

She stared at him with those dark eyes, her eyeliner still perfect, her lipstick beginning to fade. Someone had once told him that a good lover ruins lipstick, not mascara, by making love, not causing tears.

He hadn't even kissed her. He smiled at the possibility and leaned toward her. She didn't retreat. He took it as a signal of acceptance but stayed in his place, hoping, *willing*, her to reach forward.

She did. She leaned in and placed a feather-light kiss on his lips, the current running through his body too much to bear. He wrapped his arms around her and pulled her close as she relaxed into his embrace.

He kissed her then, a slow, gentle kiss, of sweetness and understanding, of acceptance and hope. She let his tongue explore her mouth as he grew more aggressive and urgent, and she matched each of his moves with equal passion and tenderness.

Then she pulled away and took in a sharp breath. "I… I should head home."

He withdrew, confused by her signals, knowing this was never going to be easy. But just because it was hard didn't mean it wasn't worth it. "Drive all the way back? But there are events in the morning."

"I'll be back."

"Stay here. Surely the boss has a room for you?"

She smiled. "There's no spare room for me. But on late days, I usually sleep in the office. There's a pullout bed. I should convince Arjun to remodel the back room as a bedroom for staff."

Avinash's heart raced as he blurted out, "Sleep in my room."

She raised an eyebrow. "What?"

He mumbled most uncharacteristically. "I meant, sleep in my room, not sleep *with* me!"

Her eyebrows seemed to skim the sky. She chuckled at his embarrassment. "No?"

"I mean, if you want…" He coughed. He was blowing it. "Everyone's gone to bed. No one will know. Your reputation is safe."

She frowned, clearly in two minds. Her phone rang, and she fumbled with her bag again. "Ma? Is Sunny okay?"

He pondered on how her first concern was always for her son. Would he ever have that responsibility, that burden, that *privilege*? Putting someone else's safety above one's own seemed so natural with her, with any parent, really. But fate had decided not to give Avinash the opportunity to explore if he could rise to the task.

He heard squawking sounds, and then she hung up.

Anila said, "There's a huge traffic jam from a fatal hit-and-run and police blockades. Ma said to stay at the chateau."

He held her hand, and she didn't pull it away. "Come on. You can't sleep on a pullout bed. Come to my room. God knows it's big enough for us both."

"But…"

"Hey! No strings attached."

They went upstairs and walked down the carpeted hallway. Besides an occasional sound of coughing and a laugh from behind closed doors, it was quiet. Avinash willed everyone to stay in their rooms. At the end of the hallway was his room, the presidential suite, decorated with ornate dark wood furniture, a four-poster bed with classy, heavy linen, and humongous flower vases and indoor plants, which the bellboy had told him Anila had picked out herself.

He opened the door and motioned for her to enter. Someone had lit the fireplace, and the room was warm and toasty. Avinash took off his jacket.

In the full length mirror, he saw her reflection right beside him, the picture of a happy couple.

He turned to her, and she blushed, dropping her gaze.

Before he could stop himself, he said, "You're so beautiful."

She gave a hesitant laugh, then looked up at him through her dark lashes. "Is that all I am to you? A beautiful woman?"

Avinash felt his heart flutter. "You're so much more. You're an enigma. You help your brother with his business. I hope he pays you well, coz this is the best retreat we've had in all these years. And you're a mom. And you're so strong. And…"

"And?" She gazed at him with those massive eyes.

"My god, I could kiss you right now."

Her voice dropped to a whisper as she squeezed her hands together. "Why don't you?"

He saw the pulse beating in her neck, color rising to her cheeks in the most enchanting way, her skin glowing in the warmth from the fireplace. She wasn't wearing the pendant.

He hesitated and leaned closer, his whole body afire. If she stopped him now, he'd die. He touched her chin and tipped up her face.

She closed her eyes. "Avinash…"

He leaned closer, "Stop me if you don't want it, too."

"I don't want to stop you." She pressed her lips to his and circled her slender arms around his neck. He moaned in agonizing pleasure, a thrill running through him, an unusual feeling he'd rarely felt before. His dalliances often ended in bed, a mechanical, physical, and biological process that gave pleasure but not happiness, satisfaction but not contentment. With Anila, his heart galloped at an unfamiliar pace. With her, he hoped for more. He craved happiness. He yearned for a future. He longed for love.

This time her kiss was possessive, harsh, *desperate*. His hands ran up her arms, and she pulled him closer.

"Hey," he said, leaning away from her. "Are you sure about this?"

She gave a half smile. "I might live to regret it, but right here, right now, this is what I want. What I need."

Her words stirred something in him. He didn't want her to regret this tomorrow. He pried her arms away from his neck. "I've dreamed about this since the day I saw you. But I can't do this if before we even start, you're already considering *regret*."

She laughed. "Are you serious?"

He shrugged and raised his palms to her. "This is totally unlike me. For me, it's always no strings attached. Strictly casual. No worries, no regrets. But with you…" His breath faltered when he saw her changing expression.

Her eyes narrowed, her body growing rigid. "But with me… why? Because Sierra was so goddamn beautiful, no one can ever compare? Because I have been married, and I have given birth, and my body isn't what it used to be?"

What nonsense was she talking about? He waved his hands in the air. "No! No. None of that."

"Then why?" she demanded, her voice harsh.

"Because you're too important."

They stared at each other, the flickering fire reflected in her lustrous eyes. She took a determined step toward him and said, "Pretend you're auditioning for season two."

He frowned.

Her lips curled into a coquettish smile. "Let's get serious now. Are you interested in the job or not?"

That was his undoing. He unzipped her dress, and it fell in a pool by her feet. He hefted her out of the dress as she circled her arms around his neck again, clinging to him, her soft, floral perfume filling his senses. He undressed her in slow, languorous moves as light from the fireplace shone on her glorious body, her unbelievably flat belly, the soft mounds of her breasts, the dark nipples that were hardening under his gaze.

She shivered. He lifted her up and placed her gently on the four-poster bed, on top of silken sheets.

Anila lay back and curled her fingers to beckon him. He pulled off his tie and unbuttoned his shirt, his hands fumbling. She sat up and helped him undress, unzipping his trousers and pulling them off him in a way that took his breath away.

"Avinash Singhania," she whispered, "You're one handsome hunk."

"Oh, now you're reducing me to a slab of meat."

"Some meat. Grade A, baby."

He grinned at her playful charm and joined her on the bed, pinning her down with his elbows on both sides of her, his hands stroking her face, his lips devouring her mouth until she moaned. But he took his time caressing her, kneading her, running his fingertips down her body in slow circles, until she caught his hands.

He paused. "What happened?"

She said, "I have stretch marks… from the pregnancy."

"Oh, baby! Who cares about that? You're beautiful no matter what."

She relaxed under his weight and ran her hands up and down his back as he continued his relentless campaign of making her his. He had remembered to bring protection. She ripped open the shiny little square with her teeth and helped him put it on, in movements so sexy he was ready to burst.

But he brought Sierra's face to his mind and controlled himself. This was different. Sierra was selfish in bed, but because of her, he'd learned to give more than to take.

Anila lay back on the bed and stared at him, her eyes pools of dark mystery, her soft, pink, parted lips whispering his name. He parted her knees with his and stroked her. She gasped and then whispered, "I want you now."

They were like an ice skating couple, synchronized and coordinated, anticipating each other's moves, holding each other for support, releasing control when the time was right. She was relentless, with an unending hunger and unparalleled stamina. When he finally rolled over in bed, exhausted, it was almost four in the morning.

19

ANILA OPENED her eyes in the darkness of the presidential suite, Avinash sleeping beside her, his heavy, muscular arm wrapped around her waist. It was warm, comforting, and protective. The fire had died down, leaving ashes in the fireplace, and from the window she could see a sliver of the moon. Shadows of the maple tree danced across the opposite wall. Anila moved Avinash's arm and crept out of bed, as he moaned and turned over. Still in deep slumber, he didn't stir.

The clock read the time as five o'clock. She had a ton of things to prepare, but most of all, she needed to get out of here before the staff started rising.

Anila dressed quickly, a smile hovering on her lips, her heart bursting with an emotion she couldn't fathom.

When Avinash had asked her if she was sure about it, desire burning in his eyes, light from the fire dancing on his square, shadowed jaw, the vein throbbing in his neck, that had been her undoing, the moment that had decided for her.

As wonderful as Vikas had been, Avinash made the act of lovemaking into an art, which was so much more pleasurable, so much more sensual and playful, a give and take instead of just arousal and release.

But what she felt was more than physical pleasure. It was an emotional and spiritual awakening, a strange contentment and belonging that she'd blocked her heart from feeling so far. Being with Avinash felt so right, so real, so perfect.

She had no regrets. In fact, what she felt was the polar opposite. She was glad he'd pursued her. She was relieved he'd persisted when she'd rebuffed him, and honored that he wanted her.

She wanted him too. With a smile, she realized that with him, it was not a season two. It could be a whole new series.

She put on her heels and crept out of the suite, scanned the hallway to make sure no one was up and about—someone could have ordered room service—and padded down the stairs. Once she reached her office, she opened the door, locked it behind her, and blew out through pursed lips. She felt like an errant teenager who'd returned home after curfew. She giggled at the thought, then went to the bathroom and freshened up. Then she opened the tiny closet and pulled out a patterned dress and changed her shoes.

She'd slept for only an hour. She reached her desk and called the kitchen. "Can you send me a pot of coffee?"

"You're here early, Ma'am."

She hoped no one had seen that her car hadn't moved all night. "Yes. Lots of things to do."

She turned on her computer and started checking off her list when a knock sounded. She was tired, and desperate for coffee. "Come in!"

The door opened, and she smelled the coffee and continental breakfast already being laid out in the foyer.

"You can place it here," she said, without looking up.

"Um…"

She faced the door. It wasn't the kitchen staff. It was Avinash. He must have showered, because he looked fresh as a daisy. Right behind him came the kitchen staff holding a tray with coffee and pastries.

She said, "Thanks." Then she looked at Avinash. The waiter seemed to take longer than necessary to place the tray on her desk. Had they noticed her car hadn't moved from its spot all night, after all? Snoopy buggers!

She stood up. "How may I help you, Mr. Singhania?"

He cleared his throat, apparently taken aback at her formality. She hid a smile. Let him brew a bit. He said, "I was just making sure the account is settled and everything is cleared."

She gave him a dazzling smile. "It's all done."

The waiter excused himself and left, closing the door gently behind him.

Avinash said, "You left last night."

She smiled and tilted her face. "Morning you mean." He blushed furiously, and she grinned. "Can't have rumors spreading now, can we?"

"Did you go home? You've changed."

She motioned to the bathroom. "I always have spare clothes in the back."

He quirked a brow. "For the off-chance you'll sleep with a guest?"

She bristled at his comment. *How dare he!* "For the off-chance that I work late and cannot get home to my family."

He lifted his palms up in surrender. "I'm sorry. That was rude. I didn't mean it that way."

"You're excused." Her eyes hardened. "Would you like some coffee?"

Stroking his forehead, he sank into the chair. "I need it."

She poured him a cup from the tray. For herself, she poured coffee into a mug that said, "World's Best Mommy." She held it between them like a shield, as if she had to make sure he knew she was a mother.

He did. "Gift from Sunny?"

She said, "Arjun's idea for Mother's Day."

He picked up the cup and took a sip. "Anila…"

"Yes? Oh, I'm sorry I didn't ask… want sugar? Cream?"

"No. Black is fine."

"Cool. I thought you were a black coffee kinda guy." She spooned in sugar and poured cream into her coffee and stirred it. Then she topped it with cinnamon. The kitchen staff knew her preferences and had added a tub of nutmeg, which she left alone.

He blurted, "Did you regret what happened last night?"

She bit her lip, trying not to smile. Then she said, "No. You?"

He grinned, relieved. "No, of course not. It was magical. So, would you like to go out with me sometime?"

"As a matter of fact, I was going to ask you. I have this event… Do you know Connor Riley?"

His entire frame relaxed. "Vaguely. Award winning photographer, right?"

"Yeah. He's the husband of the lady who made our dresses for Lily's wedding. The Rileys are family friends. My son is good friends with their daughter, Megha. Same school. Anyway, Connor has an exhibition coming up, and he invited me. My parents can't come because of a prior engagement. And I…" She looked into his eyes. "Um… I don't want to go alone."

His lips curled into a dashing smile, his face alight with twinkling eyes, mirth lines, the works. "You're asking me out on a date?"

She kept her face straight and leveled her gaze at his eyes. "Of sorts."

"What's the dress code?"

She shrugged. "Business casual."

He frowned. "Business casual, eh?" He stared at her for a few seconds, and she resisted the temptation to tell him she owned the eponymous company, and that she knew he used it. She kept her face studiously blank. When she didn't react, he continued, "Absolutely. I'd be delighted. Text me the invite with the details."

They didn't see each other for the rest of the morning, but the warm light in her heart from the night before followed her on her drive home. She rolled down the windows and enjoyed the breeze on her face and in her hair. The ocean shimmered in the distance, and the sky was somehow bluer. Far away, a cruise ship pulled away into the horizon.

Anila hummed a tune, and realized it was a nursery rhyme. She'd missed her little boy, and couldn't wait to see him.

Her phone buzzed. She glanced at it while keeping her hands on the wheel. Her heart raced as she read the message from yet another unfamiliar number.

Why do you make it so hard?

Hands clammy with anxiety, Anila took the nearest exit and parked in front of a fast-food restaurant. So Noah had found her new number, after all.

After thinking for several minutes, she decided to respond. She texted back: *Please do not contact me again.*

A prompt reply: *I care about you.*

She gritted her teeth and sent her thumbs flying over her phone: *Well, I don't.*

Then why did you bring me soup?

Had she known a simple act of kindness would be so terribly misconstrued, she'd never have done it. *I did that as a friend.*

How can I show you I love you?

She took in a deep breath and stared out the window at a family ambling out with their food. The little girl spoke in a high pitch about some TV show, and the mother laughed, while the father nudged them along, holding a box filled with fried food.

She typed: *Please honor the Cease and Desist letter.*

Ah. Cease and Desist. I'd rather Pursue and Persist. I've watched enough movies to know that showing you how much I love you will eventually break you down. You'll see.

Anila couldn't believe this. She knew she should stop and call Harrison, but her fingers flew over the screen of their own volition. *Noah, or Isaac, or whatever your name is, I do not reciprocate that emotion.*

Please stop harassing me. You're stalking me. I will have no choice but to take legal recourse.

What would you do?

She took in an exasperated breath, her thumbs flying over the screen. *Restraining order is next.*

You'd do that to a client?

What do you mean?

I am a member of Business Casual.

Again, she wondered how he'd found out about her secret website. Well, if he was such a computer geek, he'd have found a way. But she was shocked to find he was a member and she didn't know it. Maybe he was bluffing. Still, it was no point denying her ownership of the site.

She paused for a moment and then typed: *I haven't seen you in the profiles.*

His reply made her heart stop. *Amazing what cosmetic surgery can do.*

That meant she had no idea what he looked like now. She wouldn't have remembered if he had signed up as Isaac Abbott. There were so many male members on the site that it would be impossible to find him. Besides, he could be lying, trying to lead her up the gum tree, making her waste her time on the website.

She had to tell Harrison. Maybe he could have Haller sniff Noah out from the site.

Noah texted: *How would the courts agree I'm harassing you when you yourself cleared me for your website? Think of the ignominy. Your secret would be out.*

Anila's chest felt it would implode into itself as a massive sob erupted. Just the other day she had received a thank-you letter from the Air Force Wives Welfare Association. Her website was everything to her; it had given her a reason to live during the darkest times. She could not afford to lose it.

She typed: *You wouldn't.*

I don't want to hurt you or your loved ones. Even the attorney. But you give me no choice.

Her hands were shaking. *Please, I'm begging you.*

Don't beg. All I ask for you is to love me back.

Anila's stomach churned. She wanted to throw up. She wanted to cry. She wanted to wring Noah's neck. She resisted the urge to throw the phone out of the window.

Instead, she took deep breaths and turned off her phone. She'd have to turn it over to Harrison and decide the next course of action.

Her jaw set, she turned the ignition and drove home.

20

AVINASH ENTERED his office just as his phone rang. He tossed his briefcase on the desk and grabbed the phone. "Hey, Auntie Lupe. How are you?"

"Did Moyna tell you about the lease for *Lupe's Cupcakes*?"

He snuck the phone in the crook of his neck and opened the venetian blinds to let in some natural light. "Yes. I talked to the landlord. I told him you're a long-term tenant and would like to stay in the same spot. Moving over to the corner spot is not something you'd consider. But he assured me he was still in negotiations with the potential tenant of the other units in the building. He said to wait until New Year's."

He heard a loud sigh on the line. "Well, it's too late for that. I got a letter from the landlord. Now instead of making me move over to the other spot, he wants to evict me."

"He can't do that. You're a long-term lease holder. When do you renew?"

"Next month."

He settled into his leather chair and twirled toward the window to enjoy the view. "I'll talk to him."

"I already did. He was cagey, but I found out he wants to sell the building." Auntie Lupe sounded desperate. "I think he already has a buyer."

That would be a problem. But why would the new buyer want to evict a reliable tenant? "Does the buyer want to remodel or something?"

"No, the buyer wants to use my space for their business and want me to move over or leave."

"Why not just move over?"

Her voice rose an octave. "It's my first venture, Avi. I am attached to the location! It was only after that café opened that my illness started to get better. I know you don't believe in superstitions, but that's that. You have to help me."

He took in a deep breath. "Let me contact Mr. Chu again and see what I can find."

"Can you try to contact the new owner? Ask them if I can keep the same lease. I don't mind paying a higher rent, if that's the issue. This is my very first café, Avi. It gave me a new lease on life... I can't imagine moving out to any other place."

Avinash called Mr. Chu's office and told his assistant he needed to talk to him urgently. In the meantime, he dashed off an official letter on behalf of Auntie Lupe, basically asking Mr. Chu to cease and desist unless he wanted a lawsuit. He hoped the tactic would pay off. But if Mr. Chu indeed wanted to sell the property, and the new owner wanted a vacant area, there wasn't much Avinash could do. Still, no one liked the cloud of a lawsuit hanging over them; even if it came to nothing, there were lawyer fees and opportunity costs. People generally backed off when they heard of a possible lawsuit.

For the rest of the morning, Avinash worked on a couple of divorces and a family trust.

At the end of the day, a knock on his office door broke his concentration. "Come in!"

It was his secretary. She said, "Aren't you heading home? It's nearly seven."

He looked up from his draft. "Oh, sorry. I should have asked you to go. Just finishing up some paperwork."

"Need anything? Coffee?"

He shook his head. "Go on home. I know Jimmy has basketball practice."

"Thanks, boss. His team may make it to the league finals."

He grinned. "Be sure to invite me if that happens."

She smiled and left.

He turned off his computer, stuffed his briefcase with documents he'd work on at home, and slipped his laptop inside. He pushed back his chair and got up as his cell phone rang.

He smiled and picked it up. "Anila. How nice to hear from you."

Anguish dripped from her voice. "I need a lawyer."

Immediately attentive, he said, "What kind of lawsuit?"

"Oh, I hope it won't come to that."

"I mean what kind of case?"

"Um... it's for my business."

That surprised him. "Doesn't Dheer Winery already have a lawyer?"

She hesitated, making him wonder where this was going. Then she said, "Um… I have a side business."

"My mother handles all business and corporate law. She is out of town, but I'll have her call you when she gets back."

"No! I want you to represent me. Since we already have a rapport. Just like you wanted me for the retreat."

He wanted her at the retreat for selfish reasons, but she did have a point. After all, he was handling Lupe's case, which was not family law. He could handle a bit of business law.

He rubbed his forehead. "The staff have left for the day. If you'd like to make an appointment, I can have them call you. But…" His heart raced. "If you'd rather see me sooner, we could meet for dinner."

To his delight, she agreed without hesitation.

Avinash went to the bathroom, splashed cold water on his face, and ran a comb through his hair. Then he drove to an Indian restaurant in downtown LA.

He found a booth at the back of the restaurant. Anila texted: *I'm running ten minutes late. Please go ahead and order.*

Avinash ordered a bottle of red wine with chicken tikka. "Extra lemon."

In fifteen minutes, he saw Anila enter the restaurant wearing jeans and a well-fitting black T-shirt, looking like a model on a casual outing. But she was not alone. Holding her hand was her little boy, Sunny.

Avinash took in a sharp breath. This was the package, he told himself. She was a Mom. And Sunny was a cute kid.

Anila approached his table. "Sorry, I couldn't find a babysitter. Ma is in India and Papa is at a banquet, and the nanny is never available…"

Avinash stood up and shook hands with Sunny first, and then Anila. "No problem." Then he grinned at Sunny. "How are you, young man?"

Sunny grinned back, and Anila smiled. Avinash asked the waiter to bring a highchair.

He asked Sunny, "You like chicken?"

Sunny nodded, his eyes large and round. He definitely was a cute kid.

Soon, the waiter brought the wine and the plate of chicken tikka. "Careful folks, it's hot!"

Avinash said, "Would Sunny like something to drink?"

Anila turned to the waiter, her long neck exposed. She still wasn't wearing the necklace her husband had given her. Did that mean something? He hoped it did.

Anila said, "Can you bring a small glass of apple juice?"

The waiter left, and Avinash said, "Okay, tell me more about your issue."

"It's about a property I want to buy."

Was that her business? Real estate? He hid a smile. "Go on."

"I want to remodel the first floor. The tenants on the second floor may stay if they wish, but I need the first-floor tenant to vacate the property."

Avinash didn't tell her he was dealing with a similar issue, but from the opposite side. "So what's the problem?"

"They don't want to vacate."

He shrugged. "As the new owner, you'd have to renew the leases anyway. So, don't renew. But, you could offer them to move to the second floor temporarily."

Anila said, "Second floor is residential. The first floor is commercial."

He wasn't sure what she wanted the property for. If it was just as an investment, she'd be better off getting the regular tenant back after the remodel. That's what he'd advise her. "If the tenant is a successful business, they'd love to move back into the remodeled property. You could offer them that."

Anila looked flustered. "No, I mean, they can't come back after the remodel, because we want to use the entire space for the company."

"What company is that?"

She coughed. "My company."

So she did not deal with real estate alone. "May I ask the name of your company?"

She took a sip of wine and eyed him evenly. "Does that make a difference?"

It did, to him, personally. He smiled. "Not right now."

The waiter brought the glass of apple juice, and Sunny grabbed it with both hands. He took a gulp and promptly started hiccupping.

Without getting agitated, Anila took a glass of water and asked Sunny to take a sip. "Take a deep breath first. Blow it out. Then drink the water slowly until you feel another hiccup coming."

Avinash marveled at her composure. "We can draft out a letter explaining the plan to remodel under the new ownership. I see no problem."

She looked at him with those large, dark eyes. "The problem is, the current owner told me he received a letter from a lawyer asking for a year's extension. It seems they will sue me. I don't understand. They are a decent-sized privately-owned chain with shops all over town. What's the problem in moving to a different location? They're already so popular. People would drive miles to buy Lupe's cupcakes wherever they move."

Several things happened simultaneously. As the realization struck, Avinash choked on wine and coughed. Anila's phone rang. Sunny stood on his seat to grab a piece of chicken, burnt his hand on the hot platter, screamed, and spilled the red wine on Avinash's suit.

Anila ignored her phone and attended to Sunny. "It's okay, Sunny. Here."

Avinash stood up and wiped his trousers with the napkin. "I'm sorry, but I cannot represent you."

She frowned, at the same time dunking Sunny's hand in her glass of ice water. "Why not? Is it because of Sunny?" Her phone stopped ringing.

"Oh no! I adore the kid. It's just that..." He closed his eyes and sighed.

Her eyebrows knitted together high on her forehead. "It's just what?"

"I'm representing the owner of the bakery. Lupe's Cupcakes."

Anila's back stiffened. "Oh! So it's you. And may I ask what's the problem in moving to a different location? I'm willing to pay for the move, and pay six months' rent in the new place."

Avinash shook her head. "It's Auntie Lupe's first ever shop..."

"Auntie Lupe?"

He took in a deep breath, sliding back into his seat. "She and my mother were roommates. She started the bakery right after college. It's her first ever venture. She's attached to the place. She had severe arthritis, but she believes the café helped her get better."

"The café made her get better? That's preposterous."

He shrugged. "That's what she believes. Why do you want to buy it anyway?"

"I told you. It's for my business."

Avinash held his head in his hands. How much more complicated could this get? He took a sip of the wine. "Care to elaborate?"

Her face was flushed. This was not a woman who took no for an answer.

She said, "What's the point?" She straightened her napkin across her lap. "Let me put this up to you again. I really, really need the space. And I am making a very generous offer. But, I'm willing to double it. I'll pay her rent in the new place for a year. Or even, double of her rent!"

He shook his head.

She took in a sharp, exasperated breath. "Or, she could just move over to the bookstore area. Two walls with windows. It's a larger space."

"I'm sorry. I talked to my client, but she refuses to move."

"Move out or move over?"

Avinash grimaced. "Both."

She tossed the napkin on the table. "It seems we're at an impasse."

He reached over to hold her hand, but she jerked it away. "I'm sorry, Anila. Please try to understand. I'm sure there's a way to work it out."

"Oh yeah? How? This won't work out."

"This? What do you mean by this?"

Before Anila could answer, her phone rang again. Sunny had stopped whimpering, his hand still dipped in the glass of ice water.

Anila picked up the phone. "Hey, Lily. Aren't you in Chicago? That conference…"

He heard mumbled words as Anila frowned. Then she stroked her forehead and said, "Oh my God. Is he…" She swallowed hard. The shock in her face was palpable. Her lips trembled, and her eyes glistened. He was desperate to hold her, to make her feel better.

She stood up abruptly. "I… I have to go, but I need to ask a favor of you." She closed her eyes for a moment. "I know we're on opposite…"

He interrupted her. "Anila! What's the matter?"

"Can you take Sunny to Trevor's house? I mean, Harrison's. You know him, right? It will be a sleepover."

Avinash's eyes widened. That was not what he was expecting at all. "Um… Is everything okay?"

Tears flooded her eyes. "My brother's been in an accident. I have to go to the hospital."

Avinash said, "Hey, if you need me to pick something up from your house to drop off for the kids' sleepover, I'll be happy to."

She frowned. "Have you ever prepared a kid for a sleepover?"

Avinash shook his head, saddened not only because she didn't trust him, but also because he didn't trust himself. He didn't know what a kid needed for a sleepover. Nightclothes? Toothbrush? Comb? A toy? A blanket? Then a thought struck him. *Diapers?* He knew nothing about Sunny.

She stared at him with imploring eyes. "Just take him to Harrison and Laura's. I'll call them on my way to the hospital." She leaned toward her son and held him by his face. "Sunny, Arjun Uncle is hurt. I have to get to the hospital. You'll spend the night at Trevor's. Okay?"

Sunny looked excited to spend the night with his friend. But he frowned. "Is Arjun Uncle okay?"

Her chin trembled. "I hope so, honey." She turned to Avinash. "You'll need the car seat."

Avinash nodded. He had definitely not thought about a car seat. He had much to learn. Leaving some cash on the table, he rose. To his surprise, Sunny stood in front of him, arms outstretched, staring up, in the universal child's signal to be picked up.

He hesitated a moment before lifting him off the floor. The boy felt heavy, warm, and somehow comforting. Sunny wrapped his arms around Avinash's neck and rested his head on his shoulder.

Anila said, "Oh, I'm sorry, he skipped his nap this afternoon. He's tired."

The boy smelled of baby powder, his hair tickling Avinash's neck. "It's okay."

Sunny lifted his head. "I don't want to go to sleep."

They followed Anila out of the restaurant. She transferred the car seat into Avinash's Lamborghini, showed him how to securely fasten it, and got into her car.

"Dive safely!" he said.

"You too. You're carrying my precious cargo!" She waved to him and drove out of the parking lot.

Avinash turned to Sunny, who was comfortably tucked into the car seat, and surprisingly, wide awake. "Hey, kid. Do you want some ice cream?"

Sunny answered with his whole body: legs kicking the back of the passenger seat, arms jigging up and down, head nodding his assent. Avinash grinned at his enthusiasm and pulled out of the parking lot.

He drove to an ice cream parlor that was open until midnight, unsure of whether it was okay to feed a kid ice cream at night. Probably not. Sunny declared his love for chocolate, and Avinash ordered two scoops of chocolate ice cream.

The middle aged woman at the counter smiled. "Cup or cone?"

Avinash said, "Cup."

"And for your son?"

Avinash stared at her and then at Sunny.

Sunny said, "Cone, please."

Avinash gulped. Anyone looking at them would have thought they were father and son. Somewhere in the back of him mind, he knew he was trying it on for size. He kicked the thought out of his mind.

They chose a small kids' table and Sunny settled in, his eyes glittering like diamonds. Avinash squeezed himself into the seat, his knees propped high. He scooped a tiny bit of ice cream with the tiny plastic spoon. The spoon broke.

Sunny grinned and said, "You should have got a cone."

The woman at the counter laughed, came around, and gave Avinash another spoon.

Avinash said, "Cones have other issues."

"What?" asked Sunny.

"You can drop the whole scoop. Right on the floor."

"Not if you do it properly." Sunny licked his ice cream, turning his cone in expert moves to maintain the height of the ice cream to a perfect level.

Sunny seemed to derive extra energy from the sugar and talked non-stop, as Avinash's mind wandered. He scooped tiny bits of ice cream and hoped Arjun was okay. Based on Anila's panic, the accident seemed bad.

After they finished the ice cream, Sunny put out his hand to be held and Avinash smiled. The innocence of childhood, the utter trust kids placed on a caregiving adult... it felt nice. He took Sunny's hand, waved to the woman at the counter, and opened the car door. He hefted Sunny up and tucked him carefully into the car seat.

Then he drove to Harrison's house, his mind a hundred miles away, on what might have been.

21

OVER THE PAST two years since the Vegas wedding, Avinash had slowly realized that his marriage was an odd one. Sierra and Avinash seemed to lead parallel lives, like roommates with benefits. They took turns at the chores of cleaning bathrooms and throwing out the trash, but more often than not, they communicated through notes stuck to the refrigerator. She wasn't home when he returned from classes or work, and he wasn't home during the day while she lounged on the sofa eating Cheetos.

So Avinash was surprised to find the apartment empty when he opened the door in the middle of the day. He'd returned to pick up a document he needed for the last project for his law school discussion group. In just a few months, he'd take the bar exam and become a licensed attorney.

He dropped his bag on the sofa, went to the rickety desk that stood against the wall on the far corner, and turned on the flower-patterned table lamp Sierra had bought at Nordstrom to "liven up" the place. He rustled through the papers looking for the document. Cursing under his breath, he whispered, "Where the heck did I put it?"

He settled heavily into the swivel chair that always swung too far back, cursed under his breath, and rubbed his forehead. Had the paper fallen into the trashcan? Sierra must have emptied it days ago. But she often forgot. He hopped up, opened the backdoor that led to a small landing where they kept the trash until trash day.

For a change, he was happy Sierra had forgotten to throw it out. He opened it and screwed up his nose at the stench of rotting fish and moldy bread. Gingerly, he picked at the papers and found what he was looking for.

He groaned. There were coffee stains all over the document. He'd have to print the damn thing again, but their printer was out of ink.

Then his eye caught sight of an unusual piece of trash. A home pregnancy test. He frowned and picked it up. A faint blue marking announced he was going to be a Daddy.

Anxiety tore through him. He wasn't ready to be a father. He and Sierra had never discussed having children. In fact, he'd often mentioned to her how Auntie Lupe's life dealing with so many kids scared him. He'd admitted that Sonia's death weighed on his mind, and not having children removed the fear of losing them.

Still, how could Sierra keep it a secret from him?

He'd thrown out the trash when it was his turn, so she must have taken the test within the last week. He tossed the test back into the garbage bag as if it were contaminated with plague and tied up the bag. He took it down to the common metallic bin meant for the entire apartment complex and flung it into its smelly depths. Returning, he closed the back door and washed his hands.

Then he sat on the lumpy sofa he'd bought at a garage sale a couple of years ago, his head in his hands.

He was going to be a *father*.

He was going to be a father.

How in the world was he going to be a father? How could he deal with caring for a baby, the teething, the drooling, the diaper-changes, the nightly feedings, the tantrums, the constant hassle he'd seen Auntie Lupe engaged in with each child she adopted? She'd asked him to watch her baby once at the café. She went to the bathroom, and the baby had just woken up. Six-month old Maya started fussing and crying, and Avinash looked around, waiting for Lupe to appear. But she didn't.

He slipped a cloth over his shoulder and picked up the baby. She had been found abandoned in a trashcan behind a public parking lot just a day or two after birth. Harrison was the detective on the case, and when he told Avinash about it, he called Lupe. Auntie Lupe's heart bled for the unwanted, the abandoned, and the innocent, and she agreed to adopt the baby immediately. Under her care, Maya had grown stronger.

Nestled on his shoulder, Maya cooed and drooled and generally made a mess. When Lupe returned, she said, "You two look so content."

He handed her over to Lupe and the baby sat in her lap, her fist in her mouth, babbling nonsense, and occasionally giving him a toothless smile. Well, not completely toothless. She had two tiny lower teeth.

Holding her had felt nice. She was warm and sweet and heavy in his arms. Just like Sonia had felt when she'd sit in his lap and demand that he read her a book while he was trying to cram for AP exams or college courses. He chuckled at the memory.

Right now in his apartment, Avinash wondered if having a baby was such a terrible idea. His own existence was the result of an unplanned pregnancy. And a baby might change the dynamics between him and Sierra; God knew they had problems. Perhaps the baby was the bridge their marriage needed. It would be okay. They would be okay.

He stretched his legs out on the coffee table and wondered if it would be a baby girl or a baby boy. Would the baby look like him or Sierra? Would the baby be more attached to him or to the mother? Sonia had been especially attached to her mother, although her death had crushed both their parents. But in those few years that she'd been alive, hadn't she brought joy to them all?

Avinash and Sierra would move out of this shithole into a nicer place. He'd paint the nursery blue or pink, depending on the sex of the baby. Or maybe purple with a green accent wall. He'd get posters of animals, fish and dinosaurs, of the English and Hindi alphabet, of anything he or she liked, really. He'd never had any of those, having grown up with his grandparents in a strict and poor household in India.

Sierra would be home soon. He couldn't wait for her to tell him the good news. He'd pretend to be surprised. And he'd tell her, unplanned or not, this was a blessing and he was thrilled.

He'd been working as a paralegal in his family law firm and would ask to work more hours so Sierra could rest. By the time the baby came, he would have graduated already.

He called his mother's cell phone. "Ma, after I graduate and until I take the bar exam, can I work full-time in the firm?"

"Of course. I wouldn't have it any other way. Your grandfather did the same for me. After all, you'll be the other Singhania in our firm. And we have no doubts you'll pass the bar exam on the first attempt. Your grandfather wants to retire once you join, you know." His grandfather had hoped his father, Sameer Singhania, would join the firm he'd built up, but that hadn't panned out. Sameer went into politics and it was Moyna, the daughter in law, who became the second Singhania. Avinash smiled. The future looked bright.

Sierra didn't return that night. Instead, she texted him. *I'm staying over at my friend's.*

He called her number. "Are you okay?" He winced at his misjudged words the moment the words left his mouth. With her, any wrong comment would spark an argument. Like the time he'd demanded to know why she'd lied to him about visiting her aunt in Denver while she was spending the weekend with friends in Las Vegas. She'd got into a rage and somehow, at the end, it was Avinash who'd apologized.

He hated walking on eggshells around her, but that would change once the baby came.

She sounded annoyed. "What do you mean?"

"Oh, just that you've been working late at Marco's recently."

"Yeah. I took on an extra shift. Someone's got to bring home the bacon."

He was used to her stinging comments about how she made more money than he did. He was able to work only a few hours a day with his school and projects. But that was going to change so soon. It was just hormones. He let it go.

"Okay," he said. "Have fun."

22

ANILA PARKED HER car in the poorly lit parking lot and rushed into the hospital lobby. The double doors swished open, emanating an antiseptic smell. She asked the clerk at the front desk, "Is my brother, Arjun Dheer, here?"

The clerk typed the name and gave her directions to the Pre-Operative Area. "Follow the blue arrows." Anila thanked her and walked down the blue lined arrows on the shiny floor until she came to the glass door labeled "Pre-Operative Area."

Anila took in a deep breath. She had lost her husband so suddenly; she would not lose her brother. She couldn't bear it. Taking in a deep breath, she stepped inside. In front was a small desk at which a nurse sat, typing into a computer. On one side were a row of beds surrounded by screens. She heard machines beeping and people talking softly. Someone groaned.

The nurse looked up from her computer screen. "Can I help you?"

"I'm here for my brother, Arjun Dheer?"

The nurse told her in hushed voice, "Dr. Ramaswamy will take him in for surgery soon. He's the neurosurgeon."

"Can you give me any details?"

Her eyes softened. "He has a fractured skull with a subdural hematoma. Broken ribs and a clavicle. Sprained ankle. But those can wait. He is unconscious right now. Hopefully after they remove the blood clot he gets better. But you should talk to the doctor for details. You brother is in the last bed down the hall to the left."

The thought of losing him hit her like a tsunami, unleashing the trauma of losing her husband. *It can't be!* Her heart raced, and she took deep breaths. Arjun would be fine. He had to be fine.

Anila walked to the end of the corridor with beds on either side. Behind a depressing gray screen, she heard her father's voice. "Arjun, *beta,*" he said, "Please don't go. I know I haven't been a good father to you. I've been tough on you. But it's only because I know you can handle it. You can do better than I could ever imagine. Please, *beta,* forgive me. Don't go." His voice cracked.

Anila watched her father grasp Arjun's hand, his shoulders shaking from the sobs that overtook his body. Her brother lay still on the bed, his eyes half-closed, a bruise forming on his forehead, a breathing tube down his throat. His foot was in a splint, propped up on pillows, his toes poking out.

As Papa continued sobbing by Arjun's bedside, she placed a hand on her father's shoulder, understanding, at last, that he loved Arjun in his own way. Papa wasn't Arun's biological father, but the love in the shuddering voice and shaking shoulders was real.

"Papa!"

He turned to look at her and broke down in her arms. "I always told him not to drive so fast."

Barely able to stand on her own legs, she resolved to be strong for her family. "Lily said it wasn't his fault, Papa."

His voice cracked. "I love you both so much. If something happens to him, I don't know what I'd do. Your Ma will be devastated."

Anila saw a doctor in scrubs and a long white coat walk into the room. The nurse said, "Hey Dr. Ramaswamy. You look rested."

"Haha!" he said. "Worked all night last night and was back in my office at eight."

The nurse said, "But you didn't miss the game, I heard."

"Yeah. Lost a hundred bucks on that buzzer shot."

The nurse laughed. "Thanks for the bagels. We love Panera Bread."

"You're welcome. I hope they added enough variety for everyone?"

"Yes. I prefer the cinnamon swirl, and the afternoon shift is crazy about the everything bagel."

"I like the blueberry one the most."

"That's why they have so many flavors, I suppose."

The doctor guffawed, a reaction out of proportion to the humor in her statement. "True. Different strokes for different folks. So, are his scans back?"

Anila's eyes widened. The terrifying emergency for her family was so routine for the doctors and nurses. How did it feel to take care of sick people all the time? To tell family that their loved one may not survive? Or was the weight of that responsibility lessened by giving good news from time to time? Did they block the pain by chatting about mundane things like bagels and ball games?

The doctor spent some time talking to the nurse and presumably looking at Arjun's scans. Then he approached them and pulled open the screen. "Hello, my name is Dr. Ramaswamy. I'm the neurosurgeon." He examined Arjun with a small frown on his forehead.

He turned to Anila and her father and explained the procedure. "He has a concussion from the accident." He pointed to his temple. "There is a blood clot under the skull that is pressing on his brain. The surgery should not be long. Once the clot is evacuated, we will know more."

"Will he be okay?" asked Papa.

"I hope so. But only time will tell."

Anila's voice cracked. "But there's a chance?"

He smiled at her. "Definitely. I'm good at what I do."

At least Arjun had a chance. Vikas had never had a chance to recover from his accident. She tried not to think of his battered body, torn flesh, and broken bones. She choked back a sob as her eyes misted. She had to be strong. She had to. She banished the image of her husband, refused to equate it with Arjun. Her brother was breathing. He was alive. And he would live on.

The hours waiting for news about the surgery were the worst. Anila asked her father to go home. He needed his medicines, and he needed rest. Ma was flying back to Los Angeles, but it would take her almost twenty-four hours to get here. Poor Ma. How terrible she must feel, stuck in an airplane, knowing only that her only son was badly wounded, unconscious, and undergoing surgery.

It was almost eleven o'clock, and the waiting room was empty, aside from a young woman who scrolled her phone, her leg bouncing on her foot, spreading her anxiety in the air like a mist.

Anila had to distract herself. Worrying about Arjun helped no one. She pulled out her phone from her bag and called Harrison, being friendlier with him than with Laura. "How's Sunny holding up?"

"He and Trevor are in the bath as we speak. How's Arjun?"

"He's in surgery. I don't even know how it happened."

"After Avinash dropped Sunny off, I called the Sheriff. Arjun was driving at fifty miles an hour uphill on Highway 1, and a driver from the opposite side of the road swerved into his lane. Apparently he was asleep on the wheel. Some poor student driving without insurance. Arjun had nowhere to turn, it being the hillside. He turned into the shallow ditch but it was a head-on collision. The other driver escaped with just some scrapes and bruises."

Anila gripped her phone. "I'm praying Arjun makes it."

"He's a strong guy. He'll be fine. Is Lily back yet?"

"Her flight arrives in the morning."

"Hang in there."

"Thanks."

"Oh, hey! So you were having dinner with Avinash? Are you guys dating? I don't mean to be nosy, but he's a great guy, despite what you read in tabloids."

"Um..." Anila trailed off. The tension from their impasse swirled back to the forefront of her mind. "It was a business meeting. About the potential office space for Business Casual. But he's representing the other party, so it came to nothing."

"I see. You know, he seemed to enjoy spending time with Sunny. They went for ice cream."

Despite the chaos, Anila felt an unfamiliar swell of affection in her chest. She hid a smile. "I should thank him."

Harrison's voice dropped to a whisper. "By the way, there have been no more texts."

Anila rubbed her forehead. She'd given her phone to Harrison. Noah was clearly an expert at hacking, and Harrison wanted his friend Haller to use a backdoor through Anila's phone to prove Noah had defied the Cease and Desist letter. Haller gave her another phone, which would receive all forwarded phone calls, but not texts from Noah's phone. Harrison didn't want her to worry. "It's time for a restraining order." The Cease and Desist order had been mailed to the Wellington Estates address Haller had provided, but the restraining order had to be handed over in person. The order was ready to go, but Noah seemed to have disappeared, and there was no way to locate him. His house looked abandoned, there was no housekeeper, and the gardener had been paid for three months.

She said, "Thanks."

"Keep me posted about Arjun," he said before hanging up.

A nurse came and called the young woman to see her father, who was out of surgery, leaving Anila alone in the waiting room. The TV played the news about a winter snowstorm on the East Coast. Anila tried to settle deep into the chair and picked up a Time magazine from months ago. Then she tossed it back on the small table and picked up her new phone again. She dialed Avinash's number.

She heard a ring tone right outside the door of the waiting room. She turned to look as Avinash walked in, the phone to his ear. "Hello?"

She saw him and hung up the phone, a smile hovering on her lips. "What are you doing here?"

"I came to see how he was doing."

She got up from the chair. "You didn't have to do that."

He regarded her with those warm brown eyes, a dark shadow on his chin. "I owe it to Lily. And I hoped, to you."

His voice was like dark chocolate, smooth, warm, enveloping her in its silky depths. She felt color rise to her cheeks. "Oh. I was calling to thank you for taking Sunny to Trevor's."

"Oh, yeah. No problem. How's Arjun?"

"Still in surgery."

"What's the prognosis?"

The concern in his voice made her voice crack as tears stung her eyes. "I don't know."

"Hey!" he said, drawing her to him. "This is a great hospital. I'm sure he's getting excellent care here. He'll be fine."

She leaned into his wide shoulder. "Don't make promises you can't keep."

He pulled her closer and she felt his breath in her hair. "I'm sorry, Anila. I don't know what to say. What I can tell you is that my firm will sue the wazoo out of that guy."

She pulled away from his grasp and sat down. "He didn't have car insurance, Avinash. He's just a poor student. Basically penniless."

Avinash stood with his feet slightly apart, his fists clenched. "What can I do to help?"

She looked up at him. "Could you stay with me?"

They sat together on the small couch, hugging each other for comfort. He placed his jacket around her shoulders. "Try to take a nap," he said, but she shook her head.

She said, "Harrison said you were great with Sunny. I can't thank you enough."

"He was a pleasure to hang out with. I have to confess, though, I took him out for ice cream."

She smiled. Sunny needed pampering once in a while. And tonight of all nights, when the only father-figure in his life was under anesthesia with his head cut open, she was glad Avinash had taken him for ice cream. She hoped it was chocolate. She hoped it was a cone. She hoped it didn't fall off the top like it had once, on Santa Monica pier. She'd taught Sunny how to roll the cone and lick off the top with each turn so the height would remain constant and the downward pressure of the tongue would push the ice cream into the cone, not off it.

She sat there, thinking about trivial things, about the new shoes she had to buy for Sunny, Valentine cards for the kids in his preschool, and tried to figure out what to do about the tenant in the property she wanted to buy. All to avoid thinking about her brother, who had taught her the ice cream cone trick besides so many other things, and who was fighting for his life just yards away in the operating room.

Avinash grimaced. "You're not upset?"

Anila glanced at him. She was upset that Arjun was fighting for his life. She was upset that Avinash couldn't represent her in her business deal, that being on the opposite sides in the deal made it hard to remain on such friendly terms. "Upset?"

"About the ice cream."

She chuckled and shook her head. "The thing about parenting is that you know when rules can be broken. You were great. You'll make a great Daddy one day."

23

A WEEK AFTER Avinash found the pregnancy test in the trash, Sierra still hadn't shared the news with him. That Friday, he left class, went to the jewelers, and bought a pair of diamond earrings he couldn't afford. His windshield wipers swished back and forth, ineffective in clearing the rain from the thunderstorm. He parked in the carport, grabbed the gift, and scampered into the apartment, shoes squelching.

Surprisingly, Sierra was home. She was on the sofa, her feet up on the coffee table, a blanket over her legs, her long hair in a messy bun on the top of her head, holding a cup of tea with both her hands, in the way he found enchanting.

He scrubbed his shoes on the coir mat, tossed his keys on the corner table, and gave her a smile. "I'm so glad you're here! I got something for you."

Her face was ashen as the steam swirled around her face. "What?" She was curt with him more often than he cared to admit. Maybe she was hungover, as she often was. She'd be cranky and short with him and by the time she recovered, it was time for her shift. But she was pregnant; she couldn't be drunk, could she? No, this was hormones. Just hormones.

He took out the little velvet box and handed it to her. "Here."

She placed her teacup on the table and opened the box with a frown. "Is this for real?"

He grinned. "I thought I'd surprise you."

She looked up at him. "Did I miss some anniversary?" She looked so beautiful, it hurt.

"Can't a guy get his wife a gift?"

She placed the box on the table and picked up her teacup. "Is this a bribe? Did you mess around? What did you do?"

"Come on, Sierra. Do you like them?"

She gave a small smile. "Yeah, they're pretty. Thanks."

He shrugged off his jacket, hung it on the hook by the door and sat across from her. "So, I talked to my Mom, and I can start full-time the day I finish law school."

A shadow passed over her eyes, but she didn't say anything. Was she worried about the money?

He said, "The pay will be better once I pass the bar. It will be great."

She tucked the blanket around herself, as if creating a barrier. "Good for you."

"We can move to a bigger apartment."

"Yes, that's nice."

"Sierra, aren't you excited? We can finally have an extra room. We'll need one when…"

"When what?"

He ran his fingers through his hair. "I know about…"

Her eyes flashed. "You know about what?"

He got up and paced the room and came to stand in front of her, shifting his weight from one foot to the other. "Don't you have some good news to tell me?"

Sierra stared at him, her pale face serene and beautiful. He hoped it was a baby girl and that she'd grow up to look like her Mama.

He persisted. "I mean, we've been married for almost two years. We have nothing to worry about. I'll pick up extra hours at the firm, and you can start cutting back."

"Why would I cut back?"

"Sierra, I know about the pregnancy."

Her steel-gray eyes glittered like ice. "You do, do you?"

"Yes, and I know we didn't discuss it earlier. I know I said things about Auntie Lupe and all that. But this is our kid. It will be fine. In fact, it will be wonderful."

In that charged pause, she leveled her gaze at him, as if judging how serious he was. God, she was beautiful. Sierra didn't have social graces, which he attributed to her childhood in a broken family, but Avinash would teach the kid everything he knew. And with his parents and Lupe's family and Auntie Tanya, the baby would never want for attention.

And then Sierra threw the bombshell. "I had an abortion."

Those words felt like a punch in his gut. "What?"

"Yeah. This morning. That's why I'm home early."

He couldn't believe it. "How… how could you do that?"

Her voice grew cold. She spoke like she was explaining a simple concept to a retarded child. "I went to the doctor and told them I cannot have the baby."

He shook his head. "You didn't even tell me."

"So you're a doctor now? There was nothing to tell."

A shocking thought hit him. "Was… was it not mine?"

Her voice cracked. "It was yours. And how dare you imply anything otherwise?"

"I'm sorry. I'm so sorry." He wished he could take those words back, but an ache had formed in his heart, a poisonous sting that was desperate to worm its way out.

She took another sip of her tea. "It's done now. There's nothing to discuss."

Nothing to discuss? He stamped his foot. "How can you say that? This is a decision we should have made together."

"I know you didn't want kids. I made it easy. I thought you'd be grateful that I made the decision for you."

Outside, lightning struck and rain spattered against the windowpanes. As light flashed on her pallid, almost unfamiliar face, Avinash said, "But you didn't give me a choice."

"It's my body. How do you expect me to dance on stage with a fat ass and a fat belly carrying a baby no one wants?"

"A baby no one wants?" He took a stunned step back. "Do you even realize how unfair this is to me?"

"Oh, so now you wanted the baby? Well, *I* didn't. So there."

"But you cut me out of the process completely. How do you think it makes me feel?"

"Relieved, I think."

"No!" he yelled. "It makes me a fucking eunuch."

"What?"

His arms waved about the room in angry gestures. "It takes away any sense of belonging to this family. As a unit. We make decisions together. You could have told me. You could have said this wasn't the right time. I might have come around."

"'Might' being the operative word."

"Sierra, please! Have I ever disrespected you? I would have respected your decision."

"So fucking respect it now!"

He shook his head. "That's not the point... I feel so utterly helpless. You're making all the decisions in this family. Next you'll tell me we're moving to London."

"Speaking of, I had auditioned for a show last month. The leading lady broke her leg. I got the part."

"Congratulations!" He was happy for her. He was! Then he said, "Is that why you did it?"

"I'm moving to New York. It's the opportunity of a lifetime. You can come with me if you want."

"If *I* want? I... What do *you* want, Sierra? What do you want from this relationship?"

After a long pause, she said, "This relationship is as dead as the fish in the freezer."

His voice cracked. "I just can't believe it."

"I'll pack up my stuff and move out. Give me a week."

He reached out for her, pleading with her to give it a chance. To give *him* a chance. "Sierra, wait. Please! Let's try therapy, counseling, anything you want. We can fix this!"

She wrenched her hand away from him, scratching his wrist with a sharp, manicured fingernail. "You know as well as I do that there's nothing left to fix."

24

IN THE WEE HOURS of the morning after the surgery, Anila watched as Arjun's chest heaved up and down with each breath forced into his lungs by the machine, his eyes closed underneath the bandage on his forehead. The doctor had told her the surgery went well. If the damage to Arjun's brain wasn't bad, he would be waking up some time soon. She stared at him, willing him to open his eyes.

Don't leave me, Arjun. Anila had found a way to survive without her husband because she had a kid. How would Lily cope? Arjun *had* to fight to live.

She glanced at her watch as dawn cracked through the window blinds. Six o'clock. Sunny must be awake now. He'd always been an early riser like his father, forcing Anila to change her entire schedule. She didn't mind, really, she thought with a smile.

Her phone rang. After momentary panic when she thought it was Noah, she smiled to see it was Trevor's mother, Laura. "Hey, Anila."

Anila said, "You're up early."

"I couldn't sleep."

Anila knew Laura was pregnant but wasn't sure if Anila was supposed to know it yet. "Um... How have you been?"

"The usual. Baby was kicking me all night. This is the first time I felt it, Anila. It's magical."

Laura had had a series of miscarriages, following which she and Harrison had adopted Trevor. This pregnancy was accidental, and a pleasant surprise.

Anila said, "How wonderful. Congratulations. Um... how were the kids last night?"

"Harrison played catch with them in the back yard and got them really tired. Took baths and slept like logs. They're still asleep."

"I can't thank you enough."

"What are friends for? How is Arjun?"

Anila got up and stretched her back. "Doctors say he should wake up soon. They removed the blood clot. He has bruises from the airbags, broken ribs and collar bone, and a sprained ankle, but he's lucky to be alive."

"Do you want me to send the kids to preschool today? Sunny can wear Trevor's clothes, and I'll pack them sandwiches for lunch. PB and J good?"

"Sunny loves PB and J. Thank you so much, Laura. Lily's flight comes in soon. I'll go home, take a shower, and maybe a nap."

A movement made Anila stare at Arjun. He'd fidgeted in bed. Then it was gone. She slipped her phone back in her bag just as Lily walked in. She was wearing jeans and a white t-shirt, a sweatshirt tied loosely around her waist, her hair in a messy ponytail.

Lily gave Anila a long hug. "How is he?" She plopped her overnight bag on the floor.

"Not bad, considering."

Lily looked uncharacteristically frazzled. Anila had seen her after her night calls, in stressful situations, and she'd always looked composed and put-together. But today, at the prospect of losing her husband, Lily's face was drawn and pale. Anila knew how she felt.

Lily said, "I called the neurosurgeon on my way here. He said it went well. You should go home and get some rest."

Anila said, "Hey! You took a red-eye flight. You need the sleep more than I do."

Lily's voice was shaking. "I'm not going home, Anila."

Anila nodded and patted Lily's shoulder. "I understand."

Lily leaned down to plant a kiss on Arjun's forehead. His eyes moved behind closed lids. "That's a good sign."

A shadow in the doorway made them turn. It was Avinash, holding two cups of coffee.

Lily said, "Hey, you." Then she frowned. "Is there a legal issue I didn't know about?"

Anila felt heat rise to her face as Avinash gave a silly smile. "Um… no. I came as a friend."

"As a friend. I see." She stared at Anila and then at Avinash. "Is there something I should know?"

Anila said, "We were having dinner when you'd called last night."

Lily's eyebrows rose. "Ah ha! Dinner!"

"It was meant to be a business dinner, but it turns out he cannot represent me," she said, bitterly.

"And why not?"

Avinash stammered, "I'd love to, but I'm representing the opposing party."

Anila said, "He's an enemy, so to speak."

Lily grinned and took the coffee cups from his hand. "In that case, hand over the coffees. You can drink water."

He smiled and said, "Enjoy. Um... how is he?"

Anila said, "Same."

Soon, the nurse arrived to check his vitals. Arjun's eyelids fluttered, and he opened his eyes. He tried to tug at the breathing tube, and Lily promptly removed it. She said, "Hey, you!"

Arjun seemed to have trouble focusing. "Wh... what happened?"

Lily said, "You were in an accident. You're okay now." She stroked his face and Anila's stomach knotted. She hadn't had a chance to console her husband. Fate had taken him so abruptly, so cruelly. But she was grateful that fate had spared her brother.

Arjun said, "Who are you?"

A collective gasp sounded through the room, and Lily's eyes glistened. "Arjun! It's me. Lily."

"Lily who?"

Lily sobbed. "I'm your wife."

Arjun grinned. "Just kidding. How can I forget my beautiful bride?"

Lily smacked the side of his arm. "Your sense of humor can make anyone cry."

Arjun winced. "Ouch! That hurt."

"It should, you buffoon. Now's not the time for jokes. Do you recognize everyone here?"

Arjun smiled at Anila. "Hey, sis." Then he looked at Avinash and raised his eyebrows. "Are we suing someone?"

Avinash said, "No, I came as a friend. I'm glad you're doing well."

The nurse said, "He needs to rest."

Anila gave her brother a kiss on his cheek. "I should get going as well."

She picked up her bag and together, Avinash and Anila walked to the parking lot. She said, "I can't thank you enough."

He waved his hand. "Um... will I see you again?"

Her heart was pulling her in two directions. One the one hand, there was Vikas whom she loved with all her heart. But Vikas wasn't there, was he? He had set her free, but she had rejected the freedom.

On the other hand, here was Avinash, whose interest in her was clear as the lines on her hand.

She wished he could have represented her. She didn't want to be on opposing sides with him on any issue, ever. Her mind had impressed upon her heart that if she were to stay in the here and now, it was to be with Avinash. Vikas was history.

She said, "Aren't you coming to the exhibition? Or did you ditch me already?"

"Oh. I thought since I can't represent you, you wouldn't want to go with me."

She had to ignore the lawsuit for now. "On the contrary." Then she raised her eyebrows. "Oh! Was the coffee a peace offering?"

"No, I just thought you might need a pick me up." He turned to her and grinned, making her heart skip a beat. "So I'll pick you up at seven?"

She nodded and got into her car. She rolled down the window and said, "Again, thank you so much."

He smiled. "Sure."

Anila drove home and updated her father on Arjun's condition. He said, "Don't tell Arjun..."

She smiled. "That you were sobbing by his bedside? I won't."

After her father left for the hospital, she took a shower and changed into her pajamas.

But instead of taking a nap, she turned on her computer. Multiple things circled in her mind. She could push the lawsuit away for only so long. Now that Avinash was the opposing counsel, what choices did she have? She liked him. A lot. She didn't want to look for another property after spending so much time and effort on this one. Was it wise to find another attorney and fight the lease with an established business like Lupe's Cupcakes? If his *Auntie* Lupe didn't want to leave, was Anila interested in a legal battle that would surely mess with her plans? Her family would find out about her business if she went to court. It wasn't worth it, was it? Still, there was some urgency in setting up a physical location for her business; there was no denying it.

So, she had to decide whether to fight. Avinash had himself said she would probably win. Even if she did win the battle, would she lose Avinash in the process?

Was Avinash even hers to lose?

She wanted him, that much was clear in her mind. But was she just an option for him, something to play around with until something else came along? Was he serious about her?

She logged into her website and created a fake profile. Bina Kashyap. Grew up in Delhi, moved to Los Angeles after marriage. Has a five-year-old daughter. Divorced two years ago amicably. Ex already married. Bina is the owner of a small software business. Seeks companionship for business and social events. Anila thought about hobbies, and in the end she typed in: "computers and spending time with my kid." She found a profile picture of a woman from a royalty-free website.

With a deep breath, she made the profile live, using her administrative privilege to bypass the background check.

In five minutes, three names were matched with Bina's. The last one was Avinash Singhania.

Her heart racing, she sent a message through the fake profile. *Hey Avinash, the site matched us. Want to meet up?*

Anila wanted to find out secretly if he was interested enough in her to refuse a date with someone with a profile similar to hers. She had no idea what she'd do if he agreed to go out.

He answered within seconds. *I am so sorry, but I should have updated my profile to 'Inactive'. I will withdraw immediately.*

Anila typed, still posing as Bina. *How come? I'm new to the service. Did you have problems with the website?*

No, the website is great.

Oh. Did you find someone?

He replied with a smiley face emoji. *I have, maybe, hopefully, found someone.*

25

ANILA WOKE UP with a start, a tremendous pressure on her chest and belly crushing her. It was Sunny sitting astride her, a massive grin lighting up his face. "Ma, wake up!"

At once relieved and annoyed, Anila blew out through pursed lips, "Yes, *raja*?"

"Can we go to the zoo today?"

She groaned and glanced at the radio clock on the bedside table. Six-thirty in the morning. "We're supposed to go visit Arjun Uncle in the hospital." It had been two days since Arjun's surgery, and the doctors had said he would be discharged soon.

"But after?"

She raked her fingers through her son's thick, lush hair. It was time for a haircut. "Why the sudden interest in the zoo?"

"Megha said there is a baby panda. Please?"

Ugh, she thought. His persistent interest in babies of all kinds! Still, it was better than him asking for a baby sister. "Okay, okay. But the zoo opens around ten. So let's have breakfast, get ready, visit Arjun Uncle, and then we'll go."

"Can he go with us?"

"No, hon. He's in the hospital. He's getting better, but they won't let him go."

Sunny pouted. "Okayyy," he said, drawing out the word to showcase his disapproval, just like Vikas used to.

She remembered a time when they'd been married for a year. She had planned on making spicy lentil sprouts and he'd been looking forward to it. She soaked the seeds, let them swell, and then covered them with a soft cloth. But in the cool weather, they didn't sprout. Indeed, they got disgusting fungus all over them, and she had to throw it all away. She made a regular lentil soup. "It spoiled," she told him.

"Okayyy," he'd said.

Anila's stomach knotted. She knew how much Sunny yearned for a father figure in his life. Megha and Trevor had stories of their outings with their fathers, and Sunny must feel left out. Though Arjun had tried his best to take the place of a father, it was different.

After a quick breakfast, she got Sunny ready, packed a bag with sunblock, hats, granola bars, and water bottles, and set off for the hospital. She'd asked her mother to text to Myra not to come to work. Her mother had returned from India and was relieved to find out Arjun was doing well. "Ask him to move back home," she'd said.

Sunny was in a talkative mood throughout the drive, and Anila answered in monosyllables, watching him in the rearview mirror as he prattled away, strapped safely in his car seat. From some angles he looked just like Vikas. She swallowed hard. Her fingers moved to the pendant by habit until she remembered it lay somewhere in the recesses of her seat.

She felt guilty and free at the same time; guilty about wanting to forget Vikas, and free from being burdened by thoughts about him all day. Each time she thought she'd moved on, a reminder thrust itself into her mind, front and center. She had to make space in her life for something new, something different. And now with the pendant lost, it almost seemed possible.

Anila held Sunny's hand and led him inside the hospital, where they were given their "Visitor" stickers.

"What's this for, Ma?" Sunny asked.

She affixed a sticker to his T-shirt. "So no one mistakes you for a doctor."

He giggled. "You're silly."

Arjun had been moved to the surgical floor. When she entered his room, Arjun was on crutches from the severely sprained ankle. A physical therapist was explaining the rehab exercises. Lily must have gone home or to the cafeteria; she hadn't left Arjun's side since she'd returned.

Arjun saw his sister and nephew and grinned. "Look, Sunny, I am finally learning to walk. Not as well as you, of course."

Sunny laughed and gave his uncle a hug. Arjun winced, the pain from his broken ribs evident. Anila pried Sunny's hands away from Arjun.

They chatted for a while after the physical therapist left.

Arjun said, "I can't wait to get out of this dump."

Anila said, "Ma wants you to come home. Lily will soon go back to work, and you'll have no one to watch over you back at your place. So, I'll be here tomorrow to take you home. Lily will pack her stuff and stay over as well. A week or so until you can put weight on your foot."

He sighed. "Fine. Anyway, it's been a long time since I ate Ma's *pulao*."

Sunny pointed to Arjun's tray. "Are you going to eat that Jell-O?"

Arjun passed the jar to his nephew. "All yours, buddy. So what's the plan for the day?"

Sunny opened the green Jell-O and scooped out a little with a big plastic spoon. It flung over his head and landed on the floor. Anila wiped it off with a napkin and tossed it into the trash.

Sunny said, "We're going to the zoo. Can't you come with us?"

Anila said, "Sunny, you know Arjun Uncle can't go."

Right then, the door opened and Avinash walked in with a cardboard tray holding three cups of coffee. He said, "Can't go where?"

Arjun raised his eyebrows. "Hello, hello. Thanks for the coffee, bro."

Avinash handed over a cup to him. Anila declined, embarrassed to see him here, declaring his interest in her so openly, and frankly, terrified at the prospect that he thought "he'd met someone," as he'd declared on the website.

Avinash said, "What am I to do with a cappuccino with cinnamon? I drink black."

She said, "Fine."

Sunny finished his Jell-O and turned to Avinash. "Ice Cream Uncle!"

Avinash grinned. "Guilty as charged. But I didn't know you'd be here, so all I have for you is a lollipop." He extracted the said candy from his pocket, and Sunny took it happily.

Anila said, "Sunny, you just had Jell-O. Please save the lollipop for later."

Avinash handed her a cup of coffee and took a sip from his. "So," he said, "Where are you off to?"

Sunny's eyes shone as he glanced at his mother and stuck the lollipop in his jacket pocket. "We're going to the zoo. Megha said there's a baby panda. Can you come with us?"

Avinash said, "Well, I've got no meetings or any other commitments, so I'd be honored."

"Huh?" said Sunny.

"I'll be happy to go with you, if your Mom will have me."

Anila flushed a deep shade of red as Arjun sniggered. She said, "Sunny, he might have other things to do."

Avinash said, "Nope. There's nothing on the agenda for today. Nada. Zilch."

Sunny turned to his mother. "Please, Ma?"

Arjun said, "Get out of here, everyone. I need to rest." He looked perfectly rested and did not need a nap. But Anila rose from her chair. "Fine. I'll be back in the evening."

As Anila, Sunny, and Avinash walked to the parking lot, Anila said, "Are you sure you don't mind going?"

Avinash placed a hand on his heart. "Scout's honor."

She smiled. "We'll go in my car."

They drove to the zoo, as Avinash made silly faces and Sunny watched in the rear-view mirror, roaring with laughter. The smell in the car had transformed from the usual vanilla air freshener to Avinash's musky cologne. Anila's heart sang.

Sunny, Anila and Avinash walked into the zoo, Avinash holding three tickets in his hand. The little boy was too excited to know where to go first, so Anila took charge. One by one, they ticked off the boxes on Sunny's wish-list of animals to see. The baby panda was adorable, but after the first few minutes, she slept, tucked into her mother's underside.

Avinash said, "There should be a nice fast food place right around here." Anila wondered how he knew. Sure enough, they turned the corner and saw a shack with a few square tables covered by colorful umbrellas. Sunny was hungry, and Avinash insisted on buying lunch.

She said, "No, you already bought the zoo tickets."

"Please. For the pleasure of your company, allow me."

Soon, he returned with a tray filled with all kinds of finger foods that Sunny absolutely loved: chicken nuggets, fries, tater tots, and lots of ketchup. He'd bought a salad for himself and for Anila.

Later, they went to the tiger enclosure and moved on to see the giraffes and then the elephants. Sunny was sleepy and cranky by then.

Avinash said, "Let me carry him." He swung Sunny easily on his shoulders, where the boy sat, his little feet dangling, as he clutched Avinash's neck. Avinash placed his hat on top of Sunny's head.

They passed a man selling flowers, who said, "Rose for your wife, sir?"

Before Avinash could say anything, Anila waved him away and felt heat rise to her cheeks. But Avinash seemed unconcerned. And luckily, Sunny hadn't noticed. Then she thought, it was such a lovely day, and they were having so much fun. So what was her problem? Why was she so diffident around Avinash? What could possibly be wrong in wanting more in life?

Here was a handsome hunk of a man, so sweet and so tender, so loving to her son. But what if it was all just for show? What if she was a conquest for him? And as soon as Avinash got her, he'd be cruel to Sunny as her Papa had been to Arjun. *But Papa loves Arjun; he just didn't know how to show it.* Avinash was openly demonstrative in his affection. Besides, he'd never given her the reason to believe he'd betray her or her son. The muddled thoughts were giving her a headache.

Avinash said, "The petting zoo is right here. He'll love it."

Avinash hadn't seen the map, which Anila still clutched in her hand. She frowned and smiled at the same time. "How do you know about the petting zoo?"

He laughed, a deep belly laugh that made her stomach knot. "Through experience. I brought Tanya here once." He was actually blushing.

So he brought his little sister! That was a different level of adorable. "That's so sweet."

He shrugged. "But be careful of the donkey. He bites."

She laughed and said, "Okay, that's a story that deserves to be told."

"I was in high school. I'd just got my drivers' license, and Ma asked me to pick up Tanya from school because she'd be late at work. Instead of going home, we came to the zoo. Tanya loved looking at the chimpanzees. Anyway, we went into the petting zoo armed with celery and carrots. I'd busted my allowance on the trip. As she was feeding one of the donkeys, he bit her finger."

"My God!"

"He probably thought her finger was a carrot."

"What did you do?"

"She started screaming. I dropped my stack of celery, pried his mouth open and retrieved her hand. Then I spent my last bit of change on an ice slushy. I asked her to stick her hand into it like you'd done for Sunny at the restaurant. It helped a little. But she got a nice purple finger and a story she loves to tell."

Anila laughed. "Did you get in trouble?"

"Yes and no. Not for the donkey bite or the fact that we came to the zoo. But I was grounded for a week for not asking for permission to bring her."

"Would you have got permission if you'd asked?"

He grinned. "Probably not. Ma loves the zoo, too. She'd have taken us on a Saturday. Maybe she'd have let me drive."

"That's not the same as spending quality time with your sister, though, is it?"

"Nope. And despite the donkey bite, it was totally worth it."

They laughed and went into the petting zoo with Sunny, who had suddenly become alert, enjoying the ducklings, piglets and baby deer. There were no donkeys, thankfully.

Avinash's phone buzzed. He stared at the screen and said, "Do you know someone called Noah?"

Her heart sank, and her knees seemed to give way. "W… what?"

He shrugged. "It's a text. He's asking if you're with me." He looked up at her and frowned. "Anila, what's wrong?"

"My God!" Anxiety tore through her as her heart raced and blood pooled to her legs. She felt faint. She sat down on a small kids' bench, and Avinash settled beside her. That look of concern on his face made him vulnerable to Noah's attacks.

If anything, Avinash had earned the right to hear the truth. And keeping it bottled up inside her was making her sick. So she told him everything, about Noah, about the texts, and the stalking.

Avinash's eyes glinted with anger towards Noah, with concern for her, and she could barely look at him for fear of breaking into tears. Her voice caught in her throat. She jutted her chin toward his phone. "That's who this guy is."

Avinash clenched his teeth for a moment. Then he said, "I'll break every goddamn bone in his body."

She said, "Even Harrison hasn't been able to find him yet."

Avinash let out a sharp breath. After a moment, put an arm over her shoulders. "Why didn't you tell me before?"

She shook her head and wrung her hands. "I didn't want to bother you. No one knows. Not even my family. I don't want to scare them."

"But Anila, they care about you." Avinash gritted his teeth and typed in a message as Anila peeked over his shoulder: *Leave her alone.*

Oh, you are with her, then?

Do you understand the meaning of cease and desist? You're facing a lawsuit now.

Oh, I know my rights. I have a hot shot lawyer too.

Go to hell.

Is that a threat? Oh, I shouldn't worry. I know all about you. Dumped by your wife. Tell Anila I'm sorry her brother got hurt. It went out of control.

Anila gasped. What did that mean? Had Noah caused Arjun's accident? Noah wasn't the driver, because the driver was a young guy, maybe twenty years old.

Avinash put his phone away. "I'll take care of it. I'll have Harrison talk to the driver. Let's get back."

A giant sob erupted from Anila's chest as Avinash held her in his arms. She whimpered, drowning in self-pity and self-loathing. "If Vikas hadn't died, I'd have stayed in India, I'd never have met Noah and this would never have happened. Arjun almost died because of him."

Sunny ran back to them, two ducklings following behind him. "What happened, Ma?"

Anila couldn't speak. Avinash said, "Nothing important, Sunny."

Sunny tugged at his mother's arm. "Why're you crying?"

Anila looked at Avinash with imploring eyes, begging him not to scare her little boy. Avinash clenched his jaw. "She's missing your father. Sunny, hold my hand. Let's go home."

26

THE ELEVATOR DOORS dinged open, and Anila found herself in the plush lobby of the Law Offices of Singhania and Singhania. Classy décor of pale grey and cream, tasteful paintings and photographs, real plants in large planters, plush furniture, and a beautiful Kashmiri throw rug decorated the space. A young receptionist sat at a massive desk, the US flag and awards and honors of various kinds on a wood panel behind her. Before Anila said anything, the receptionist nodded and got up from her seat. "Ms. Mallik? They're expecting you."

Harrison had said they had new information on Noah and wanted to discuss the next course of action. Avinash's office seemed like a reasonable place to meet because Anila didn't want her family to worry; Arjun was recovering at home, and Lily had taken extra time off. Sunny refused to go to preschool with so many people at home, and Anila had volunteered to help out at the Winery Chateau. That's where her family thought she was, at this moment.

Anila was led down a carpeted hallway adorned with expensive art to a large office with a massive window overlooking the downtown skyline, with a glimpse of the ocean to the west. Harrison was already there. She couldn't help but notice how dashing Avinash looked in his suit, the necktie loosened, a faint shadow on his jaw.

Someone brought in three cups of coffee and a plate of cupcakes, which Anila thought looked like Lupe's. Was this some sort of gentle pressure for her to back off from the lawsuit? But Avinash had been nothing but direct with her. She shook the thought away as he gestured her to a chair across his desk. Harrison stood, leaning against the wall.

Anila took a sip of coffee, her eyes flicking from Avinash to Harrison, waiting for one of them to speak.

Avinash nodded to Harrison. "Tell her."

Harrison took a deep breath. "It's your nanny, Myra. Her brother is Noah's gardener. She's been telling him your whereabouts and what you wear, whom you meet. Anything she's overheard."

Her jaw dropped. "My God. My own nanny? Who watches my kid, pretends to care for him! I can't believe it."

Avinash said, "Better believe it."

Anila said, "I'll call the agency for a replacement right away. What about the driver, the guy who hit Arjun?"

Harrison tapped the table. "That's where it gets interesting. The driver is the nanny's boyfriend."

Anila clapped her hand to her mouth. "She never mentioned a boyfriend. Why? Why did they do it? For money?"

Avinash said, "Noah paid them, sure. But he's paying for Myra's ailing mother's hospital bills. He told them his mother died at home because he couldn't afford better care, so he understands their predicament."

Her voice quavered. "He pays their mother's bills in exchange for killing my brother?"

Harrison shook his head. "They were just supposed to scare Arjun. Arjun would tell you how he almost had an accident, and Noah would tell you it was him."

"How can Noah think I'd want to be with him after he threatened my family?"

Harrison said, "He's not right in the head, Anila. He knows you aren't into him. He'll do everything in his power to terrorize you."

Anila clutched her forehead. "Will they prosecute the driver?"

"Yes, but I think we should wait. If we make it public, Noah goes underground. Right now, Alex, the driver, has been released from custody. He's under surveillance. I've got the department looking for Noah. But he's really good at hiding. No one knows what he looks like or where he is."

Anila said, "He said he had cosmetic surgery. Did you have any luck with the driver or the gardener to get a picture profile of Noah made?"

Harrison shook his head. "They never saw him. They communicated through texts. Money transferred to the hospital from an off-shore account. But I doubt if he wants to hurt you."

Anila said, "I don't care about me. I'm worried about my parents and Sunny."

"I'll have a couple detectives near your house. Don't worry. Your parents won't even know."

"Arjun is still recovering at home. I'm worried about him, and about Lily. Oh God! What a mess!" Anila heaved a sigh, her eyes shining.

Avinash came around the massive desk and wrapped his arm around her shoulder. "It will be okay."

Harrison said, "Trust me. We'll get him." Then he paused and stared at her. "Anila, I have to tell you. He sent another text. He said he'd be at the exhibition."

"My God! Then I shouldn't…"

"No, you should not change your whole way of life for this creep. But don't go alone." Harrison spoke firmly, but kindness shone through his eyes.

Anila blushed, and Avinash clasped her hand across the desk. "I'm taking her."

Harrison nodded approvingly. "Great idea. You'll be safe with him."

"I won't take Sunny with me."

Harrison raised his hand to stop her. "Myra has told him you're going with Sunny. If you change any plan, he'll suspect something, and he'll disappear, and we'll lose the chance to nab him."

"Oh God, how am I going to do this?"

Avinash said, "I'll be right beside you."

Anila frowned. "He'll get even more jealous."

Harrison said, "The idea is to make him show himself."

Anila breathed out through pursed lips. "Okay. But I really don't want to take Sunny."

"I understand, but…" He hesitated. "Don't change plans, or he'll figure it out. I'll be there too, with a couple plainclothes officers."

She stared out the window as a jet flew across. Vikas had once said every time a pilot took off, there was a danger he wouldn't return. And yet they flew day after day, night after night. *It's called being brave,* he'd told her. If Anila didn't set an example for her son, how could she honor Vikas's memory? And Avinash and Harrison would both be there.

She had to see this through. She nodded. "Okay."

Harrison and Avinash exchanged a glance. He said, "Sure you're up to it?"

She nodded. "I need to be free. But there is no way I'm letting Myra anywhere near my son. I'm firing her. I hope that doesn't alert him."

Harrison said, "Tell her with so many people in the house, Sunny wants to stay home with them. Something like that."

With that, he left the office.

Anila rose as well, but Avinash circled around the desk and stood right in front of her, blocking her way. He leaned in, planted a kiss on her lips, a slow, gentle, reassuring kiss. And while she'd been thinking about Vikas moments ago, this didn't feel wrong. She felt no twinge of guilt, no spark of regret. When he pulled away, she sighed, content.

He stared into her eyes. "I thought you needed that."

She smiled at him. "I did."

"We're going to catch that son of a bitch, Anila. I promise you that."

27

ON THE EVENING of the exhibition, Anila hefted Sunny's slippery form out of his bath, wrapped him in a fluffy towel, and dressed him in a crisp new collared shirt and a pair of trousers. She was still tempted to leave him home with her parents, but Harrison was right. She'd better stick to the plan to avoid alerting Noah.

Anila had fired Myra the night before. What a traitor she'd turned out to be! How could Anila feel safe entrusting her child to someone who'd give up the intimate details of her employer to the highest bidder? Though Anila had considered confronting Myra about it, she finally told her simply that she no longer needed her to come.

Myra, in her usual skinny jeans and tank-top, her hair in a ponytail, and fake eyelashes with goopy mascara, looked more alarmed than disappointed. "If you're unhappy with how…"

Anila said, "It's not that. Sunny wants to spend time with his Uncle Arjun and Aunt Lily." She hoped she sounded authentic. She told her parents the same story but hadn't told Sunny yet.

Myra had left the mansion with an extra month's pay, which Anila hoped would cool her off.

Anila affixed the top button of Sunny's shirt. He winced and scratched the back of his neck. "This is itchy, Mamma."

She smiled and patted the collar down and adjusted the tag. "Better?"

He said, "Where's Myra?" This routine of dressing him was usually done by the nanny.

Anila buckled the new leather belt around Sunny's tiny waist and said, "She won't be coming anymore."

"I didn't like her," he said. That was news to Anila. How come she didn't know he didn't like the nanny? A pang of guilt thrummed in her heart. Had she focused too much on her business and neglected her son? "Why not?"

"She is always on her phone. She won't play catch."

"I've seen her playing with you."

"Only when you looked."

Anila frowned. "Why didn't you tell me before?"

Sunny shrugged in the typical child's way of not having an answer.

She said, "You know, Sunny, if anyone, *ever*, says something to you that you don't like, or does something you don't like, you must tell me." A prick of worry crept in her mind. If Avinash ever made Sunny feel less, she would boot him out of her life. Not that she thought Avinash was the type, but as far as Sunny was concerned, she was the Mama Bear.

He said, "Okay."

Anila sighed. "Well, Myra is gone now." She towel-dried his hair and ran a comb through it. "You need a haircut, but you're still the most handsome boy in the world."

His face glowed. "More handsome than Ice Cream Uncle?"

She laughed. "Absolutely."

His voice rose in pitch as he asked, "More handsome than Arjun Uncle?"

"Yup."

He stared at his mother. "More handsome than Papa?"

Her breath caught in her throat. She hadn't thought about Vikas for a full day. It was a new feeling, this sensation of peace in her heart, the absence of the numbing pain Vikas's name wrought for the last three years. She saw Vikas's smiling face in her mind. Sunny had only seen photos of his father and had no idea how much alike they were in looks and in temperament. "You look just like him." She kissed his forehead as the door-bell rang.

Anila was already dressed in a knee length purple dress with black sandals, with amethyst earrings and bracelet, her hair tumbling down to her shoulders in gentle waves.

She took Sunny downstairs and opened the door. Avinash stood in the doorway in a very trendy tuxedo, a bouquet of roses in his hands. "For you."

Over his shoulder, she saw his red Lamborghini parked in the driveway and groaned inwardly. Did he have to show off his fancy car? Wouldn't it enrage Noah? And then she saw the new child's car seat in the back and smiled. Avinash sure was considerate.

Avinash handed her the flowers. She thanked him and asked him to come inside. As Sunny chatted with Avinash, she arranged the flowers in a vase and picked up her purse. "Shall we?"

She tucked Sunny in the new car seat in Avinash's car and closed the door.

Avinash reached for the handle on the passenger-side door. As both stood outside the car, he dropped his voice. "You look ravishing. I could spend all evening taking photos of you. But I would not put them up for exhibition."

She said, "Oh yeah?"

"Yeah. Just for my viewing pleasure."

She raised her eyebrows.

He flushed a deep shade of crimson. "That came out creepy. Sorry. I just meant to say you look wonderful." He scoffed in his self-deprecating way. "I tried to be creative, and it obviously didn't work."

She smirked. "Obviously. But thanks."

He coughed. "Um… Shall we?" He pulled open her door.

She laughed and got into the car. "Let's go."

"Yes, Ma'am."

The traffic was not too heavy on a Saturday evening, and just twenty minutes later, they stopped in the parking lot of the downtown building where the exhibition was scheduled. The sun was setting in the west, and the buildings were mostly dark.

Anila held Sunny's hand, and they got into the elevator with a few other people, all dressed well, all presumably going to the exhibition, since it was a weekend and offices were closed. She scanned their faces, searching for Noah. An elderly, wealthy couple in designer suits, a middle-aged woman wearing a damn tiara, a young couple who looked like art students. Innocuous.

The elevator glided to a smooth stop. They stepped out onto the terrace. A blast of cool breeze ruffled her hair. Overhead the moonless sky darkened. Cleverly placed lights illuminated large photographs all around the terrace, setting the space aglow in ethereal golden light. At the entrance was a bar attended by a young, handsome barman, probably a frat boy from a local college making an extra buck.

"Champagne?" he asked.

Avinash placed a ten-dollar bill in the tip jar and first asked for a glass of apple juice for Sunny, then picked up two champagne flutes. He handed one to Anila and their hands touched, sending an electric current through her.

"Nervous?" he asked.

She shrugged. His awkward compliment earlier had relaxed her somewhat, but being so close to Noah and not knowing what would happen had raised her hackles.

Sunny spotted Megha and tugged at his mother's wrist. "Can I go with Megha, Mamma?"

She smiled. Sunny called her "Mamma" when he wanted something badly. Anila glanced at Megha's nanny, an older woman with graying hair tucked in a neat bun, wearing a string of pearls and a scoop-neck pastel dress. Sunny knew her well. Anila hesitated, glanced around the terrace searching for Noah. People still streamed into the terrace from the elevators. Not finding anyone who looked suspicious, she relented and led Sunny to Megha's nanny, Avinash following behind. "Isn't Trevor here?"

She said, "No, he wasn't feeling well. It's just Megha."

If Trevor wasn't feeling well, did that mean his father, Harrison, wouldn't show up? A moment of panic gripped her until she saw Harrison across the terrace. Anila nodded. It would be easier for the nanny to keep an eye on just the two kids.

"Watch them."

The nanny nodded and smiled, as if telling Anila, *of course I will.*

Avinash whispered, "Maybe Noah got scared and won't show up after all."

"I don't know what to wish for… There's a hope we'll catch him if he shows up. But I'll die of anxiety if he doesn't."

Avinash squeezed her hand. "I know. Stay close."

Connor Riley walked over to them, his hands splayed in pleasure. "You made it! These photos are selling like hot cakes." His eyes glistened in the reflected light from the photographs. He looked youthful, exultant.

Anila forced herself to smile. She was genuinely happy for him, but the situation was making her antsy. "I knew they would. You remember Avinash, right?"

Connor shook hands with Avinash. "The famous lawyer? Of course!"

Avinash pointed to the row of photographs, of buildings viewed from odd angles, of wildlife in unexpected moments, and of children playing. He said, "I'll pick up a few pieces for my office."

Anila said, "I'll do the same for my… for the chateau." She had been about to say, "my business," but caught herself in time.

Connor beamed. His wife, Juhi, approached them. "Anila, I told you purple is your color. Brings out the natural glow in your skin. I'm glad you listened."

Anila wanted to tell her the "natural glow" was her from anxiety, but she said, "Thanks. You're glowing yourself."

Juhi grinned and stroked her flat belly. "It's the baby and the hormones. Let me borrow Connor for a bit. There's some freakin' billionaire who wants to buy the whole black and white section, the ones with the stairwells. He has questions."

Connor raised his eyebrows. "Questions?"

Juhi grinned. "He wants to know what they mean."

He looked incredulous and shook his head. "They're stairwells."

She giggled. "He needs to know where they're from, what they mean, the deeper meaning of life and that kind of stuff. Make something up, will you? He'll bid higher if he gets to talk to the hotshot photographer. Our kids' future will be secure."

They laughed, and Connor left with Juhi, hand-in-hand. How nice it was for Juhi and Connor to be in such a sweet and complementary relationship. How nice to have someone with you in the most crucial time in your life.

Avinash nudged her. "Hey! Where are you? Your mind is far away."

She looked at his warm eyes and paused. Then she smiled. "No, I'm here." She really meant, *you're here.*

Anila turned her attention to the photographs. It was amazing how focusing on different areas in a scene created depth. She was particularly engrossed in a photo of distorted reflections in an Italian style fountain, when someone bumped into her.

"Sorry!" the man said. "I didn't see you there." He was short and balding, *and definitely not Noah.*

"No problem," she said with a smile. "It's easy to get distracted with the photos. So stunning."

"Yes, it is. Enjoy your evening." He turned away and Anila watched him, unsure if he was one of Noah's minions, meant to distract her from Sunny. Her gaze darted around until she saw Sunny and Megha giggling about something. Megha's nanny was talking to an older man, and their body language was definitely on the flirtatious side, the nanny touching the man's forearm as she threw her head back laughing at his joke. Anila hoped she would stay focused on watching the kids.

From across the hall, she spotted Harrison again who gave her a quick nod. He'd said there would be two undercover cops, working freelance as detectives slash bodyguards. She scanned the terrace for anyone who looked like a cop, someone with short, cropped hair, but saw no one who might be her savior. But then, she couldn't see Noah either.

A chill went up her arms and settled in her heart. She took a sip of the champagne. As it burned down her throat, she felt herself gaining courage. She could deal with this. She was the widow of a brave soldier. She could face this.

Just as she started walking to the kids, someone tapped her shoulder. It was a tall man, definitely taller than Noah. "Don't I know you from somewhere?" He spoke in a British accent, and was about her age.

"I'm not sure." *Are you Noah wearing insoles to raise your height?*

But it turned out he was just trying to get her number. She motioned to Avinash and said, "My uh…" She coughed. "My fiancé here is trying to buy some pieces for his law office."

Hearing the words "fiancé" and "law office," the man sauntered off. Anila sighed. Was she supposed to live the rest of her life watching over her shoulder?

From across the terrace she saw Harrison in conversation with someone who didn't look like a cop, with straggly long hair, but a fit physique and a brisk manner. She caught Harrison's eye and nodded. He nodded back and jutted his chin toward the back of the terrace at another man, a bit taller than Noah, with the same build, but different facial features.

Noah had said he'd had plastic surgery. Could this be him?

There was only one way to find out. Knowing Harrison had her back, she decided to take it into her hands. Her heart hammered in her chest as she walked up to him with unexpected bravado. "Hello." She extended her hand. "I'm Anila. I'm friends with the photographer, and if you have any questions about a piece, I can have him talk to you."

He smiled. "I'm Pierre." His accent was French. But it could be a fake one, like Noah used to use back during the course. He circled his arm around the waist of a woman standing next to him. "Ah, zees is my wife, Gladys."

The woman was wearing a silvery clinging designer dress— Valentino probably-- and Jimmy Choo shoes. The woman smiled at

Anila and turned to Pierre. "Darling, let's bid on that one with the camels."

Pierre smiled at Anila, bowed his head, and walked away with his wife. *Not Noah.* She scanned the terrace as she heart slowed to its usual beat. She spotted another man, about Noah's build, staring at her from across the room. He looked nothing like Noah. And therefore, it must be him. She took a deep breath as her heart raced once more. She stuck her chin up and marched up to him. The man stared at her with startled eyes.

"Hey, you," she said, giving him her most dazzling, flirtatious smile, and poking a finger in his chest for added effect.

"D… do I know you?" he stammered.

"It's me, Anila. Noah, right? From the course?"

"I… my name is Tom."

She stared into his eyes, a deep blue, different from Noah's hazel eyes. *Contact lenses.* She tilted her face and said, "You're right, you know. I finally get it. You do love me. Why would you go to all that trouble if you didn't? No one's ever done so much just for me. And after a lot of thinking, I've realized that I feel the same way about you."

He turned pink and started stammering. Avinash showed up behind her and held her elbow. "Excuse me," he said, smiling at Tom. "My sister didn't take her meds today."

Poor Tom walked away stiffly.

Avinash turned Anila around and whispered, "What the hell are you doing?"

His breath was sweet, with a hint of champagne and olives. She sighed, tears threatening to roll down as she began to tremble, her nerves jangling at each movement around her. "I can't take it anymore. He's here somewhere. God knows what he wants."

"He wants what I want. You. And I'll make sure he doesn't harm a hair on your head." He took her champagne flute from her and handed her a glass of water. "Drink this."

She gave him a feeble smile and took a sip. "He also wants to hurt my family. My son. Speaking of…" She scanned the area. There were fewer people than before. She spotted Megha's nanny still talking to the older gentleman. But the kids were gone.

"Where's Sunny? And Megha? Do you see them?"

Avinash raised himself on tiptoes and looked around. "I don't see them."

And all of a sudden, the lights went out, plunging the terrace in darkness.

28

ANILA FELT AVINASH'S hand grip her arm. "Don't worry. The generator should come on soon."

It didn't.

Anila pulled her phone from her bag and switched on the flashlight. People around them had the same idea and turned on theirs, blinding each other with the flashlights' sharp, focused intensity.

Anila's heart thudded against her ribs. Where was Sunny? Why did the electricity cut off right now? There was no such thing as a coincidence. She was sure Noah was behind it. He certainly had the skill to hack into any grid.

Or maybe she was truly paranoid. *God, let it be me being paranoid.*

A commotion rang out as people started panicking. "Where's the generator?"

"Why didn't it turn on?" "What's going on?" "Call the utility company." "Is there a blackout?"

People jostled and shoved in overall panic. Someone shouted, "Hold it. I'm calling the manager. Just stay where you are!"

Anila had still not seen Sunny or Megha. Was it any use finding Connor and Juhi to join in the search since their daughter was also missing? But they would just get more hassled. This was their event, after all. She looked for Harrison, but again, without luck.

She craned her neck to hear her son's voice. Surely he was panicking too, and calling for his mother? But she didn't hear him.

"Sunny!" Anila called out in the dark, her voice rising in panic. "Sunny! Megha! Where are you?"

Megha's nanny came to her, her eyes widened. "They were here a minute ago."

Anila shouted, "Go look for them!"

The nanny nodded, her features ghostly in the stark light from Anila's phone. "I'll check the bathrooms."

Anila and Avinash walked to the door leading to the elevator and stairwells. Sunny loved to punch buttons in elevators. Had he and

Megha somehow got into an elevator before the electricity went out? They must be stuck and terrified! She considered phoning Harrison for help. But there was no signal. She scowled. This was Noah, all right. The cell tower was just blocks away, and the signal had been strong all over the terrace.

Avinash said, "There are two stairwells. I'll take the north one. You look in the south."

She nodded, her eyes wide.

"Hey!" he said, grabbing her by the shoulders. "We're going to find them." It was Avinash telling himself rather than assuring her. She bit her lip and nodded.

Avinash opened the door to the north stairwell and disappeared into the darkness, the door thudding shut behind him.

Anila turned around and bumped into the woman in the silvery dress. She asked, "Did you see two little kids?"

The woman pointed to the south stairwell. "I saw them go that way."

Anila murmured her thanks and opened the heavy stairwell door. She heard a scuffle. She pointed the flashlight down the stairs and took a step down as the door closed with a bang.

She shouted, "Sunny! Megha! Are you here?"

A hand grabbed her by the neck and another covered her mouth. She smelled a perfume, an expensive one, one that she had smelled not too long ago. She struggled in the grip and realized it was Pierre. Her entire body tingled with fear. She tried to open her mouth, to shout for help, to bite him, but he tightened his grip further. Her phone clattered to the step below, the flashlight blinding her from the floor.

A voice whispered in her ear, making her shudder. "Anila, don't worry. You should know I'd never hurt you."

Noah could change his appearance, put on an accent, but he had revealed himself in the way he said her name. *Anilla.*

She struggled and twisted in his repulsive grasp as he released the hand from over her mouth. She wanted to scream for help, but realized he was responsible for making Sunny and Megha disappear. Best to play his game for a little while.

Her voice came out hoarse. "What do you want?"

Pierre... *Noah* ... smirked. In the light from the floor, she could see the fine scars below his jawline where he'd had cosmetic surgery. It was eerie. She hoped Avinash or Harrison would show up soon. All she had to do was bide her time.

Finally, he spoke. His voice was also unfamiliar. Had he done something to his throat? Was that even possible? Or voice lessons? "I overheard you talking to that guy."

She didn't know whom he was talking about. Probably Avinash. "And?"

He held her tight by her waist, his breath hot upon her face, her neck, and her hair. "You said you loved me. Is that true, Anila? After all this time?"

Anila swallowed hard. She had no choice but to play along for a while. She dropped her gaze and steeled herself. "Yes, I've had a lot of time to think. I do realize the lengths you went to get me. You're right. You've been right all along."

His eyes softened. "Do you like the way I look now?"

She said, "I don't care how you look. I never did. It's who you are on the inside that matters." She prayed he would buy that. If she could only turn him around so his back was to the stairs, she could find an opportune moment and shove him down the stairwell with all her might. Then she'd run for the door.

As if reading her mind, he pushed her to the edge of the step. "You and I should be together."

"I... I couldn't agree more. But you're hurting me, Noah. Let me go."

"I let you go once. I cannot do it again."

She forced herself to relax in his arms, her toes at the edge of the step, and turned her face up to him, staring at his eyes, then at his lips, desperate for him to drop his guard. He took in a shuddering breath and leaned in to kiss her.

Repulsed, she closed her eyes, hoping he would not perceive her shudder. Then he pulled back, and she let out a sigh, relieved he had not kissed her.

He said, "What about Avinash?"

It took her all her resolve to run her finger down the side of his face. "He's just a friend."

He leaned in to kiss her again, but she placed her finger on his mouth. "But first tell me, how you managed it all. Did you cut off the electricity?"

"Yes. Manipulated the grid. They won't even find out."

The glee in his voice sickened her. "And the generators?"

He grinned, his straightened and whitened teeth glistening. "Hacked."

"And the cell towers?"

"Yes. Yes. Aren't you impressed?"

She took in a deep breath, wishing she could have taped his confession. "You did all that for me?"

His eyes smoldered. "Yes. I'll do anything for you."

She frowned a little, pretending to be jealous. "Who is the woman with you? The one you called your wife? Gladys?"

"Just an actress I found. A nice Valentino and Jimmy Choo pumps, and she was mine for the evening."

She forced herself to smile. "Noah, if you truly love me you must know how much I love my son. He's gone missing in the darkness. He must be terrified. Will you help me find him?"

Noah took a deep whiff of her hair, and she shivered. "Your son is fine. He is with that girl, safe."

"Please let me go to him. I need you to do this for me."

He took in another quivering breath. "Let me kiss you first. You owe me that much." He pulled her close to him and she could feel his disgusting body, his revolting desire press against her.

Noah planted a rough kiss on her mouth, and she let him. She had to. He bit into her lip, and she hid a sob, swallowing a trickle of salty blood. She forced her tongue into his mouth to stop him from hurting her. He quivered.

She would stop him if he did anything more. If he tried to grope her, she would kick him in the balls and make a run for it. But she needed him to tell her where he'd taken Sunny and Megha. Tears stung her eyes in anxiety and anger as Noah devoured her mouth, his breath coming in raspy and hot.

29

AVINASH POINTED his cell phone flashlight down the dank stairwell, stepping over cigarette butts and bits of trash. He heard a whimper. And then a faint sound of someone sobbing. His voice cracked as he shouted, "Sunny! Megha!"

A small voice said, "I'm here."

Avinash took the steps two at a time and went down two floors. He saw the little girl sitting on the step, tear tracks shining on her cheeks, her eyes reflecting the light like a cat's. She was alone. "Megha? I'm Avinash Uncle. Your Papa's friend."

Knowing she was safe now, Megha sobbed harder. He extended his hand, but she didn't hold it. He came to sit beside her on the dusty step, trying to comfort her. She reminded him of Nina. "Where's Sunny?"

Megha pointed down to the stairs. "There."

"Let's go get him. Hold my hand."

"I can't walk. My foot hurts."

He pointed the light at her swollen ankle and said, "Did you twist it?"

She nodded. She smelled of candy cane. He stuck the phone in the crook of his neck and stood up. "I'll carry you." He hefted her in his arms. "Why did you come into the stairwell?"

Her breath was warm in his neck. "We were bored. The lady in the silver dress said there were more kids here."

Who was this lady in the silver dress? Avinash had a memory of someone dressed like that, and wondered if she had anything to do with Noah. She must, because there were no kids down a stairwell. It was clearly a distraction. "Where's the lady?"

Megha said, "She shut the door and didn't come. So we went down and down."

"I'm here now. It's okay."

"But Sunny is stuck, and it's my fault."

He felt a pang of pity for the poor child. He patted her back with his free hand as the cellphone flashlight danced on the walls in eerie patterns. "It's not your fault."

He felt Megha's tears brush against his cheek as she sobbed. "Sunny wanted his papa. So I told him a trick."

Avinash took the steps slowly now, holding the little girl in his arms, wondering if she knew Sunny's papa was dead. "What trick was that?"

Megha said, "Once, my head was stuck in the railing on the stairs in my house, and Daddy took me out. He told me it's the job of the daddy. But Sunny said he doesn't have a daddy. I told him to stick his head in the railing, and his daddy would come."

Avinash closed his eyes momentarily, moving the phone to his other hand. "And he stuck his head in?"

Megha nodded. "He couldn't get out. And then it became dark. We were scared. We shouted. Then I went up the stairs to get my daddy, but I slipped in the dark and hurt my foot." She was very loquacious for a four-year-old.

On the stairs below, Avinash saw Sunny's huddled form. "Hey, kid. You doing okay?"

Sunny's voice was muffled. "I'm stuck."

How silly kids could get! He remembered the time he and his friend Rafik tried to make it rain by yelling at the sky all afternoon on the hot terrace, returning home with hoarse voices.

Avinash placed Megha down and asked her to hold the phone with the flashlight pointing to Sunny. He saw the boy's shadow occupying half the opposite wall, a lock of hair dangling in front of his face, his little chin trembling, the bars on either side of his head.

Avinash tried to turn Sunny's head this way and that, but it was stuck firmly between the bars. How the heck did he even get in? There was no cell signal, and he couldn't call 911. He could go back and get help from someone on the terrace, but he didn't have the heart to leave the terrified kid or kids alone.

There was no way except to pull at the sturdy metal struts.

He tugged and pulled and strained, but to no avail. His phone pinged. Was there a signal now? He looked at the screen, but it was the phone warning that his battery was low.

Sunny had turned his face toward Avinash. In those wide, terrified eyes, Avinash also saw the faith a child puts in a trusted adult. The way Nina looked at Stella. The way Sonia had looked at her big brother Avinash.

He had to find a way to help this kid. His head was stuck, and no help was coming.

As a young child back in Bombay, he remembered once when Rafik's father's car had stalled and he'd asked the kids to push. They'd pushed with all their might, but it hadn't budged. Rafik had said, "I'll count to three, and on three we're going to push like our life depends on it. One, two, three." The car rolled forward and started with a shudder.

Avinash closed his eyes and gripped the metal bars. He counted out loud. "One, two." He took a deep breath and said, "Three."

With a tremendous groan, he tugged hard at the struts, and they bent a tiny bit. Encouraged, he started another count, joined in by Megha and even Sunny. They had faith that Avinash could do it. He just had to find that faith in himself.

He heaved and panted with the counts until his hands went numb. The struts became loose enough for Sunny's head to finally escape the trap.

Sunny pulled out his head and turned to him, his face glowing in the dim light from the phone. His eyes were red and flooded.

Avinash pulled him close to his chest. "It's okay. You're safe."

His phone flashlight went out, and they were plunged in darkness. He held both the kids close and hoped he'd be able to find his way back up to the terrace.

Above them, they heard voices, and Megha called out, "Daddy!"

Another phone flashlight swung downward, outlining two figures in an eerie light. It was Anila, her eyes wild, her hair disheveled, the Frenchman gripping her arm. Avinash's eyes lingered for a moment on Anila's bruised lips as he wondered what the Frenchman was doing here.

Anila dropped to the floor and hugged the kids, sobbing. Avinash tapped her shoulder and she looked up, her eyes widened in panic. He could barely discern her mouthing, "It's him."

Anger rose through Avinash. This was the man that had tormented Anila for so long and almost killed her brother. Avinash sprang up, leapt up two stairs, and grabbed him by the throat in an action so fast and so sudden that the man had no time to react.

As Noah gagged and began frothing at the mouth, steps sounded above them.

Even in the dim light from Noah's fallen phone, it was clear that help had finally arrived.

Harrison said, "Is that him?"

Behind Harrison, another plainclothes officer pushed a woman in front of him, her hands tied behind her back, as strong flashlights crisscrossed in the stairwell, blinding Avinash. But he could tell the woman was the supposed wife of the Frenchman. The woman in the silvery dress who had lured the kids down the stairs.

He tightened his grip on Noah's throat as he gurgled, turning purple.

Harrison said, "Let him go, Avinash. I've got it from here."

Avinash released his grip and shoved Noah toward Harrison, who handcuffed him as he read his Miranda rights.

The cops led the two criminals up the stairs, as their footsteps echoed above them. In the pale cone of light, the little group gathered closer together. Anila held Sunny in a tight grip, sobbing, shaking in relief.

"I'm fine, Mommy."

She didn't let him go. "What happened? Why did you come here?"

Megha pointed upward. "That silver dress lady sent us here. Sunny stuck his head in the bars so his daddy could get him out."

Peeking over Anila's shoulder, Sunny asked Avinash, "Are you my Daddy?"

"What?" said Anila.

Before Avinash could answer, lights flooded the stairwell. Anila looked at her son's face in astonishment. Then she said, "Oh my God! You're bleeding." Dark red stains covered her son's neck and cheeks and the collar of his new shirt.

From behind her, Avinash said, "It's not his blood."

He splayed his hands to reveal deep cuts and blood streaking across his wrists.

Her eyes grew wider. "How?"

Avinash jutted his chin toward the bars on the stairs, now bent out of shape, blood marking the places where Avinash had pried them apart. She stood up and took his hands in hers. "I don't know what to say."

He smiled. "You don't have to say anything."

Anila found a scarf in her purse and ripped it into two. She tied each part to Avinash's injured hands, his blood smearing over her cold fingers, as he whispered, "Thanks."

From the stairs below, Megha asked, "So, are you his Daddy?"

Avinash felt heat rising in his face as Anila trembled. If this didn't qualify him for that role, what could? But she stayed quiet. Her silence slashed through his chest like a lance, hurting more than the wounds on his hands.

Megha said, "Where's my Daddy?"

Anila turned to her and said, "They must be up on the terrace."

Avinash hefted Megha in his arms and said, "Her ankle hurts."

They left the stairwell together, the air of unanswered questions and unexplored possibilities heavy between them.

30

AVINASH DROVE into Wellington Estates to drop Anila and Sunny home. It was almost ten o'clock. His hands throbbed from the cuts he'd sustained, Anila's fragrant scarf offering some relief. She had offered to dress the wounds with antiseptic in her house, but he didn't want her family to find out. No doubt her son would soon tell everything that happened, but he didn't want to be the reason Anila had to explain Noah to her family, especially now that it didn't matter, since Noah would no longer harass Anila.

Sunny had fallen asleep halfway back, exhausted from the craziness.

Anila said, "At least let's go to urgent care. You don't know what was on those bars! It might get infected. You'll need a tetanus shot."

"No. I'll be fine." He'd said, his mind on the events that had transpired in the past hour.

When Sunny had asked, "Are you my Daddy?" it had taken all his will power not to answer. God knows he wanted to be Sunny's Dad. But until Anila asked, he had to stay away, take a step back, retreat. And retreat was not his strong suit.

He held the door open for Anila, and she took Sunny out of the car seat. He waited until they went inside and then turned his car around. Driving out, he called his friend's number. "Rafik, still awake?"

Rafik's voice was heavy with sleep. "Avi. What's up?"

"Can I come over?"

Without hesitation, Rafik said, "You're always welcome. I'll have *kahwa* ready."

In half an hour, Avinash was seated in Rafik's living room, sipping hot, flavored *kahwa* tea. Rafik's wife was visiting her parents, and the place was quiet.

Rafik was in his standard garb of *kurta pajama*, pillow creases still showing on his cheek as he pretended to have been awake. "So!" said Rafik, placing his bone china teacup carefully on a shell coaster.

"So," said Avinash, taking another sip.

Rafik eyed him with calm. "You want to tell me what's going on?"

"Why do you think something's going on?"

Rafik nodded at his friend. "Your crumpled tux. Your ashen face. Disheveled hair. Flowery, blood-stained scarf on your hands. Did you kill someone?"

Avinash burst out laughing. "What if I did?"

"I'd help hide the body. You know that."

"And if it's something else? Like a kid who wants me to be his daddy, but I'm not sure if Mommy wants me?"

Rafik paused, then answered with a small smile. "If you want to be his daddy, you should tell the Mommy. I'll make sure the Mommy knows what a great dad you'd be, and that she'd be stupid to pass up the chance."

Avinash was quiet for a moment. "You don't know if I'd be a great dad."

Rafik took a sip and smiled. "I've seen you with Tanya, whom, incidentally, I saw with a boy at Starbucks."

Avinash's eyes widened. "She's seventeen! Who's the boy? I'll kill him."

"See?" Rafik grinned. "I lied. So…"

"So."

Rafik brought out some antiseptic and bandages and opened up the blood stained scarf. "Deep cuts you've got here. Want to tell me what happened?"

"Nope."

"Is this the same woman you'd talked about? Anila Mallik? I've heard about her."

"Yeah."

"So why don't you ask her?"

"It's complicated."

"Okay?"

"I'm representing Auntie Lupe in a property dispute with Anila."

"So what?"

"If we continue with the lawsuit, I'll lose even if I win. Don't you see that?"

Rafik shrugged. "There are plenty of lawyers in town. Lupe can find another one."

"You know I can't do that."

"Tell me how you got hurt, Avinash, or I'll tell your mother."

Avinash laughed. In a childish, mocking voice, he said, "I'll call your Mommy!"

"I'm serious."

Avinash knew he could not avoid it any longer, so he told him the gist of the story as Rafik dressed his hands in clean bandages.

"All done," said Rafik, patting the bandaged hands.

"Thanks."

Rafik stared at Avinash. Then he said, "*Inshallah*, things will work out. Now go back home and get some sleep. You look like shit."

31

ADRENALINE COURSED through Anila's veins through the rest of the evening and the night. A tumult of emotions assaulted her: disgust at Noah's predatory embrace, relief from being finally free of him, gratitude that her son was safe, and appreciation for Avinash's presence of mind, and his sheer strength and will to save her son. The speed with which he'd grabbed Noah's throat when he realized what was happening had rendered her speechless. The ease with which he lifted Megha up, and the very fact that he did lift her up, a child hurt and in need of help, just as hers had been, made Anila choke back a sob. If he was helping Sunny just to worm his way into Anila's heart, would he have shown compassion for Megha?

Little did he know he had already wormed his way into her heart. Not wormed. *Bulldozed.* That was the effect of his larger than life personality. You couldn't ignore it, let alone resist it.

Avinash hadn't asked about her bruised lips. He must have known Noah had forced himself upon her. And she had allowed it so she could find her son. She felt dirty, disgraced.

She entered the mansion. Luckily everyone was asleep, and no one asked about the blood on Sunny's clothes. She put her son to bed, washed out his shirt, and took a long soak in the tub, scrubbing off any remnant, any shred of Noah's touch, willing herself to forget he had ever kissed her.

She closed her eyes, and all she could see was Avinash, his flushed face, his bleeding hands, his tousled hair. His eyes when Sunny had asked if he would be his daddy. Anila swallowed back a sob.

How had things become so convoluted? Here she was, wanting to be with Avinash, and Sunny wanted that too. But it was complicated. For one, Avinash hadn't answered Sunny. Anila had stiffened up, terrified of his answer if it were to be a rejection. She could handle it, but could Sunny?

If Avinash did want a relationship with her, what could he have said anyway? *Yes, I'll be your Daddy?* That would have been too awkward.

This was between Anila and Avinash to figure out. Did he really want her when her son came as a package deal? Could he really, truly love another man's child?

And the big issue loomed over her. He was representing someone who wanted to sue Anila. Was it best if she tried to find another location for her business? But the place was perfect!

"Aargh!" she shouted in the bath.

A phone call interrupted her thoughts. She got out of the tub, wrapped herself in a towel, and picked it up. "Hello?"

"Anila Mallik?"

The voice was unfamiliar. Was it the police? She frowned. "Who is this?"

"This is Rafik, Avinash's oldest friend. Do you have a moment to talk?"

She had heard Avinash mention Rafik's name. "Is he okay?"

A laugh. "Yes. And no. Can you meet me for a coffee?"

Anila glanced at the radio clock. It was well past midnight, but this must be urgent. But what if this was a trap? "I'm not sure that's a good idea. Tell me what you want over the phone."

He sensed her hesitation. "Look, I know about Noah. Avi told me earlier. You have every reason not to trust me, so ask me something about Avi that only his oldest friend would know."

Anila sighed. "Fine. Where did you meet him?"

"We became friends on the first day of school. My father used to run an organization *Dosti ke Haath.* Avi and I used to help out together."

"When did he come to Los Angeles?"

"He was fourteen. He had a rough time."

She took in a deep breath. "Okay. I'll meet you." Anila got dressed and drove out to the small overnight café Rafik had picked, which she'd never visited before. It was a quiet night, and besides a policeman, whose presence made her feel safer as she waited for a stranger, the place was empty. She ordered decaf.

Soon, the doors dinged, and a man entered. He looked about Avinash's age. He was wearing dark jeans and a golf shirt with a dark jacket. He nodded to her and approached. "Hello, I'm Rafik. Thank you for agreeing to meet me. I know it's late."

She got up and shook his hand. "Nice to meet you. So what's this about?"

The waitress came over, and he ordered decaf as well. Then he turned to Anila. "Do you know about Sonia?"

Anila had heard the name during the holiday retreat, and had thought it was Avinash's wife. But his wife was Sierra. She shook her head.

Rafik told her about the little sister Avinash had doted on, and how she'd died, how Avinash had sworn never to become a father to avoid the hurt. And then about Sierra, on how she got an abortion without telling her husband, and how it almost broke Avinash.

Rafik stared at her over the rim of his coffee cup. "He built a wall around himself. Impenetrable. But it seems you've breached it."

Anila swallowed hard. "Why are you telling me this?"

"I don't know how you feel about him. But he's the best friend, brother, son, and husband a person could want. And I know he'd be the best father." He smiled and pointed to his hands, drawing imaginary lines with his forefinger where Avinash had sustained the wounds. "I heard about the vacancy."

His comment made Anila smile back. "I don't even know if he wants the job."

"Believe me, he does."

She took a sip of coffee and regarded him. "He didn't answer when asked."

"How could he?"

She replaced the cup, frowning. "It's complicated."

He nodded and said, "Yes, his Auntie Lupe. She's like family to him. See his dilemma?"

"You mean I should look for another place for my business?"

He shook his head vehemently. "No, not necessarily. You're a businesswoman. He's a lawyer. You're both smart, successful people. I'm sure you can work it out." With that, he got up. "I'm sorry, but my wife's plane lands in a few hours. She'll wonder what I've been doing if I show up unkempt. I need my beauty sleep."

She glanced at her watch that read two o'clock. "You should tell your lawyer friend he has the best lawyer. You." She marveled at how lucky Avinash was to have a friend like Rafik.

Rafik smiled at the compliment. "I'd do anything for him. And he would for me. And I think for you, too."

They left the café together. Anila massaged her temples as she drove back home. Rafik's words revolved in her mind. *I'm sure you can work it out.*

But how?

When she was young and got into a fight with Arjun about some trivial thing, Ma would always find a solution that made everyone happy. Ma always said, "You just have to look ahead for the best outcome and figure out how to reach it."

Back at home, Anila tried in vain to sleep, but tossed and turned until the bedside radio clock read 4:30 AM. A mockingbird began his morning song, and Anila turned over in bed. Sleep itself was a distant dream.

Staring at the gently dawning sky through her window, she toyed with her problems. What was the best option? That she could use the bookstore for her clients, but Lupe could keep her bakery. She imagined her clients meeting in the bookstore. Doing what? Reading books? What had she been thinking? She scoffed at herself as a solution presented itself.

She grabbed her phone and sent Avinash a text. *Want to meet for coffee?*

He'd get it when he woke up and maybe agree to meet her.

The answer came within seconds: *Can't sleep either?*

She smiled and answered, *Nope. So is it a yes or no?*

What, now?

Why not? Since you can't sleep either.

I was planning to go on my morning run. Want to join me? Sunrise in Griffith Park is spectacular.

She grinned. *Sure.*

She told her surprised mother she was going for a run and to watch Sunny when he woke up. The sky was turning pink when she parked her car and saw Avinash driving in. He waved to her.

She noticed fresh, clean bandages on his hands. They jogged side by side in the chill of predawn, and she knew he was slowing his pace to match hers. The fog dissipated near the crest, and treetops became visible at last. She'd saved her stamina for the steep inclines and sped up over the last turn to the top.

"Hey! Not fair!" He laughed and caught up with her as the sun rose, a blood red sphere suspended over the horizon.

She bent over, hands on her knees, gasping for breath, and then sat down on the grassy knoll to enjoy the view. A misty haze covered the valley, the tips of downtown buildings beginning to pop into sight, glinting in the sun.

Avinash settled beside her, and offered her a bottle of water, which she took gratefully. Instead of looking at the view, he turned to her.

Color rose to her already flushed cheeks as she handed him the bottle back. "Thanks."

He came closer and gently touched her lips over the swelling where she was still sore. His voice was soft. "I wanted to kill him."

"I know. Thanks for not doing it. He isn't worth it."

He smiled and nodded. "So here we are."

"Here we are."

"What did you really want to talk about?" he asked. "Or you really just craved some coffee?"

She turned to him. "Tell me about your Auntie Lupe."

"Like I told you before, she was my mother's roommate in college, and they are still best friends. She suffered from severe rheumatoid arthritis from a young age, and *Lupe's Cupcakes* was her first business venture when she started getting better. She couldn't have children of her own and has adopted six."

She needed to know what Avinash thought about adopting children. "How do you feel about that?"

"I couldn't understand it at first. But with the fifth one, I started seeing why she does it. She has so much love to give. Kids need a Mommy. She wants the job."

Anila's heart swelled with joy. "I think I've found a way out of our dilemma."

"We had a dilemma, did we?"

She turned to him, frowning. "Didn't we? With Lupe's?"

"Ah." He leaned back on the grass, supporting himself on his strong arms, not even wincing as his palms touched the ground. "So you won't buy the building?"

She said, "No, I'm still buying it, but she doesn't have to move."

His face lit up. "Oh? That's great. She'll be relieved. That place means a lot to her. Can we go over and tell her today?"

She placed a hand on his forearm. "Wait. There's more."

His eyebrows rose to the sky. "More?"

"Lupe could expand."

"What do you mean?"

"At the back of the bookstore, there's a tiny nook, enough for two or three tables. That south nook will be reserved for my company clients, where they can meet and mingle. The entire bookstore area with be an extension of Lupe's café. But she'll have to offer her café services to my clients as and when they meet."

He gave a short laugh. "She'll be thrilled, I think. But I'll have to check with her."

Anila turned to stare at him. "Make her agree, Avinash. It's my final offer."

He nodded. "Is she paying rent on that area?"

"Nope. It's a freebee." She smirked. "Because I have a rapport with her lawyer."

He quirked an eyebrow. "You do have a rapport with her lawyer. So what's your company anyway? Or can't you tell me still?"

She smiled, hugged her knees and turned to him again, as his face glowed with dawn. "It's an online thing."

He tucked a stray strand of her hair behind her ear in an act so sweet and so intimate that warmth flooded through her.

He said, "What's the name?"

"Um… it's called Business Casual."

He started laughing. "I know the company. But I never knew I knew the owner!"

She plucked at the grass around her and tossed it around. "Not many people know. It's embarrassing, really. I'm a widow, who was never interested in dating, running a fake-dating site."

He held her hand in his. "It's not fake. I've heard great reviews. In fact, I recommended it to a couple of friends."

"Thanks."

He blushed a little and brushed his hair out of his eyes. "I have a secret. I've been using your company for years."

It was the perfect time to tell him how she'd snooped on his profile. "I know."

"You looked me up?"

It was her turn to blush. "Yeah."

He nudged her and said, "And?"

"And I have a secret too. I made a shadow profile, and guess who the program matched me with?"

His eyes widened. "So you're Bina Kashyap? Why did you do that?"

"I'm sorry. I don't know why I did it. Maybe to check if you'd go out with someone with that profile. Single mother who owns a business. But I preferred your answer."

He pretended to wipe sweat off his brow. "Phew!"

She smiled a sheepish smile. "Our profiles match, Avinash. I trust the algorithm I created. And I know things are complicated. I was married before."

He swung an arm around her shoulder and tugged her close. "So was I."

"My husband died."

"My wife is as good as dead to me."

"I have a son. Who wants and needs a sibling. I had such a great time growing up with my brother, and I want that for him."

Avinash said, "Yeah. I got a sister when I was a teenager, but it was a riot."

She said, "So."

He grinned. "So?"

"I mean, it'll be different, and it might be hard. But we could work through it."

He paused.

She stammered, unsure of his intentions. "We can be friends. We could date." What if Rafik was wrong about him? Did he even want her? Had she been too forward? Did he realize that the so-called vacancy wasn't just for a dad, but for a lover, a husband, a life partner?

As the sun rose, a jet flew overhead, and she took in a deep breath.

Avinash said, "You think about him every time a plane flies by."

She stared at his face, at the skyline, her whole world reflected in his eyes. "Yes, I can't help it."

"I know you'll always love him. And that's okay." He stood up and waved at the sky.

She giggled and stood up, as both waved to the jet plane as it flew away.

He took in a deep breath. As if reading her mind, he said, "Are you ready to move on?"

A weight seemed to rise from her shoulders, and she felt free, relieved, hopeful for what lay ahead. She nodded.

He smiled. "After the whole thing with Megha and Sunny…. When he asked if I was his daddy, all I wanted was to tell him yes."

Relief washed over her. "Really?"

"But I couldn't tell him that because I didn't know what *you* wanted. So, Anila, do you want me?"

She nodded, joy blossoming in her chest, vanquishing the last shred of doubt.

He paused. Then he said, "I can't replace Vikas."

She smiled at him, her answer coming from the depths of her heart. "You don't have to."

"I'm not trying to replace Sunny's father. I only promise to love him with all of my heart."

Anile felt tears sting her eyes at the words of this magnificent, kind, and loving man. She let out a half cry, half laugh. "Two things come to mind. One, Sierra is the stupidest woman alive. And two, you need to have Rafik on retainer."

"What's Rafik got to do with this?" he asked, tilting his head in amusement.

She flashed him a smile. "You don't want to know."

He kissed her gently then, tipping up her face to him, and she melted into his body. This felt right, so right. And even though Vikas's face popped up in her mind, he was smiling his blessing. She would always love Vikas, but she had fallen hopelessly in love with Avinash, and it was time she opened her heart to possibilities, to the future, to happiness.

Avinash pulled back a little, and she felt his breath on her face. "And," he said, "one day, not too far in the future, Sunny could have a sibling."

"Oh yeah?"

"I mean, with me as the dad. Only if you want."

She laughed. "You lawyers, always making sure every detail is discussed, every loophole smoothed over. Every "i" crossed and every "t" dotted."

He grinned and wagged a finger at her. "I see what you did there."

She laughed.

He persisted. "So? Do you, Anila Mallik, take me, Avinash Singhania, as a lawfully devoted boyfriend?"

She made a solemn face. "I do."

"Things not moving too fast for you? I mean, it's perfect for me. I've never been happier. I've never been so certain."

She said, "At this stage in my life, I'm not for taking things too slow. I know you well enough now. I've checked your references, that is, your friend Rafik. Lily and Harrison say you're a good man. Sunny adores you. I like you."

"Just like?"

She rolled her eyes. "I sort of love you. So yes, I'm ready. I'm ready for more."

Flocks of birds rose from the trees and flew across the sky, twittering and squawking. Spring was around the corner. Bees buzzed on the wildflowers that had started to appear on the hillside, vibrant with the hope of new life.

Avinash's eyes widened like a child. "I've been waiting to hear this forever, Anila. I love you too." He grinned and paused. "In fact…" He pulled out her tattered, blood-stained scarf from his pocket and ripped out a thin shred.

"What's this?" she asked.

He tied the silken length around her finger. "A promise and a question. Do you, Anila Mallik, take me as a fiancé, until marriage do us join in eternal bliss?"

She laughed. "Yes, you ridiculous man. I do."

He took out an imaginary pen from his pocket and smirked. "Shall we sign the deal?"

She tossed the imaginary pen over her shoulder. "Some deals are written on the heart." She waved her finger with the blood stained scarf in front of his face. "In blood."

His eyes twinkling, he swooped in to kiss her.

THE END

Note from the Author

Thank you for reading this book. If you enjoyed reading it, please consider leaving a review on Amazon.com, Amazon.in, and Goodreads. If you'd like to get updated on new release information, do sign up for my newsletter on my website, www.sunandachatterjee.com

I would love to hear from you. You can find me on Facebook or email me at sunandajoshichatterjee@gmail.com.

Best,
Sunanda Chatterjee

About the Author

Freelance author, blogger, and ex-Indian Air Force physician Sunanda Joshi Chatterjee completed her graduate studies in Los Angeles, where she is a practicing pathologist. While medicine is her profession, writing is her passion. When she's not at the microscope making diagnoses, she loves to write fiction.

Her themes include romantic sagas, family dramas, immigrant experiences, women's issues, and medicine. She loves extraordinary love stories and heartwarming tales of duty and passion. Her short stories have appeared in anthologies, short-story.net and induswomanwriting.com.

She grew up in Bhilai, India, and lives in Arcadia, California with her husband and two wonderful children. In her free time, she paints, reads, sings, goes on long walks, and binge-watches TV crime dramas.

Acknowledgements

Special thanks to Shivani for her help in the story outline during our long walks and for graciously spending her precious free time to edit this novel. Thank you for being my confidant, my best friend, my daughter.

To my parents for always being proud of me.

Other books by Sunanda J Chatterjee

Sins of the Father
The Wellington Estates Series Book 1

Police Officer Harrison McNamara grew up with a silver spoon in his mouth. The former Wellington Estates heir has dedicated his life to taking criminals off the streets. But when he goes undercover to expose a blackmailing scheme, he meets a freelance model who may hold a key to his past.

For psychologist Laura Carson, freelancing as a model is the perfect bridge until she can set up her practice. But her modeling agency isn't what she expected. Encountering the enigmatic undercover cop might be everything she's ever wanted—and everything she must avoid.

As Laura and Harrison grow closer, their past threatens to destroy them. Trapped in an unending cycle of guilt and blame, can they find a way to bury the sins of the past for a future of redemption and love?

Book 1 of the Wellington Estates Series, *Sins of the Father* is a stand-alone romantic saga.

Look forward to Old Money, Book 2 of the Wellington Estates Series.

Old Money
The Wellington Estates Series Book 2

"Families are made from love, not DNA," said her father.

Fashion designer Juhi Raina has always struggled with her identity; an Indian-American, she straddles two worlds, haunted by salacious rumors of her family. After a break-up with her fiancé, all she wants is a little distraction. But the handsome photographer threatens her uneasy status quo, forcing her to question her past.

Wellington Estates heir-turned-photographer Connor Riley shuns his family's wealth and abhors all form of pretense. He is mesmerized by Juhi's simplicity, and Juhi is drawn to his candor. The two misfits make a perfect match. But being with Juhi brings challenges Connor may not be ready for.

The past unravels, revealing secrets that may be best left unopened. Can Juhi and Connor look past the deceit and shame to reclaim their love?

Book 2 of the Wellington Estates, "Old Money" is a stand-alone romantic saga about heartbreak, loss, and finding forgiveness despite all odds.

Fighting for Tara

How far will a mother go to save her child?

"I have no use for a baby girl. Get rid of her tonight!" He towered over her as she cringed in fear.

But Hansa, a thirteen-year-old child-bride in rural India, refuses to remain a victim of the oppressive society where a female child is an unwanted burden. Instead of drowning her baby, Hansa escapes from her village with three-month-old Tara.

Hansa soon discovers that life as a teenage mother is fraught with danger. But a single lie opens the door to a promising opportunity far from home.

Just seven years later, Hansa finds herself fighting for Tara's life once more, this time in an American court, with a woman she calls 'Mother.'

Will the lie upon which Hansa built her life, defeat its own purpose? How can she succeed when no one believes the truth?

A story of two mothers, two daughters and a fight to save a child, *Fighting for Tara* explores the depth of love and motherhood.

Shadowed Promise

A sassy, sexy, sweet romantic saga with secrets and politics…

Moyna, an orphan, has been brought up by a domineering aunt to believe she brings bad luck to those she loves. During riots in Bombay, Moyna promises to protect her dying cousin's baby and makes a hasty decision that would return to haunt her years later.

Sameer, the happy-go-lucky son of a successful lawyer in Beverly Hills, falls in love with Moyna, who remains secretive about her past and insulates herself from love to protect others from her unlucky curse.

At the cusp of political victory, Sameer faces increasing gun violence and death threats leading to an FBI investigation. But his greatest challenge comes when a shadow from Moyna's past threatens to destroy their future.

What hope do they have with the media hungering for a scandal?

A story of friendship, redemption, and forgiveness, *Shadowed Promise* is a journey from blind faith to triumphant love.

The Blue House in Bishop

Alisha has left the Indian Police Force with a broken heart, her wish to bring criminals to justice, unfulfilled. When she agrees to be a friend's 'pretend' fiancée and travels to Bishop, California, she has no idea the decision will transform her life.

Haunted by his failed mission and failed marriage, Duke Wilcox has left the Special Forces, and an accident leaves him recovering in his friend's house in Bishop.

Alisha falls hopelessly in love with Duke, whose troubled past prevents him from opening his heart, especially in the presence of their mutual friend.

But when a mysterious woman appears with a baby, Alisha's cop instinct kicks in. Is this woman who she claims to be? Why is the FBI after her? And how is she involved with a Colombian Drug lord?

A story of loyalty, camaraderie, and love, *The Blue House in Bishop* is a romantic suspense that brings four strangers together in a quest for self-discovery and justice.

The Vision

"You have been given a gift! Use it!" the guru said.

All Divya wants is to become a great pathologist and save lives, something she must do to redeem herself for a childhood blunder. But when her wish for a "good eye" comes true, she starts getting visions of the future. Terrified of her predicament, Divya wonders if the guru is right or if she's losing her mind.

Her estranged lover Krish follows her to Los Angeles, complicating her life as she struggles with her new-found ability. Krish claims he has only ever loved Divya. Then who is the woman Divya keeps seeing in her visions?

As premonition and truth begin to blend, Divya struggles to retain her sanity. Krish warns her that playing with the future distorts cosmic balance and could eventually hurt her. But Divya plunges headlong into what she believes is her duty, helping those she can with her visions.

But will her gift become her nemesis? Will she ever find redemption, or will the attempts consume her?

Lost and Found, a collection of short stories

Just when you think it's smooth sailing, life throws a curveball.

A servant becomes the master.

Family secrets are revealed in unexpected moments, and we find ourselves caring for the generation that cared for us.

In this eclectic mix of cross-genre tales, families fall apart and come together, true love finds a way, and societal hierarchies threaten to topple.